Rescued to Be Messy

A SECOND CHANCE SWEET ROMANTIC COMEDY

MESSY LOVE ON MANGO LANE

DINEEN MILLER

CHAPTER 1

Zane

"Whoever said what you don't know can't hurt you was an idiot. Here, on the beach, you have to know everything. A life may depend upon it."

Spring training—my favorite time of the year. Why? Because every lifeguard here, whether new or seasoned, is driven by commitment. And for the next four weeks, the newbies are mine to train, examine, and decide if they're cut out to be part of a program I've worked eight years to build, design, and fine-tune.

"Lifeguards, pick your trainees and break into teams. You know the drill."

The sun has peaked and burned off the residual coolness of the morning, bringing in the humidity with a vengeance, and summer has yet to start. Four of my best lifeguards are on task today to help train the newbies and are as drenched in sweat as their trainees. Even I'm feeling the heat as sweat trickles down my back faster than my moisture-wicking shirt can keep up.

After watching the drills, I lower the clipboard that has the full list of trainees with my notes for the day's performance and signal to Nick, my right-hand man and assistant, to take over.

He gives me two thumbs up and his signature grin, which has more teeth than a shark.

With that, I launch up the steps of lifeguard tower number one (we have four total on Mango Key, all painted different colors to stand out—red, green, blue, and yellow) to jot down some ideas for a youth lifeguard program I'd hoped to get started this summer. I've worked on the plan for weeks, not to mention the years the seed of this idea spent growing in the back of my mind.

But something's still missing. I want this to be a strong program, like the one I designed for Mango Key Beach, and Mayor Stringer has given me free rein to develop it. And it's not just about making the mayor of Sarabella happy.

Theo used to be the head lifeguard of the program and took me under his wing when I joined at the tender age of twenty. Two years later, he shared his plans to enter the political arena with me as his replacement as head of the lifeguard program. Eight years later, we have one of the most recognized programs in the state of Florida and up the East Coast.

Speaking of which—or who—Theo Stringer's name streams across the top of my phone.

I tap the accept button. "Hey, Theo."

"How's the training going?"

"Good. They're working hard."

"I can see that."

I step out onto the small outer deck of the tower in search of Theo. "Where are you?"

"At the pavilion. Can you join me for a few minutes? I'd come your way, but walking on the beach in a suit and dress shoes is really not doable."

With a chuckle, I head down the steps and hit the sand. "Sure. On my way." I signal to Nick that I'm heading up to the pavilion.

Mango Key Beach is composed of finely ground quartz,

which makes the sand feel cool to the touch, no matter the time of day. And I never tire of the feel of that soft white sand between my toes. I've heard some tourists compare it to snow powder. I'll take their word for it.

As I approach the pavilion, I notice Theo isn't alone. A young man—more like a teenager—shifts from one foot to the other next to him. I shake hands with Theo as I reach them both. "Come to watch the new string of trainees?"

"Yeah, we wanted to check things out." He gestures to the kid. "This is my nephew, Isaac. He's my sister's son. He wants to join the youth program."

I shake hands with Isaac, who has a mop of tightly cropped dark brown curls and a smile I'm sure the girls at school take acute notice of. "Hi, Isaac. Why do you want to be a lifeguard?"

Theo grins at Isaac. "Zane always gets right to the point."

Isaac shrugs. "I love being on the beach, and I like helping people."

I purse my lips and nod. "Those are good reasons to start with. I love that you want to join the program, but I'm not sure we'll have it up and running this summer."

Theo's expression turns hesitant. "That's part of what I wanted to talk to you about, Zane."

I've known Theo long enough to know what his silent signals mean, and whatever he has to tell me must be a doozy.

I shift my focus to the boy and gesture back at the group on the beach. "Hey, Isaac, why don't you go and watch the training? Tell Nick I sent you down, okay? He's the one leading the exercises."

Isaac nods and takes off, kicking up sand as he runs.

After making sure he connects with Nick, I turn back to Theo. "What's on your mind?"

Theo tucks his hands into his suit pants pockets, pushing the flaps of his jacket back, which must be sweltering at this point as the morning sun has launched higher above us. Sweat beads above his brow and his gray-sprinkled sideburns are glistening.

"It's about the youth program. I did some research and found a program I think you'll like."

"But I've been working on some designs and thoughts of my own."

"I know, but you're spread a little thin lately, especially after that hurricane last year. This should take a load off."

As much as I don't want to admit it, he's right. I have been spread a little thin lately. Hurricane Phillipe blew in with a vengeance last fall and did a lot of damage not only to the beach but also to the local businesses downtown, which is just a mile or so from the shore. My team and I not only worked hard assisting in the restoration of the beach but also did a lot of volunteer work to help the business community recover.

Sarabella is a small town with a big tourist industry. We've learned to look out for each other over the years. Because of that, we recovered faster than any other city on the coast that Phillipe ravaged. I'm proud of our community, and I don't hesitate to help when and wherever needed.

And I feel the same way about creating a youth lifeguard program that will make a difference here in Sarabella. This has been a part of my vision for the lifeguard program almost since the day I first joined almost ten years ago.

However, I trust Theo, and, if he's vetted this program and approves, then the least I can do is check it out. "Sure, I'll look it over."

Theo holds one hand out, something he does when he shifts into reassurance mode. "I'm certain what you have will fit well with this program. You and the designer have a lot in common."

I'm not sure what he means, but I do sense an implication here. "How so?"

He glances away for a moment. "I sent the program information to you this morning. Should be in your inbox. Take your time reading the material…but not too long."

Theo's not usually one to be vague, but I'm a team player, and, like I said, I trust him.

I nod. "Sounds good."

Theo grins. "I'm glad you're on board. This is important." He sends a pointed look toward Isaac. "I want the boy to have a chance."

Again, I sense something stirring beneath the surface, like rip currents that catch a swimmer off guard and turn deadly if not navigated properly. Sarabella needs something to support and encourage our teenagers in a world that's becoming more and more challenging to navigate. That's a big motivator for me to get this program up and running.

Right now, I can tell it's not the time to ask about the situation with his nephew because Theo is waving at Isaac to come back, but I suspect there's more going on here than meets the eye.

I give Theo a bro shake and a pat on the back. "I'll get right on it."

Isaac reaches the sidewalk somewhat winded, his cheeks pink from the effort. Sweat beads on his brow. But I can see a spark in his eyes that tells me the kid is interested in a big way.

"Like what you see?" I ask more to confirm my suspicion than anything else.

Isaac swallows and shrugs. "Yeah, it slaps."

Theo rests his hand on Isaac's shoulder. "That means he approves."

I grin at Isaac. "I figured. Great meeting you, Isaac." I bump elbows with the boy and wave to Theo as they leave.

Since I know Nick has the beach covered, I head to my office in headquarters, curious to see the details of this program Theo found. His email is simple—just a brief explanation about the attached document. I tap the PDF and wait for the first page to appear.

And there it is, a simple title—Lifeguard Youth Program. Right to the point. But it's the author's name that crashes over me like a killer wave and spins my head so hard I can't tell up from down.

The memories of her sandy blonde hair, hazel eyes, and peachy scent rise quicker than high tide and wash away my conviction that I was over her.

The one who got away…

Callie Monroe.

CHAPTER 2
Callie

"Are you sure you want a third wheel around? You two are still newlyweds." I glance at the phone framing my best friend Emily's face and fiery red hair. I still love how she turned the one feature she got teased the most about growing up into her greatest feature. She's like a natural-born Emma Stone.

"It'll be fine. Aiden's totally on board, too. And he's going to be pretty busy with the renovations for the coffee shop."

"But he knows it's just temporary, right?" I throw another pair of jeans into one of my suitcases, think better of it, and replace it with two more pairs of shorts, and throw the jeans in one of the boxes on the floor. Spring may still sit on the cool side in LA at the moment, but Sarabella will already feel like a sauna. Eight years may have passed since I lived there, but I remember the humidity well.

"Of course." Emily's face grows larger on the screen as she leans in.

Aiden's voice trickles in from somewhere behind Emily. "Take as long as you need, but not too long."

His chuckle punctuates Emily's eye roll. "He's just kidding."

Hands full of more items to add, I stop packing to stare at

Emily's miniaturized face. "Seriously, I can stay in a hotel until I find a place. Mayor Stringer already offered to cover the cost."

"No, it's fine. It'll be great. Your room is ready. I'll see you when you land." Emily waves goodbye.

"See you soon!" Once the connection ends, I slump onto the bed. The sounds of my two roommates binge-watching their latest zombie series filter in, enticing me to leave the mess of my half-packed life for a little fun. But I did that all week, and now I have to pay the price. I still have to pack all this stuff in my car tonight so I can get an early start in the morning, and I haven't even finished sorting what's going with me and what's getting donated or claimed by my roommates.

For the most part, I'm excited about this new adventure. I've loved LA since the moment I arrived eight years ago, and I've had a blast building a youth lifeguard program that's widely used in Southern California and spreading up the coast. And two years ago, when an unexpected offer came to consult on a new television series about lifeguards, I jumped at the chance to try something totally new. Old fans of *Bay Watch* were eating up *Wave Watchers* like candy.

But, to be honest, I've had my fill of drama, particularly with the show's star, Jake Ward. He seemed like a great guy at first—down to earth and real. Until I figured out it was part of his persona, Jake Ward, that he created for Hollywood and looked nothing like his true identity, Ward Jacobson.

Our short-lived romance fizzled after the first season, and from then on Jake has treated me like I'm part of some plot to prevent him from realizing his full creative potential, when in reality, I was keeping the numbskull safe in the water. Give the guy a handbook and some general instructions, and he immediately thinks he's the expert. So much so he nearly caused his acting double to drown when he interrupted filming to argue with the director about the accuracy of the scene.

And like clockwork, whenever Jake's latest fling fizzles out, he shows up at my door, trying to rope me into renewing our relationship, if you could even call it that. His idea of romance was ordering pizza and critiquing the latest episode of *Wave Watchers*, which usually entailed complaints about how editing downplayed his best features or disregarded his *unique* interpretations of the script. (And no, the writers aren't a fan of Jake Ward either, as you can imagine.)

So when my former lifeguard trainer and mentor, Theo Stringer, replied to my email about the possibility of creating a youth lifeguard program in Sarabella and offered me a job, I jumped at the chance to get out of town for a while and get away from one self-centered TV star who believed his own press about his heroics.

No joke. The guy helped an overheating extra on set find cold water, and instantly he's a real-life hero and can't stop talking about how he rescued her from heat stroke. Of course, you can dig up all kinds of social media images of him at dinner with her that evening, along with headlines that made me want to puke.

Wave Watchers' Jake Ward's Heroics Turn into a Fairytale Romance

With a juicy quote from the Beach Bunny, "He saved my life, then saved my heart."

Blech! Major pukefest.

Yep, Jake knows how to take any situation and turn it into his latest great performance.

As soon as filming for the second season ended, I breathed an enormous sigh of relief that may have been audible halfway up the California coast. The thing is, Jake did flings, not relationships. And I didn't aspire to be one of those, so I ended it and gave notice to the show's producer along with a recommendation for my assistant, Debra, to take my place. As a fellow lifeguard, she can more than handle the task and jumped at the chance.

But to be honest, I have another motivation for going back to Sarabella.

A tall, blond-haired, and blue-eyed head lifeguard, who I

once thought was my other half. That was until I discovered my need to venture out of the small Florida beach town where I started my career as a lifeguard. Zane had no desire to leave Sarabella, and I had no desire to stay. So I felt I had to leave to explore distant shores.

Literally.

I took off for California and never looked back. Not much, anyway. Not until I returned last year as maid of honor for my best friend Emily's wedding.

And saw Zane…

Something shifted in me that day. But then the wedding wound up postponed because of a hurricane. I hustled back home, pushing away a string of memories and thoughts about him that made my heart pound harder than an angry shore in a storm. How could I still have feelings for someone I hadn't seen or talked to in eight years? Though not for lack of trying. I did try to stay in touch with Zane after I left, but he stopped replying to my texts not long after I moved to LA.

Even after I returned home, I couldn't shake thoughts of him invading my mind at the most random moments, especially when I was working on the beach. Maybe I just need closure, and, based on Zane's reaction when he saw me in the flower shop and promptly left without saying hello, maybe he does, too. (I'd hoped to clear the air when I returned for Emily's wedding a few weeks later, but Zane wasn't there, allegedly because of a lifeguard training on the Florida East Coast, but I have my doubts.)

But there's the part of me that wants to explore the possibility of a second chance with him. I've had eight years to explore and go on some pretty amazing adventures up and down the California coast. But lately, I find myself wanting something more, something more meaningful in my life, something lasting.

And someone to share it with.

Maybe that could be Zane. We had great chemistry in the

beginning—both impassioned to create and build a stellar life-guard program from the ground up. Our romance with the beach turned our friendship into something more between us that last summer we were together, which may have been a mistake. I don't know.

I do know I miss his friendship. I always have.

All I can say is, back then, I wasn't ready to stay in one place, and Zane couldn't see going anywhere else. Especially when Theo made it clear he had an agenda for politics and had his eye on Zane as his replacement in the lifeguard program.

I knew then Zane would never leave Sarabella.

So I left and I guess I broke his heart. I still feel horrible about it, and I want to make amends, especially since we're going to be working together again.

As far as the part of my heart that keeps popping up with its own ideas of what could be, I'll leave it in the sand dunes for now.

But if Zane can forgive me, there could be something there again.

Maybe...

If not, I'll return to LA before the end of summer with my tail between my legs. Or better yet, try something new. There are tons of beaches up the East Coast that I've yet to explore.

One of my roommates pounds on the door before bursting in.

"Hey, I didn't say you could come in." I hold my hands out, one holding a couple of my favorite swimsuits and the other my best pair of goggles and a bottle of sunscreen.

Lana shakes her hands up and down for dramatic effect. "Sorry, but you have to see this."

I wave her off. "I don't have time to watch any shows. I have to finish packing."

"It's not a show. It's news."

After I toss those last items into my one remaining suitcase, I follow her out into the living room. My roommates switched from zombies to Hollywood News at some point, and now I can see why Lana barged in.

There, on the beach with the Santa Monica Pier Ferris Wheel in the background, is Jake kneeling down, holding out a ring big enough to be identifiable even in the video. The guy actually had it in him to propose marriage? But to who?

After moving closer to the TV, I must look like an idiot, standing there with my mouth hanging to my knees. "Are you kidding me?"

Lana rubs my arm. "I'm so sorry, Callie."

I snort. "I'm not. She can have him." She, as in my assistant, who Jake was clearly seeing while he was dating me.

With a shake of my head, I go back to packing. Part of me almost feels bad for the woman. He'll most likely trade her in for the next bright and shiny thing to enter his purview.

But he's never asked any of his love interests to marry him before. And while we were together, any time I brought up the future, he would redirect the conversation. So what changed?

Or was it just me?

I growl and stomp back into my room to finish packing. So what if Jake is engaged? What do I care?

I don't. Not one bit. That's my story, and I'm sticking to it.

CHAPTER 3

Zane

This is it. The moment I've been dreading since yesterday. Time to dig into Callie's program.

Quite frankly, I'm not entirely sure why this is so hard for me. It's just a manual for creating a lifeguard youth program. But I know as I read, I'll *see* Callie. I'll *hear* her between the lines—her heart and soul poured into something she's passionate about. That's just who she is.

And that concerns me more than a shark sighting, to be honest, because I'm afraid I'll wind up feeling all those *things* for her again.

I rub my hands down my face. This is ridiculous. I'm making a bigger deal out of this than it needs to be. Callie and I haven't talked in eight years—not since she left town, and I considered our relationship over. Seemed easier at the time to not keep in contact, so I stopped replying to her texts.

But the wiser, older me knows that was an excuse. I couldn't go back to just being friends when it came to Callie. And I hadn't given her much thought until I saw her last year at the flower shop the week before Hurricane Philippe blew in. I didn't even know she was in town for Emily and Aiden's wedding, which wound up being postponed.

We didn't talk then either. As soon as I saw her in the shop, I turned around and left.

I know, I know. A pretty shallow thing to do, but seeing her that day brought up so many memories. And unexpected feelings I thought I'd left in the past. So when they rescheduled the wedding, I made sure I had a good reason for not attending. Not a moment I'm proud of.

But now she's showing up in my life again. Not her, technically. Just the youth lifeguard program she designed, which I have to say is brilliant. But I'm not surprised. Callie always was one step ahead of the game when thinking outside the box.

I think that's part of the reason we made such an excellent team when we trained together. We had the same ideas and goals but approached them from different angles. Our synchronicity earned us the label of 'power couple,' especially when our friendship shifted into more.

Maybe that's what wrecked it for us. We should have stayed friends.

Regardless, Callie still would have left. She wanted to explore new places, other beaches, and go on adventures. Sarabella didn't cut it. I can totally see why California appealed to her.

She used to joke that since her name sounded the same as what Californians call their state—Cali—that she was destined to live there one day. I just didn't think she'd wind up serious about it, especially after all the dreams we shared about the future, which included a youth program.

I guess in that sense, she and I were polar opposites. I'm a hometown guy who enjoys knowing what to expect each day. That's not to say I don't like a little fun and excitement, but exploring new places isn't where I get pumped. I save that for the beach and working out. Or spending time with my family and friends. Connections are important to me.

I'm over halfway through reading the materials when the two-way radio next to me squawks. "Zane, is Tanner up there?"

I leave my desk to do a visual sweep of the main room. The break tables are empty, as are the locker and workout areas. After checking the time again, I pick up the radio. "No, he hasn't clocked in yet."

My gut clenches. Tanner's thirty minutes overdue. I had high hopes for the guy, but over the last three months, he's been repeatedly late and quick to lose his patience. Two complaints from beachgoers about his confrontational behavior are sitting on my desk, waiting for an explanation, which I'd hoped to settle today.

Guess that's not happening, nor is my attempt to study Callie's program and figure out how to best implement it here in Sarabella. As much as I don't want to admit it, Theo's right. Her youth program has all the pieces I've been missing and more.

"He's a no-show here."

I push the talk button. "On my way."

After slipping on my whistle and slinging my rescue tube over my back, I lock the main door and jog the short distance from the pavilion toward the lifeguard towers.

Nick meets me at the top of the steps. "Thanks for the relief."

"No problem. Sorry to hear Tanner bailed."

"Second time?"

"Third and last." I hang my tube next to Nick's below the left side of the roof.

Nick lifts his chin, then shakes his head. "That's too bad."

"It is what it is." And the part of the job I hate. Thankfully, it doesn't happen often.

Nick hands me the binoculars and points inside the tower. "I'm getting some water. Need some?"

"Thanks, but I'm good." I scan the section of beach from tower one on my left to tower three on my right. Tourist season already wound down, but schools let out last week, repopulating the beach with a batch of new and younger faces. Mango Key

Beach is in full swing today, both on the beach and in the water. Some sailboats are skimming out as well.

Movement to my right catches my attention. A young woman in a red bikini standing at the water's edge waves at me, smiling. Ever since that show *Wave Watchers* became a hit, we've had a regular stream of interest and curiosity. Sometimes too much because it interferes with our duty. And the show is so lame. Not realistic at all, in my opinion. Just another soapy drama with sand, sun, and tanned actors better suited to a model runway than actual work.

I give her a tight smile and nod before diverting my gaze back to more important observations. Not to say I didn't appreciate her attention, but when I'm in charge of making sure everyone leaves the beach safely, I don't have time for distractions.

As I pan back to my left, I see a flash of red. Bikini Lady is thirty feet out and waving again, but then she goes under and doesn't come right back up. I lift my whistle and start blowing as I grab my rescue tube, which alerts Nick to keep watch while I go in.

When I hit the sand, my whistle parts people like Moses parted the Red Sea. Bikini Lady comes up, but she's sputtering and going down again.

I splash in and start swimming. As I reach her, I push my tube in front of her as per protocol. She's already flailing toward me and reaching for it.

"Ma'am, I'm a lifeguard here to assist you. Do you need help?" We're required to say this when we approach someone who appears to be in distress, but she's already flailing toward me.

She spits out water. "Yes, please!"

I show her where to grab the tube. "Hold on here and here."

She does what I ask as I swim to move behind her, keeping alert to any sudden shift in her demeanor. A panicked swimmer can take an unprepared guard down with them, and the number one rule in the water?

Do not endanger yourself in order to save another person.

"Okay, you're doing great. Just relax and lean back. I've got you."

Once I have her in position, I swim to shore with her in tow. Nick jumps in to help carry her to dry sand, where we lay her down for further assessment.

I run my hands over my head to get the water out of my hair and crouch nearby. "Ma'am, you're fine now."

"Thank you." She smiles at me as she sits up. "By the way, my name is Daphne."

Nick gives me a certain glance that says what I'm thinking— she swam out too far intentionally for a little attention.

Still, I keep my tone congenial yet professional. "Daphne, you need to be more careful out there. Don't swim out so far next time, okay?"

She nods as I offer my hand to help her up, which she grabs, but then wraps her arms around my waist after she stands and hugs me. "I'm so grateful. Thank you."

Holding my arms out from my sides, I stand there a moment, keenly aware this rescue has turned into a flirt session. And as I'm about to push her away, I hear a voice I'd recognize anywhere.

"I see nothing's changed much since I was here."

I follow the voice that leads to Callie, who's standing a few feet away with her tanned arms crossed over an athletic white tank with LIFEGUARD across the front. A pair of red shorts accents her long legs that are equally tanned. A plume of sandy blonde hair bobs on top of her head, and her hazel-green eyes look more golden in the sunshine. The smirk on her face leaves no doubt about her opinion of what I can only imagine this scenario looks like. I disentangle myself from my clingy rescue.

Daphne, aka Bikini Lady, frowns, then looks over her shoulder. "Who's that?"

Takes me a moment to say anything because my jaw has undoubtedly hit the sand. "Callie? What are you doing here?"

With a pointed glance at Daphne, Callie strides closer, puts her hands on her hips, and raises her delicate brows. "I could ask you the same thing."

CHAPTER 4
Callie

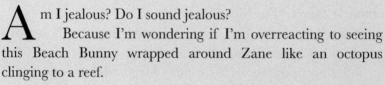

Am I jealous? Do I sound jealous?

Because I'm wondering if I'm overreacting to seeing this Beach Bunny wrapped around Zane like an octopus clinging to a reef.

I push a big smile onto my face to disguise the rhetoric spewing in my head and extend a hand to the cute guy standing to Zane's left. And I turn on the charm—two can play this game. "Hi, I'm Callie Monroe, your new youth lifeguard program director."

Cute Guy does a double-take. "Our what?"

Zane reacts in kind at the same time. "My what?"

His expression is total confusion, and now I'm wondering precisely what Theo left out of their conversation. I didn't expect to have to fill Zane in on the details of my hire. Something I'll have to address with Theo when I see him.

"Youth. Program. Director." I enunciate each word carefully in case he still has water in his ears. But also to make him squirm a little. Serves him right for running out of the flower shop that day without so much as a hello or long time no see. Or how about a simple acknowledgment that I exist? I guess those unanswered texts are still sitting in a sensitive place in my heart.

I'd hoped Zane and I would have stayed friends after I left, but instead, he kind of ghosted me.

"No need to be snippy," says the Beach Bunny, who now has her hand wrapped around Zane's right bicep, drawing my attention to the tattoo on his upper arm—a red cross with the words 'Team Lifeguard' arced over it.

Zane disentangles himself from the Beach Bunny before launching up the steps of the tower. "Finish it up, Nick."

Is he bailing on me yet again?

Beach Bunny pouts at me, then sets her sights on Nick, who's looking at me with intense curiosity. I don't remember him being here when I was, so I'm guessing he doesn't know about the history between Zane and me.

He extends his hand, bringing my attention to the same tattoo as Zane's. "I'm Nick."

Team Lifeguard? First, I'm impressed that there's a team mentality at work here, which, I admit, surprises me. And second, I'm curious to see if the other lifeguards have one, too.

"So I gathered." I shake Nick's hand, noticing his other arm has some kind of tattoo that wraps around his entire bicep. But first things first. I point toward the tower. "I'll go chat with Zane while you make sure she's *fine*." I accentuate that last part with a smirk. I've seen more of this kind of thing on the set of *Wave Watchers* than I'd care to admit.

Zane's standing at the railing, scanning the shore with a pair of binoculars. His blond hair's cropped shorter, and his shoulders are broader than I remember. He's like a wall of muscle standing watch.

He always did that quiet strength thing so well. Still does, it seems.

"So, no welcome back, or hey, Callie, it's been a long time?" I'm standing on the top step like I'm waiting for permission to enter the premises.

Well, I refuse to play this game. I'm here to stay, and Zane will have to get used to me being around again. I signed a contract with Theo—Mayor Stringer—that keeps me here for the duration of the summer. After that? That depends on how well Zane and I can work together again.

I step onto the landing, making sure I'm still in his peripheral vision. He lowers the binoculars just enough to look at me with eyes the same crystal blue as the ocean on a really clear day.

"Hey, Callie, it's been a long time." Sarcasm drips off his deep voice like condensation on a soda can sitting in the sun. And I'm not surprised he left out the welcome-back part.

He returns to scanning the beach, utterly ignoring me.

"Well, it was great catching up. I think I'll go check out headquarters. Theo said to make myself at home."

I reach the bottom step and turn around. "By the way, when I let Theo know I was here, he said he'd be right over to make sure we're on the same page. I'm sure he'll be more than happy to listen to whatever concerns you—we may have."

Zane lowers the binoculars as Nick joins him.

"Daphne is fine. I'll fill out the report."

As Zane hands him the binoculars, he checks his watch. "Next shift is about to come in. Can you manage for a few minutes?"

"No problem." Nick's quick glance my way tells me this guy is Zane's right-hand man, the spot I most likely would have filled had I stuck around. The problem was I had no desire to be his right hand. Or a man, for that matter. I'm perfectly happy in my own skin.

I wanted to be a partner, not his shadow. And back then, that's what it felt like I would be—Zane's shadow, which is now literally eclipsing mine on the sand as I make my way back to the pavilion.

And now he's running past me? Seriously? Like I said before, two can play this game.

I pick up my pace to a jog and take the lead. "What's the matter, Zane? Behind on your spring training?"

He lengthens his stride, which is his advantage. I may have long legs, but his are more muscled than mine. And I mean *muscled*.

He huffs past me. "Nope. Train all year long is my motto."

Oh, yeah, I forgot about those. The man always loved his mottos. Guess that hasn't changed, either.

Zane reaches the office door a few feet ahead of me and leans against the wall, arms crossed and only slightly winded. "What about you, Cal? Has LA made you soft?"

Hearing him use the same nickname he used to call me does weird things to my heart, which is already about to beat out of my chest. I slow to a stop and bend over with my hands above my knees as I catch my breath. Sweat trickles down the sides of my face.

What a lovely picture I must make, but I asked for it. "Hardly. I keep up with teenagers. I'm just not used to the humidity anymore."

He lifts his chin, about to shoot something back when the door opens.

Theo flicks his gaze between us. "Well, I see not much has changed between you two."

Zane gives me this scathing look I'm sure relates to what I said about the Beach Bunny.

I so want to add a retort, but I remind myself that I'm eight years older, and I've matured. I'll take the high road this time.

Instead, I smile and pat Zane on the arm. "Just a little fun between colleagues. He beat me fair and square."

Theo drags his focus to Zane. "Good, then let's make this official and get things started, shall we?"

As Theo steps back and gestures inside, Zane does the same to indicate I should go in first, which I do. He's still a gentleman at heart, which is nice to see.

A rush of memories hits me as I take in the lingering scent of sunscreen inside. One thing I always loved about the lifeguard headquarters here is the openness of the main area that serves as a break room with a studio-style kitchen on one wall and tables set up for breaks and training. Where a lounge area used to be is now filled with lockers and workout equipment, something Zane always said they needed to help the team stay in top shape.

The main office sits toward the back, and if I remember correctly, the door to the left of that is the storage closet Theo said could be converted into an office for me. I told him to hold off on that until we knew this situation would work out long-term. But now that I know that Theo didn't even tell Zane about me coming, I'm having some serious doubts about how well this is going to work out.

As I walk toward the fridge to grab a bottle of water, I hear Zane whisper something to Theo. I have no desire to eavesdrop, so I make sure I'm noisy enough to mask what he's saying despite the inner me that's screaming to hear what I suspect Zane is grousing about.

Most likely, the same thing on my mind, too, so I go ahead and say it as I turn around.

"So, Theo, did you forget to tell Zane I was coming, or is this your idea of fun?" I take in the two of them standing there, staring at me. Theo seems at ease, while Zane has his arms crossed and appears closed off.

"What?" I hold my hands out, the bottle of water in one and the cap in the other. "Did I miss something?"

Theo grins as he shakes his head. "I'm just so glad to have you back, Callie. Feels like old times."

Judging by Zane's brooding expression, he's unhappy with the situation, and now I'm second-guessing my plan to move back to Sarabella. I pull a chair out from the nearest table and slide into the seat. "Feels good to be back. I forgot how beautiful it is here."

Zane pulls out a chair, spins it around, and sits with his arms resting on the back. "It always has been."

Did he mean that as a dig? I close my eyes to resist the urge to roll them. On the off chance I'm just being overly sensitive here.

Theo clears his throat, which brings me to full alert. He's now sitting across from me with his hands together on the table. "Callie, I'm sorry I didn't tell Zane you were coming, but I know Zane would have fought me about it."

I start to say something, but Theo holds his hand up to stop me. "And I didn't tell you I wasn't planning to tell Zane for the same reason."

Zane and I both stare at Theo like we're waiting for the punchline.

He continues, "You both would have argued with me and refused to work together."

For the second time in two days, my mouth drops open. "You don't know that."

Theo shoots a quick glance at Zane. "I heard about what happened at the flower shop last year, so I'm pretty sure I'm right. Besides, I know you both. You're two of the best lifeguards in the country. And this youth lifeguard program is important."

Zane's expression softens some. "Okay, then, let's make a plan."

Again, I resist the eye roll. The man always did like his ducks (or seagulls since we're on the beach) meticulously lined up. But seagulls are notorious rapscallions.

Theo turns to Zane. "Did you have time to read through Callie's program materials?"

Zane straightens in his seat, his hands resting on his knees. "Most of it. It's…brilliant."

I almost choke on my water. Brilliant? Did he say brilliant?

Hands held up, he looks at me with genuine appreciation. "What? I can understand why it's been so successful in California."

If I'm not careful, I'll turn into a puddle on the floor. I drop my gaze, feeling exposed. "Thanks. I appreciate that."

Theo has this pleased expression on his face, like a proud

father. "I know you two will make a great team. Just like you did before." He pushes back from the table and stands. "I've already spoken to a reporter at the Sarabella Tribune about the program and gave her a copy of Callie's program so she can write a piece about it, which will also include instructions for applying for the program. She's coming next week to ask you two some questions and to get a few quotes."

I jump out of my chair to chase after him as he heads toward the door. "Wait, that's so fast."

Zane comes alongside me. "She's right, Theo. We need time to figure out how we want to structure it."

Theo nods. "I understand, but I think you already have all the elements you need. Callie's program is sound, as are your ideas, Zane. Summer break is about to start, so I'm counting on you two to make this happen. Kids like Isaac need this program as soon as possible."

With that, Theo leaves us alone in a room with a view of the beach and a tall order to implement my program, like yesterday.

I sigh. "Who's Isaac?"

"His nephew."

"Oh. What's going on?"

Still staring at Theo's retreating form through the glass door, Zane shakes his head. "I have no idea."

He doesn't say anything else, and he won't look at me either.

This is way more awkward than I'd hoped. I guess I somehow thought something of our friendship would have survived. Guess not. "Okay, so where do you want to start?"

If we're going to use mottos, I would say mine has always been 'give it a shot and see how it goes.' That's not to say I operate all loosey-goosey without a clue of where I'm going. I just prefer to leave a lot of room for things to fall into place organically.

But I know Zane operates better with a plan, and since I'm the more flexible one, I figure moving in his direction first will help get the beach ball flying. And Zane seemed open to making a plan earlier. That's something, right?

However, he's still not saying anything. Arms crossed, he just stands there with his chin tucked, lost in thought.

Baffled, I appeal to his take-charge side. "What, no plan of action or thoughts on how we should proceed?"

He swivels his head to look at me. "Why did you come back, Callie?"

I'd hoped to avoid that question a little longer, but here we are. I open my mouth to say something but only stutter. I'm not ready to tell him how much seeing him last year affected me. Nor do I have any desire to share the ridiculous details of my failed relationship with a self-absorbed TV star.

He drops his arms to his sides. "Next shift is about to arrive, and I have a lot to do this afternoon. Let's regroup in the morning."

Before I can say anything, not even a simple 'okay,' he strides into his office and shuts the door.

I let out the breath I didn't realize I was holding. This is going to be much harder than I thought, but I'm here now, and there's no turning back.

Besides, I've never run from a challenge, and I don't intend to now. Because that's what this feels like now, a challenge. Somehow I have to get Zane to understand I'm here to stay this time.

I stare at his office door. "Challenge accepted, Zane Albright."

CHAPTER 5

Zane

K ade spots me as I press the barbell up. First shift is on the beach, including Callie, who I assigned to shadow Nick today so she can get a feel of how we operate. I want her to understand how our team operates first before we structure the youth program. Building unity in my team has taken years, and we work well together. Smooth like a sailboat when the wind catches the sail, and she glides through the water.

She was hesitant about the arrangement and started to argue with me, which I totally expected she would. But then she backed off and agreed. Callie always did have the ability to surprise me more than anyone I've ever met.

"What happened after Theo left?"

I grunt as I push the bar up. "I asked her why she came back."

"What did she say?"

"Nothing. So I left." But her unspoken answer still haunts me. And I think my fear of what her reason might be is what made me walk away and hide in my office. I didn't want to know. Not yet, anyway. Seeing her was enough of a shock for one day.

"You just left?" Kade studies me as if I'm one of his metal projects gone wrong.

I grunt as I push the bar up again. "Yeah, there wasn't anything else to say."

"Where is she now?"

"I told her to shadow Nick today. She needs to get a feel for how the team operates." I don't know why I feel this need to justify my actions. Okay, maybe I kind of do. I don't know how to be around Callie anymore without feeling like I'm on guard against the storm of emotions still brewing inside of me.

"Wow, you two really need to sit down and hash things out."

"Not likely." I push up my last rep as Kade guides the bar back to the hooks.

"Why? You're both adults. Seems like a simple thing to do."

I sit up and towel off my face. "Nothing has ever been easy with Callie."

Kade gestures for me to get up, so we can exchange places. "You're not exactly the easiest person either, Zane."

That's the one thing I appreciate most about Kade. He shoots straight with me. "I know, but things didn't end well between us eight years ago. Who wants to revisit the past?"

"What exactly happened between you two?" Kade lies back and positions his hands on the bar.

"Not that much." I stand in position behind his head.

"Not buying it. Try again." Kade hefts the bar and starts his reps.

Kade's been my best friend for close to six years now, which is why I asked him to come work out with me at headquarters today. He's the one person I think can help me make sense of this situation, but opening up about what went down is still challenging.

"We trained and worked well together. Shared a lot of the same ideas about expanding the program. And then she moved away."

He snickers. "I think you left out the middle of that story."

"What do you mean?"

"The part where you two got close."

"We were good friends." At Kade's signal, I help guide the barbell back into the hooks.

"Friends don't react to each other like you two did that day in Mandy's shop."

"Okay, we became more than friends. Maybe that was a mistake."

Kade sits up, then turns and stares at me like he's waiting for me to say more.

Which I don't. Like I said, I'm not great at talking about this stuff.

"That's it? Did you stay in touch?"

"Callie wanted to, but I didn't see the point." I hold my hands out.

Kade grabs a pair of dumbbells and hands me one. "Like I said, you two need to talk."

Guess I opened myself up for this. Might as well face it. "She didn't want to stay in Sarabella."

"And you didn't want to leave."

"No way. Theo was training me to take his place so he could run for mayor. All the dreams we had for this program were suddenly moving into place. I couldn't leave." I pause as my gut clenches. "But she did."

He shrugs. "And that made you angry."

"Who said I was angry?"

Kade puts the dumbbell down and turns to face me. "The way you left the shop that day—that was anger. You may have let Callie go, but you didn't forgive her for leaving."

I finish my reps as Kade moves on to doing planks. He may be right. Being around Callie again brings up all these old feelings I thought I'd dealt with. When I see her, part of me wants to kiss her, while the other part wants to throw sand in her face, like a child in the sandbox throwing a fit.

Not a pretty picture. At all.

The door swings open, and in comes Callie, holding on to Nick as she limps in.

I almost drop the dumbbell before running over to where Nick helps her sit down. "What happened?"

Nick moves to one of the kitchenette cabinets. "Jellyfish."

Callie is holding her ankle, grimacing and hissing through her teeth. Tears are streaming down her face. "I didn't see it and stepped right on it."

Seeing her like this twists my gut into knots. "Nick, where were you?"

Callie puts her hand on my arm. "It's not his fault. He was on the tower doing his job. I went down to the water to cool off."

Nick puts a bucket under her foot and pours vinegar over the spot that's red and inflamed on the side of her instep. "Couldn't see it from the tower, or I would have warned her."

I grab a container we have set aside for this kind of thing and fill it with hot water. After setting it on the floor, I examine her foot for any stingers and then help lower her foot into the water.

She hisses through her teeth as her toes touch the water, but she doesn't stop. Once her foot is immersed, her expression starts to relax, which lets me know the hot water is doing the job.

"Just let it soak for a while."

"Thanks."

I nod and then focus on Nick. "Sorry, man."

"No problem. I'll head back out and put the purple flag out, just in case." He grabs a bottle of water before he leaves.

Kade pats me on the shoulder. "Maybe I should go, too. Let you *tend* to business."

I catch his meaning and swallow my retort. "Yeah, thanks."

Kade heads to the door. "Hope you feel better, Callie."

"Thank you. Tell Amanda I said hello."

He gives her a nod. "Will do."

Now that we're alone, that awkwardness hits me square in the chest again. Except this time Callie's injured and needs help. And I'm feeling very protective of her, which I find unsettling.

So, I do what I know I'm good at—taking care of business. I shove down all those feelings and get down on one knee in front of Callie to check her foot.

"How's it feeling now?"

"Better." She swipes her hands over her cheeks. "I hate those things."

"Pain level?"

"A two."

"Good. Just keep soaking it, okay?" I sit down on one of the nearby chairs.

She nods. "Thanks."

"No problem."

The strained silence between us makes me fidget.

"I'm fine, you know. You can leave." There's an edge to her voice, which confirms she's feeling better.

"I'm on the clock today." I lean my elbows on my knees and stare up at her.

"Oh." She drops her gaze and licks her lips, drawing my attention to them.

Memories of kissing Callie race through my mind as if they happened yesterday. I clear my throat and stand up. "I'll get a towel."

"Thanks."

After grabbing one from the cabinet, I hand it to her. Her fingers brush mine as she takes it, and again, all those old sensations rush in. How can I still feel this way toward someone I haven't even spoken to in eight years?

After drying her foot, she stands but lets out a small yelp and starts to fall back onto her chair, which won't be a soft landing because these chairs are bare bones basic. And hard.

Instinctively, I reach out and grab her around the waist as she holds onto my shoulders. The scent of coconuts and peaches slams my senses and floods me, and I seem unable to let her go.

She tilts her head up. "That was close. Thank you."

Hmmm, too close. "Happy to help."

Callie tilts her head. "You always were back then, too."

I'm not sure what she means in light of the question I see sitting in her eyes. Is she asking me if I want to start something with her again? Or is she reliving old times like me? Either way, this is too close for my comfort at the moment.

Though reluctant to let her go, I step back. "I'm still the same guy, Callie."

She nods as a smile tugs at the corner of her mouth. "Thanks for not peeing on my foot."

I laugh. "I'm no Chandler."

She grins. "Good. 'Cuz I'm no Monica."

CHAPTER 6

Zane

Close to sixty applications cover the table in front of us. Teenagers from all over the area had applied—way more than I expected from the fluff piece that ran in the Sarabella Tribune. I reach for another application at the same time Callie does. Our hands bump as we reach for the same one.

"Sorry." Callie jerks her hand back.

I slide the application in front of her. "No need to be sorry."

"Thanks." She blinks and gives me a shy smile, something I don't recall her ever doing in the past. When I first met Callie, her boldness and sense of adventure drew me to her. Nothing about her back then fit under the label of shy.

But this is different, almost as if she's overly cautious now. I can't help but wonder what kind of experiences she's had over the last eight years that would cause that. Or who she may have been involved with. Or is it because of me? Heat spreads up the back of my neck at both thoughts.

"You're welcome." I tug another application in front of me.

A tentative peace has formed between us over the last couple of weeks, which makes me hopeful that we can pull this thing off. Not sure if the jellyfish encounter embarrassed her somehow or if the joke about me not urinating on her (which, for the record, I don't advise) broke the ice somewhat, but we seem to be on the same page, at least for now.

"What about this one?" She pushes the application she finished in front of me.

I give it a quick scan. "This one qualifies, too. Almost all of them have so far. I don't see how we can run the program with this many, not without hiring more lifeguards. And we don't have the time or the resources for that."

"I agree. How about we start with twenty and put the rest on a waiting list?"

Her suggestion makes sense, but I'm still not sure about the numbers. "Maybe. But do we pick the best suited, or first come, first serve?"

"Both."

I tilt my head, waiting for her to expand.

Callie gathers the applications and shuffles them into some kind of order. "Let's start over with them in order of the date and time stamp they applied online and filter out the ones that don't quite qualify, either because of distance and/or availability. When we reach twenty, we'll have our first crew."

"Crew? I like that."

"That's part of the program. You divide the group into teams, which I call crews, and assign them names. Kind of like Harry Potter."

I frown. "To create competition? Is that a good idea?"

"They won't be competing to stay in the program. They'll be competing to earn points, which will give them rewards, like an extra swim break or to pick the snacks for the following week. Most of the activities I created are designed to build a team mindset. Others to help them understand their own strengths and abilities."

"Yeah, I noticed that in your outline. I had some of the same thoughts jotted down in my notes when I was trying to plan a program."

Her face lights up. "Can I see them?"

"See what?"

"Your notes? What you have so far. I'd really like to see them."

"Um, sure. Just a sec." I head into my office and grab the folder I'd slowly added notes to.

When I return, Callie's already sorting the applications into two piles. "This will make things much faster. These are the first twenty applicants." She taps the stack on the left and then points to the rest. "And those we can draw from to replace any in the first group that don't qualify."

"Great." I hand her the folder as I sit back down.

As she reads my notes, I scan the first application, one I've already read and know won't be a good fit for the program. The applicant missed the part that said they had to know how to swim already. At least they were honest and admitted that they didn't.

"This is really good." Callie points to one of my favorite notations. "A mentoring system…I never thought of that."

"Just made sense. Theo was like that for me…us. Made a big difference. I just couldn't figure out how to make the numbers work. I want the program to be voluntary for the life-guards, and so far, I have ten guards on board, counting you and me."

"Then we'll double up."

Now I'm feeling skeptical again. "How would that work?"

"We use a rotation system. That way, each kid will get time with his or her mentor, especially if we integrate it into the program with delegated time."

Something sparks in me over what we're building. If we can keep working together like this, the youth program could wind up even better than I expected. "That could work."

Callie touches the tattoo on my bicep with her fingertips. "Teamwork…I noticed Nick has one, too. Do all the lifeguards have one?"

I pause, relishing the sensation of her touch. "Some. Not all.

I leave it up to them, but even if they don't, we work with that mentality. That we're a team. I've worked hard over the years to ingrain that into the program."

The main door swings open, and Nick walks in with Graham and several other guards to clock in for the afternoon shift. That's when I notice Tanner walk in behind them and head to the schedule board.

Jaw clenched, I shove back my chair. "Excuse me a moment."

Callie puts her hand over mine on the table. "Anything I can do to help?"

"No, I'll handle it." I walk over to where Tanner is standing with a confused expression.

He turns around and confronts me. "Why am I not on the schedule?"

"Let's go talk in my office."

Once inside, I close the door and sit in one of the chairs in front of my desk. I gesture to the other one. "Have a seat."

Tanner pulls the chair back some before he sits. "Fine, let me have it. I know I screwed up."

"Care to tell me what happened?" I lean forward, resting my arms on my knees.

"My car broke down." Tanner is staring at his hands in his lap.

"And your phone?"

"What about it?"

"Did it break, too?"

Tanner shakes his head and finally meets my gaze. "No, sorry. Just got caught up with getting a tow truck and forgot to call and let you know."

I sit back, unsure whether or not I believe him. "Tanner, this is the third time this has happened. Not to mention the two complaints about you sitting on my desk. I'm sorry, but I have to let you go."

He's jittery and bounces in his seat. "But I need the job."

"I understand that, but the work we do here is life and death. If you don't show, that puts a strain on the team and compromises our ability to do our jobs out there. This isn't a game."

"I never said it was," he snaps back.

"But your actions do. I told you after the second time that you were on probation. I'm sorry, but I have no choice."

Tanner sits there a moment, then, like a waterspout, shoots out of his chair and bangs out of the office, making enough noise to bring total silence to the outer room.

I rise to follow and catch only his back as he huffs out the main door. The rest of the team is silent as they look to me for what's next. "Tanner is no longer part of the team. I'll find a replacement for him as soon as possible."

Most nod or express their regret that he didn't work out before returning to their various stages of prepping to relieve the morning shift.

Nick walks over to me. "You okay?"

I cross my arms and nod. "Yeah, just part of the job I hate. Wish it had worked out better."

He pats me on the shoulder. "Me too, but you did the right thing. Lives matter."

"I know, but it still stinks."

Nick glances over his shoulder toward Callie, who has her head bent over the applications. "How's that going?"

"Pretty good, actually. We'll settle the applicants today and send out notifications. You ready for this?"

"Are you kidding? I was born for this." He laughs.

"Just don't live up to your last name."

Nick has a name you'd expect to see on a movie poster. Nick Lawless, the lifeguard who breaks all the rules. Except he doesn't. Most of the time.

"Very funny." He saunters out the door with the rest of the team to hit the beach.

That's when I realize Callie's watching me. Or is she checking out Nick?

And why does that thought make me want to slam my office door, too?

CHAPTER 7

Callie

I'm ready to pass out when I get back to Emily's place. After reading all those applications, playing a kind of collegial two-step with Zane (which worked out better than I expected, by the way), and a few hours on the beach, scoping out the best places for the youth program to operate during training and drills, I'm feeling more like a beached whale than a woman of thirty.

Emily smiles at me as I walk in. "You're just in time for dinner."

At the mention of food, my stomach growls so loud Emily's eyes widen. "Wow, when's the last time you ate?"

I pause in thought. "Lunch? Maybe?" I drop my gear by the door and drag myself to the table. "I'm beat."

"I can see that." Emily disappears into the kitchen for a moment and then comes back carrying a glass of ice water and a plate of food, which she sets down on the table in front of me.

"You're my hero." I start with the glass of water and chug down half, which tells me I didn't drink enough fluids today.

Emily giggles as she returns to the kitchen.

"Where's Aiden?" I lean to the left to get a clear view of the hallway to see if he's lurking there.

"At the coffee shop. One of his employees was a no-show."

"Hmmm, that seems to be a common theme this week." I finish the rest of my water.

Emily walks back in, carrying a second plate and another glass of ice water, which I eye right away. "Why? Did something happen today?"

"Zane had to let a guard go for the same reason."

"Wow, that's rough."

"Third offense, from what I understand."

Emily cringes. "Wow, again."

"Yeah, tough day for Zane."

She takes my glass and heads toward the kitchen again, calling over her shoulder as she walks away. "How was your day?"

"Good. We went through the applications and picked twenty for the first group. Out of sixty applications. We have a waiting list now, too."

"That's great!" Emily returns with my glass filled with ice water and a full pitcher, which she sets on the table. "In case you need more."

"You're a goddess."

She sits. "Thank you, Phoebe."

I giggle with her. "We should binge-watch *Friends* again."

"Aiden hates that show."

Mouth hanging open, I drop my fork. "What? Why? The man owns a coffee shop, for crying out loud."

"Exactly. He says he runs one all day. He doesn't want to watch one on TV."

"I guess I can understand that, but I still think he's missing out on a good thing." I shovel a large bit of fettuccine into my mouth and groan. "Speaking of good things, this is spectacular."

"You're so hungry, anything would taste good."

"Maybe, but still. This is amazing!"

A comfortable silence sits with us as we eat. Emily runs back to the kitchen to grab the salad she left in the fridge.

After filling our bowls, she settles into her seat again. "So, how are things going between you and Zane?"

"What do you mean?" I know what she's asking, but I will do anything to avoid this conversation, even if it means eating with my mouth open, which I know Emily hates with a passion.

"You know perfectly well what I mean. Are you two *getting along*." She turns her head, brows raised.

And I don't miss the implication. "We're colleagues. And we're working really well together. Kind of like old times."

"How old?"

I give her a wicked stare. "Not that old."

"Well, shoot. You just crashed my day."

"Why? What were you expecting me to say?"

She shrugs. "I don't know. Maybe that some sparks are reigniting between you."

I hold a hand over my mouth full of food as I laugh. "Awww, aren't you the romantic?"

"Hey, I'm a married woman now. I have to live vicariously through you."

I swallow and point my fork at her. "Are you telling me the romance has already died between you and Aiden? Maybe I need to move out now."

"Noooo. It's not that at all." She tosses her red hair back off of her shoulders.

"I'm just kidding, you know."

"I know. But I'm talking about that new relationship romance. You know, the squiggles in your stomach, anticipating whether things will turn into *more*."

"More?"

"Yeah, you know, a relationship that involves hand-holding and kissing."

"Zane and I have a relationship already."

"You do?" She lights up like a kid playing in the sand for the first time.

"Yeah, we're colleagues."

"I mean a romantic one."

"I know what you mean, and we tried that already, remember? I'm absolutely fine with being just his colleague." Well, not really, but I'm not telling Emily about the sneaky bit of hope I carried all the way from California with me.

"Fine. Whatever."

Now I'm feeling a tad guilty for bursting her bubble. But hey, I can't open up that place in my head yet, let alone my heart. Zane and I need to rekindle our friendship first.

"Seriously, Emily. Zane and I are fine. I'm sure, over time, we'll become friends again."

"Or more." Her voice is confident as she says this.

I snort, but inside I'm swooning just a little at the thought of feeling Zane's arms around me. I remember feeling so safe with him. No matter what came up, I always felt secure when he was in the picture.

"Do you want more fettuccine?" Emily holds her hand out for my plate.

"Yes, please." But in truth, it's not more fettuccine I want.

It's a six-foot-two, blue-eyed lifeguard who still manages to rock my world.

CHAPTER 8
Zane

The sound of my whistle blast resonates over a patch of beach occupied by a group of twenty teenagers, varying in age from sixteen to eighteen, whose expressions range from expectation to excitement. This is the moment I've dreamed about for years, and now it's real.

"Okay, everyone. Today will be about getting familiar with the beach."

Most of these kids grew up on Mango Key, which is the first hurdle I have to overcome. Familiarity leads to assumptions, and assumptions can make a lifeguard sloppy.

As I'm about to expand, Callie looks like she's about to jump in and say something, but I keep talking. "I know. You've probably spent more time than most on Mango Key Beach. However, what you don't know is that the beach is always changing."

She lifts her brows like she's asking if she can speak now.

I give a short nod. Trainings are my domain, except for the rare occasions I ask Nick to assist, so sharing the role is new territory for me, especially on the first day.

"Right. The better you know your environment, the easier you can recognize when something is amiss."

Feeling a good tease, I tilt my head toward her and lower my voice. "You think they'll know what that word means?"

Lips pursed, she continues to stare forward. "What word?"

"Amiss."

The slow swivel of her head to look at me is my first sign that I've set off her prickly side. Guess she's not in a teasing mood.

She lifts her sunglasses and makes it official. "Seriously?"

Her hazel eyes look especially fierce with the sun, making them look more greenish yellow like a wolf.

And now I'm a lifeguard on guard.

After dropping her sunglasses back in place, Callie steps forward and goes through the drill of what the whistle blows mean while I stand back, arms crossed, and appreciate the view, which isn't just about the beach at the moment. Callie's matured, grown curvier, and her long legs are more defined and toned.

Nick shuffles through the sand and stands next to me, hands on his hips. "Already ruffled her feathers on the first day?"

"I asked her if she thought the kids would know what the word 'amiss' means."

He smirks. "Even I know what that word means."

"Just trying to keep things light." First-day jitters and all.

He studies me for a moment. Nick does a pretty good job reading a beach, like reading a room. And people. Me, especially.

"Quit worrying. We've got your back." He pats his lifeguard tattoo, then lifts his chin toward Graham, who gives us two thumbs up. Eight more lifeguards spread out, watching and waiting to be called into action. Pride expands my chest at the sight of them standing at attention with expressions that mean business.

Once Callie finishes the whistle lesson, she goes through a series of bursts to test their knowledge. Isaac appears fully invested as he shoots his hand up to answer each time. Then I notice several of the other students pointing at him and whispering to each other as they laugh.

As Callie continues, I make my way around the perimeter toward the three boys, who seem distracted by Isaac. "Gentlemen, is there a problem?"

They jerk away from each other so fast one of them stumbles in the sand. "No, sir."

"Good, then pay attention."

"Yes, sir," says the one who appears to be the leader. The other two nod their heads.

I continue my circle around the group to return to the front. As I reach the opposite side, Isaac meets my gaze, but his expression is borderline stormy before he snaps his attention back to Callie.

When I return to my place up front, she gestures to me. "Zane will explain our flag system." She slaps the flags into my midsection, making me grunt.

You know what they say about paybacks…

I lift each colored flag one by one and explain their meaning and how they're used in combination, all the while keeping Callie in my peripheral vision.

Which means I'm very aware of Nick standing close to Callie and making her laugh, and it's not just the sun beating down on my shoulders that's making me hot.

Once finished, I blow my whistle again, bringing all—and I mean all—eyes on me. "Now we'll assign teams."

That's Nick's cue to come forward with the clipboard with the team assignments. I stand back as he calls out names, assigning five trainees to two lifeguards until there are four groups.

Callie blows her whistle this time. "Great! Trainees, your first assignment is to work with your lifeguards, first, to get familiar with your group, and second, to come up with a team name."

Nick joins Graham with the team they're in charge of, which

I made sure included Isaac. Whatever is going on there, I want to make sure someone has the kid's back. Especially after what I witnessed passing between those three boys, one of whom wound up in Isaac's group.

"Did you find out what those three were up to?" Callie has her head tilted toward mine, and the light breeze fills my nose with her peachy scent.

"No, just being boys, I assume. But I'll keep them in my sights."

"Me, too."

I don't miss the concern in her voice, which sends this warmth through my chest. She cares as much as I do about these kids. Plus, seeing her in her element is doing crazy things to my head, so I keep reminding myself we're just colleagues.

Nothing more. And just for the summer.

There can be nothing more between us.

She gives her whistle a short blow. "As I point to each team, shout out your name together."

Callie points to the first team on the left, which is Isaac's and Nick's team.

"Lifeguardians of the Galaxy!"

Needless to say, we all pause for a chuckle on this one. And judging by Isaac's pleased expression, I'm guessing he's the brainchild behind the idea.

"Nicely done." Next, Callie points to the next team.

"Wave Runners!"

I'm almost certain that one's an homage to *Wave Watchers* because this team, comprised mostly of girls, went flippy when they found out Callie used to work on the show.

Then to team three.

"Skimmers!"

And finally, to team four.

"Stingrays!"

After Callie finishes writing on her clipboard, she lifts her attention back to the group. "Well done, teams. Great work today. Trainers, finish things up with a swim with your team and have some fun. Tomorrow, we'll begin with drills, so get a good night's sleep, and be sure to eat a healthy breakfast in the morning that's protein based. Not sugar."

A few groans meet this. I'm guessing they're the Pop-Tart eaters.

Once they finish, a guard from each team hands Callie a sheet of paper as they pass by us. The exodus of guards and teenagers jogging to the water draws a fair bit of attention from the crowd. Several bystanders even clap. Sarabella is a small town, so word gets out fast about new programs and changes. Some of those bystanders might have come out today just to watch us train.

Callie blasts me with a smile that gives the sun competition. "That was awesome!"

I can't help but grin myself. Her excitement is contagious. "Yes, it was."

She checks her watch. "I want to get T-shirts made so we can have them ready by the end of the week."

"T-shirts?"

"Yeah, with the team names on them. Helps build a team mindset. I had the trainers get shirt sizes for each trainee. Thought it would be a great reward for their first week."

In our planning, the subject of T-shirts never came up, but I'm intrigued. "More brilliant ideas from Callie Monroe."

She double blinks. "Thanks. I assume that means you approve?"

"Completely." I didn't intend to say this with a tone that expressed my appreciation for more than just her ideas, but when she's standing this close to me, filling my senses with her peachy fragrance mixed with the scent of coconuts from her sunscreen, it's like a truth-serum cocktail.

A distinct blush spreads across her cheeks, making her freckles stand out. Our eyes lock for a moment, and that same tug that drew me in when we were dating overwhelms me again.

Nick jogs up to us, breaking the moment. Sea water is streaming down his head and face. "Hey, I think we may have a slight problem on our hands."

My gut clenches as I suspect it involves Isaac and those three boys. "Isaac?"

He nods. "One of the boys said something to him, and Isaac shoved him. That's when I intervened."

Callie glances at me as she exhales. "Where are they now?"

"I sent the other boys up to the pavilion to wait for their ride. Isaac's still by the water. I figured you'd want to talk with him."

I lift my gaze over Nick's shoulder and spot a slumped form sitting at the water's edge. Then I settle my focus on Callie. "I'll talk to him one-to-one so he doesn't feel like we're ganging up on him."

"Okay. We'll chat with the boys at the pavilion." Callie clasps my forearm. "This kind of stuff happens with teenagers. That's not an excuse. Just a reality."

I nod but say nothing as she and Nick jog together toward headquarters. A part of me would rather be where Nick is, but Isaac is more important right now. Once I reach him, I sit down on the sand next to him and hang my arms over my knees.

Silent, Isaac continues to dig rivets with a white seashell.

I squint against the sun as I swivel my head to study his expression. "Want to tell me what happened?"

He shrugs one shoulder, appearing casual except for the unmistakable flash of pain across his face. "Nothing much."

"Nick said you shoved one of the other boys. What did he say to you?"

Isaac keeps his head down. "I don't want to talk about it."

"You sure? I might be able to help." I put a hand on his shoulder for reassurance.

He shakes his head. "It'll just make it worse. Mark's a jerk."

The pieces fall into place—the group of boys I instructed to pay attention during the training. "Yeah, I kind of noticed."

Isaac finally looks at me. "That's what I mean. You told them to stop talking about me, and then he took it out on me. It always works that way. Even at school."

"Always? What's going on, Isaac?"

He gets to his feet, brushing the sand from his hands. "I have to go. Uncle Theo's waiting for me."

I'm tempted to follow him up the beach so I can talk to Theo, but I'm concerned that could make Isaac feel even more uncomfortable. A phone call later will work better. Theo can more than likely speak more freely that way as well.

A wave rushes up the sand and almost reaches me, signaling the rising tide and the impending shift change. Duty calls.

But first, a quick dip to cool my head off before I head back to the pavilion. I'm in no mood to see Callie and Nick hanging out.

CHAPTER 9
Callie

J ust when I thought I could control my attraction to Zane, he goes and does something endearing, which makes me kind of fall for him a little more again.

Yeah, I couldn't resist watching him for a moment as he sat down next to Isaac. Nick continued to the pavilion to chat with the other boys before their parents picked them up while I waited for Zane to return.

When Isaac jogged up the beach toward the pavilion, Zane stood, but he didn't come up as I expected. Instead, he dove into the water and swam freestyle toward the south end of the beach. So I went to headquarters in search of Nick, who said the boys were already gone by the time he got back up there. That talk will have to wait until tomorrow, which could prove more detrimental than beneficial, depending on how we handle things. Hopefully, Zane's talk with Isaac will help us understand what's going on.

I'm guessing Zane's feeling the situation with Isaac pretty deeply, judging by the way he strode and dove into the water. But that's the thing with teenagers. Life's always deep for them. My first year was like living in a soap opera with all the drama until I finally learned to stay objective in order to help them through whatever issue they're struggling with. That's when I noticed I had more influence, and things smoothed out.

Zane may not realize this yet.

I just hope he'll let me in a little, so I can share some of that wisdom with him.

Sitting at a table near the workout equipment, I chug down the rest of my water with electrolytes and check the window again for a glimpse of Zane's return. My notebook sits open in front of me, one page filled with notes. My usual routine after a training—examine the day's events for what went right and what could go better. Isaac's name sits alone on the next page as I think about what to write there.

"He'll be back any minute. He knows the shift is about to change." Nick stands by one of the weight machines with a small towel over his shoulder.

"Am I that obvious?"

Nick flashes a toothy smile. "That you're still stuck on Zane?"

I can feel the prickle from the middle of my back rise up my neck. "No, we're just colleagues and old friends. I'm just concerned about how things went with Isaac."

Nick lifts his chin imperceptibly as he tugs the towel off his shoulder. "Sorry, my bad. I just assumed."

"You know what Zane says about making assumptions?" I grin in an attempt to lighten the situation.

Thankfully, Nick takes the hint and grins. "Makes us sloppy. That guy has a motto for everything."

"He always has."

I point to the tattoo on Nick's left arm. "Mind if I take a closer look?"

"Not at all." He leans on the table, bringing his arm closer. The words 'Team Turtle' integrate into a tribal-looking design of a bale of sea turtles wrapping around his arm as if they're swimming. Small swirls integrate the design to mimic water.

The design fascinates me. I run a finger over the words. "Why Team Turtle?"

Nick leans his head over to look at the design, bringing his face closer to mine. "I'm part of the sea turtle patrol that the aquarium organizes every year. We have to protect the little guys. Make sure they have a chance."

"Aww, I love that." My reaction makes him grin like a Cheshire cat. If I weren't focused on Zane, I'd probably flirt a little.

The main door swings open. Zane pauses in the doorway when his eyes land on me, then flick to Nick, who's still leaning on his hands on the table next to me.

Zane's expression is like watching a storm build offshore. I'm guessing he's not thrilled that Nick and I are in close proximity at the moment. He grabs a towel off the shelf by the door and rubs down his head and bare shoulders.

I have to say, watching his muscles flex as he does this has my heart beating in my throat. The man is like the statue of David but better. If my water bottle weren't empty, I'd hold it against my neck and cheeks.

When he walks into his office, I jump up and follow him in. "How'd it go?"

"How'd what go?" He stands behind his desk and picks up a piece of paper as if he intends to read it, but I know he's trying to appear disinterested.

Years back, whenever Zane was in a mood, he would become evasive, forcing me to tug the issue out of him. Guess that hasn't changed.

I better grab the rope tight on this one. "With Isaac? Did you find out what happened?"

"No, he didn't want to talk about it. But he did refer to Mark in a way that tells me this isn't the first time they've had a run-in."

"Could this be part of what Theo was talking about?"

He wraps the towel around his waist and sits down. "I don't

know, but I'm going to find out." He picks up the phone, then looks at me as if he's waiting for me to leave.

The prickle returns. Fine, I'll bug off and let him take charge. So much for the team mentality applying to me. "Great. You can fill me in later."

I don't wait for him to reply—just leave and return to my notebook to jot some notes on a new page. About Zane and his need to always be in charge and take control. And how he can be easy-going one minute and grumpy the next. Like the rainy season in Florida—sunny one minute and stormy the next.

The man gives my emotions whiplash.

But he's also caring and loyal. To a fault sometimes. He'll work himself to bare bones for a cause if you give him one, and I suspect that's what Isaac is becoming for him.

Which puts me on a sandbar with deep sides, with the welfare of a young man on one side and the success of this youth program on the other.

And right now, I'm not sure which side to dive into.

As I'm spotting Nick on the barbell, Zane's door opens, and he waves me in. I signal Graham over to take my place and make my way to Zane's office. When I enter, he sits behind his desk and gestures to one of the seats on the other side.

I feel like I'm back in the principal's office, about to be scolded for something I considered a simple risk. Life is just more interesting that way, ya know?

"I just got off the phone with Theo." Zane's mouth is a straight line, so I'm guessing he's not thrilled about the outcome of the call.

"Does he know what's going on with Isaac at school?"

"How'd you know it had to do with school?"

I hold my hands out. "Zane, I've worked with more teenagers than there are people on the beach at the moment."

School is out for the summer, and the beach is packed. However, I'm not exaggerating. I've been doing this for a long time.

A small grin cracks his stiff expression. "Right, of course. Then you may be the one able to help Isaac most because he's not letting Theo in either."

"What about his father?"

Zane shakes his head. "They're divorced, and he lives in another state. Not much contact there, *thus* why Theo has stepped in to help."

I put my finger to my cheek and mock a confused expression. "Thus. I don't think I know what that word means. Care to enlighten me?"

He sits back in his chair, which squeaks with his movement. "Very funny."

But he *is* grinning. Mission accomplished.

I lay my hands on his desk and push to a stand. "Okay, then how about you set up some time to spend with Isaac? Maybe he'll open up."

He stares up at me. "Me? You just said you're the one with all the experience with teenagers."

"Yes, but his biggest need right now is a male influence." I wave my hands down my sides. "And in case you didn't notice, I'm not."

His eyes make a slow study of me as one side of his grin ticks up higher. "I've definitely noticed."

If they made something like sunscreen for blushing, I'd have to buy stock in the market. Even Jake didn't make me blush as much as Zane does. "That's beside the point."

He snaps forward in his seat and stands. "I beg to disagree."

I frown. What game is he playing? And why am I getting so flustered? "You beg to disagree?"

"Yes." He gestures at my midsection. "You're the one who made the point that you're not a man. I simply agreed."

I press my fingers against my eyes to let the wave of frustration pass. The man is being insufferably silly and sexy all at once. I call no fair!

After a lengthy inhale to slow my racing heart, I drop my hands. "Isaac needs you, Zane. Not me."

He drops his chin. "I have no experience dealing with a teenager."

"True, but you were one once. And you have a great father. Draw upon your own experiences there."

A warmth comes over his expression. "You remember my dad?"

"Yeah. And Sally. I always envied you, your parents."

"Things still not good with yours?"

I tip my head back because I'd rather stare at the nonde-script speck on the ceiling instead of watching Zane's reaction to what I'm about to share with him. "Let's see…Dad stopped talking to me after I told him to stop trying to run my life like I was one of his cadets. And Mom's still the dutiful military wife who's convinced everything would be just fine if my father and I had a little chat." I make air quotes to emphasize the last word.

"I'm sorry." His voice is gruff with emotion.

"It is what it is. I keep thinking—hoping once Dad retires, things might get better."

He nods but stays silent. I am, too, because, after that info dump, I don't know what to say. Zane already knows how my father felt about me becoming a lifeguard. 'Wasting my life' was the exact phrase. Even the recognition I received for the youth program I developed didn't sway his opinion much, and the gig with *Wave Watchers* just confirmed his opinion that my work is frivolous.

Probably best to just leave before I spew more. I turn toward the door and force my voice to sound upbeat. "I better get going if I want to get those shirts ordered. Unless there's something else you wanted to talk about?"

Like why we're both dancing around the attraction that's very much alive between us? But I don't think Zane has completely forgiven me for leaving. And frankly, after talking about my parents, I don't have the energy to deal with whatever this is between us.

"No, go ahead. I'll see you tomorrow." His expression appears almost crestfallen like he had more to say.

I pause for a moment, waiting. Maybe Zane *does* want to talk about it but doesn't know how?

He sits down and studies the paperwork on his desk again.

That settles it, then. The moment is gone, and I have better things to do at the moment than rehash the past.

Or wonder what Zane wanted to say but didn't.

CHAPTER 10
Callie

Sarabella may be small, but you can find just about anything here if you look hard enough. Except when you discover the only shop in town that does apparel embroidery is closed.

Permanently.

I stare at the 'For Lease' sign in the window and let out a breathy sigh.

Seriously bummed, I tug my phone out to search for another location, even if it means I have to drive off the peninsula. However, that will put a major kink in my plans for the rest of my day, which included a workout (if you don't use it, you lose it, right?) and a quiet evening with Emily and Aiden.

And that reminds me, I need to find a place to live. Staying with my best friend is fun, to a point. But I can tell Aiden has reached *that point*.

As I scroll through store listings on my phone, Emily's face and name shows up on my screen. "Hey, you, what's up?"

"I wanted to let you know that Aiden and I are going away for a few days." The tentativeness in her voice is unmistakable.

"What's up, Em?" Hand on my hip, I swivel away from the store of disappointment and scan the cute shops and businesses along Mango Lane.

"Aiden wants to go to this coffee shop he read about in St. Augustine, so we thought we'd make a trip out of it and see the sites."

"No problem. I'll water the plants and whatever else you need."

"Well, here's the thing…"

I knew something was up. "Yeeees?"

"We have termites—bad—and the place needs to be tented for a few days."

I shudder inside. Bugs are the one thing I have little-to-no tolerance for. Needless to say, one of the benefits of living in California was the lack of palmetto bugs. I shudder again just thinking about them and conclude this is confirmation that I need to find new digs.

"Lovely."

"I'm sorry."

"No worries. I'll figure something out."

"The company will be here first thing in the morning. I feel awful doing this to you, Callie."

"It's okay. Complicated seems to be the theme of my day. I'll deal."

"What's going on?"

"I had this wonderful idea to get personalized T-shirts made for the kids, but Ted's Ts isn't there anymore."

"Yeah, after Hurricane Phillipe, he decided to leave Florida. For good."

"I can understand that." Somehow I find that amusing. Me, personally, I'll take a hurricane over an earthquake any day. At least you get a heads-up on those. I've only experienced a few minor shakes during my years in California. I don't want to push my odds, you know?

"What about Amanda's shop?"

"I thought she just did flowers and gift items."

"No, she's turned her place into a real hub of service items, too. If she can't do them, she could probably tell you where to go."

"Great idea. Thanks, Em."

"Hope that makes up for making your life more complicated. At least a little bit."

"I'll take any help I can get. And don't worry about the house. I'll grab my stuff and find a place to stay tonight." Tomorrow is my day off, and I have no desire to be up at the crack of dawn. Nor do I wish to sleep in a place overrun by wood-eating bugs—who knows what they do at night.

This thought brings a shudder that shakes my entire body and makes me grunt. Good thing I already hung up with Emily. That would make her feel worse.

If memory serves me right, Amanda's shop sits at the other end of Mango Lane—a shortish walk from where I'm standing. Might as well hoof it and make that part of my exercise for the day. At the rate things are going, I may not get that workout in after all.

The bells jingle as I walk in, and the memory of seeing Zane for the first time in eight years overwhelms me. I didn't expect a warm hug that day, but I thought he'd at least say hello. So when he took one look at me and then shot out the door, I was kind of devastated. Takes a lot to bring me to tears, and that one moment made me weepy for the rest of the day.

But then Hurricane Phillipe roared in, and other priorities took over. However, that day has lingered in the back of my mind ever since. And part of the reason I reached out to Theo, suggesting Sarabella might benefit from a youth lifeguard program. Great for the small-town image and all that.

"Callie!" Amanda comes from the back room, a big smile on her face. "Aiden mentioned you were back in town. How's it going?"

Her expression says what she's not saying—*with Zane*…

"Great! Today was the first day of training with the youth, and overall, it went pretty well."

"No hiccups?" She's still fishing.

"Nothing to do with Zane, if that's what you're asking."

She tilts her head. "That obvious?"

I nod. "And understandable, considering you two are like brother and sister. I promise to be nice to your brother."

"Not too nice, I hope." She giggles. "Sometimes, he needs a good thump on the head to set him straight."

Have I found an unexpected ally? I glance down. "Yes, he's still stubborn as ever."

"Understatement of the year. So, what can I help you with?"

"Any chance you do personalized T-shirts?"

"Not here in the shop, but I have a vendor I work with who's great."

The tension in my shoulders eases. "How fast can you get them done?"

"Probably within a day or two. Will that work?"

"That's perfect." I go over the details with Amanda as she fills out the order form online with the vendor she uses.

"There. That was easy. Anything else I can help you with?"

"How about a hotel recommendation? Em and Aiden have termites, and I need a bug-free place to crash for a few nights."

"How about The Sandpiper Inn?"

"New place?"

"Kind of. It's right next door to The Turtle Tide restaurant. They might have a room available. This time of year, they get booked up fast, but you can try."

"I'll check it out. Thanks, Amanda. You've been a lifesaver today."

She laughs. "Lifesaver to a lifeguard. That's a new one for me." She walks to where I'm standing and gets that sisterly concern thing going again. "Have you and Zane had a chance to talk about things?"

"Things?" I know she means well, and I consider Amanda a friend. But I can't even talk about this stuff with Emily yet.

She smiles and gives me a hug. "Zane will come around. Just give him time."

One can only hope. But my question is, come around to what?

As I reach the door to leave, Amanda calls my name. "What are you doing tonight?"

"You mean besides finding a place to rest this weary head?"

She tilts her head as she lifts her brows. "Care to join me for dinner?"

AFTER LOADING ALL my stuff into my car—boxes too because the whole bug thing really wigs me out—I wave goodbye to Emily and head to…wait for it…

The home of Sally and Jacob Albright's, aka Zane's parents.

I said yes to Amanda's invitation to dinner before I found out the *where* and especially the *who*. It's not that I don't like Zane's parents. Quite the opposite, actually. Before I left Sara-bella, I spent a fair bit of time at the Albright home.

Especially when Zane and I started dating.

Sally became like a second mother to me, and surprisingly, she understood my desire to move to California. But that was a long time ago, and I haven't done a good job keeping in touch. I tried at first, but then, over time, I felt like I was being intrusive, asking how Zane was doing because he stopped replying to my texts. Then I just got plain busy with my new life.

But tonight, I get to indulge in Sally's famous baked spaghetti, a dish that became my measuring stick for every spaghetti dish I have eaten since first experiencing hers—a fond memory I've treasured over the years.

Of course, I had to ask if Zane would be there, too, which gave Amanda the wrong idea. I just would like to be prepared, you know? Since this will be the first time we've spent time together in a nonbusiness setting. I'm a tad nervous. That's all… really…

But why should I be, right? This is just a dinner with old

friends. I can do this. Goodness knows I picked up some mad diplomatic skills over the last two years working as a consultant with the cast and directors on *Wave Watchers*. Many a time, I wound up mediating between Jake and the director. I think that's when I knew my time there was over.

That or risk losing my sanity once and for all.

Funny…I think this is the first time I've even thought of Jake in at least two weeks.

Before I can knock, the door swings open, and Sally yanks me into a hug.

"So good to see you!" Her excitement blasts in my left ear, but I don't mind. Sally not only makes the best baked spaghetti, she's also a world-class hugger.

"Good to see you, too. Hope I'm not crashing the party."

As we part, Sally gives me this no-nonsense look that's filled with genuine care, and I'm struck by how much I've missed this.

"Are you kidding? You *are* the party, Callie. I'm so glad you're back. I'm sure Zane is, too." She steps back and turns sideways to bring all attention to her son, who's standing there with his arms crossed (as always) with a smidge of a grin that I'm sure is either his sense of decorum or to make his mother happy. Or both.

From the living room, Amanda waves and smiles at me, as does Kade.

Then Jacob walks up and gives me a brief hug. "When Zane told us you were back in town, I was surprised. But I'm glad you're back."

"Why surprised?" As soon as I say it, I want to yank the words back. Jacob isn't a big talker, and I can already see the a smidgen of panic in his expression. Like he didn't see that question coming and didn't know what to say.

Then he shrugs. "After you left, Zane told us he didn't think you'd ever come back to Sarabella." He joins the others in the living room, along with Sally, which leaves me standing there with Zane, whose arms are still crossed.

"Didn't think I'd come back, huh?"

He does a quick shake of his head. "Nope."

I decide to push the moment and step closer to him so I can lower my voice just for his ears. No need to feed the natives. "Everyone seems happy that I'm back. Except you."

His arms move to his sides at a snail's pace as a range of emotions I'm unable to interpret shifts across his face. "Because I'm pretty sure you have no plans to stay."

CHAPTER 11

Zane

H er peachy scent fills my nose as I breathe Callie in. She's
close…too close.

"I never said that." Her voice is borderline steely.

"No, but I assumed once the youth program is established,
you'd return to LA at the end of the summer. Doesn't *Wave
Watchers* resume filming then?"

I had no intention of having this conversation while
standing in the entryway of his parents' home with everyone in
the living room watching us. But here we are.

Thanks, Dad. Way to go, opening that can of worms, which
is appropriate considering my father owns a nursery and land-
scaping business.

"No, actually, I don't. I gave notice before I left."

My mother calls us to the table for dinner, preempting my
reply, which leaves me feeling somewhat peevish at myself for
being an idiot. I should know better than to make assumptions
—something I hammer into my lifeguards.

But I did, and now I have a surfboard-sized foot hanging
from my mouth.

Mom and Dad take their places at the ends of the table.
Like the excellent hosts they are. Kade and Amanda sit on one

side, which leaves the other two chairs for Callie and me. The reality that I will be sitting next to the woman, whose very nearness makes me squirm, sets my body on high alert.

And the worst part? She seems to know this and is enjoying every minute of it. Every time our arms brush, it's like I get zapped, so I move away, which brings a mischievous glance from her.

Every. Single. Time.

My mother darts her gaze between Callie and me. "How'd things go today?"

"Great," says Callie, just as I say, "Okay."

Callie glances at me, but I drop my attention to the meatball that's calling my name and shove it into my mouth.

She tilts her head as she expounds. "Overall, it went really well. We just had a minor hiccup with a few of the boys."

Mom's happy demeanor shifts to concern. "Was Isaac one of them?"

I swallow my half-chewed meatball. "What made you think Isaac had anything to do with it?"

Mom stares at me as if I've said the most ridiculous thing possible. "Did you forget Bettina and I are friends?"

Theo's wife. Maybe I kind of did, but that's beside the point. I run a hand down my face. "It just happened today."

"She came into the shop today, and we chatted for a while. She's really concerned about Isaac."

My mother owns The Pink Hibiscus, which is a clothing boutique on Mango Lane. She's owned and run it for years, so she always has a leg up on the latest news and occasional gossip in Sarabella.

Callie leans into the conversation. "Does she know what's going on with Isaac?"

Distracted from eating, my mother continues to twirl spaghetti on her fork. "One of the boys at school seems to have it out for him. Sounds like it has something to do with a girl."

"Doesn't it always," I mutter under my breath, but Callie's

kick under the table tells me I spoke louder than I thought. When I look up, Kade shoots me a warning glance, but I can tell he's trying not to laugh.

I clear my throat. "Did she happen to say the boy's name was Mark?"

Callie frowns at me. "You think it's the same boy?"

"Could be."

Sally shakes her head as she twirls her fork again. "She didn't mention any names. Just that she thinks they're both interested in the same girl."

"That'll do it." Kade pipes in, which garners him an elbow poke from Amanda.

Kade locks mirthful eyes with me for a long second, confirming I have a comrade at arms.

The rest of the dinner continues with light talk and concludes soon after, which I'm grateful for. Sitting so close to Callie, feeling the warmth of her so close, turned into a bigger distraction than I expected. So when we moved to the living room after dessert, I made sure I chose a chair and not the couch where Callie sits, nestled into a corner.

My mother talks us into a round of charades for the next half hour until I notice Callie yawn. She has this sleepy, peaceful expression that creates a pocket of warmth in my chest.

After we guess Amanda's word, I rise from my seat. "I better get going. Tomorrow starts early for us."

Amanda turns to Callie. "Did The Sandpiper have a room?"

Callie shakes her head. "No, their last room just went to someone here for the entire summer, so I made a reservation at the Best Western."

"That's not even on the peninsula."

"I know. I should have taken Theo up on his offer to arrange something for me. But it's just for a night or two until I find something more permanent."

My mother steps into the conversation, and I suspect she's

shifted into problem-solver mode because that's what she's great at. "What's wrong with Emily's place?"

"Termites." Callie and Amanda answer at the same time, like two sisters who've known each other a long time. And that's what this evening has felt like. A family gathering that Callie has always been a part of. She fits in now just like she always did.

The realization dumbfounds me for a moment.

"Why don't you stay in Zane's old room?" As my mother says this, my father is nodding in agreement.

Callie hesitates. "I don't want to put you guys out."

Mom makes her signature *pftt* sound and waves her off. "Don't be silly. You're like family. Stay as long as you want or need. It's way more convenient than staying at the Best Western."

Callie rises to her feet. "Well, in that case, yes. Thank you. I really appreciate it. I'll go get my stuff out of the car."

My mother does a light clap of her hands. "Good. Zane can help you."

Mom shoots me a look to make sure I do as I'm told. Like I'm still a teenager with pimples and a bad attitude, which I have to admit, I kind of behaved like one tonight. I consider myself a confident guy. Not much ruffles my feathers because, like my mother, I'm a problem solver. Much less waste of energy that way.

But since Callie showed up, I've been off my game. And I don't like it.

As I walk out the front door, my mother's eager voice pipes up again.

"Callie, before I forget. You have to come to my birthday party next month. We're planning a big shindig at The Turtle Tide."

"I'd love to. Thanks for inviting me."

"Of course. It's going to be so much fun. And I'm hiring a band, so wear your best party dress and be prepared to dance."

Callie's laughter follows me down the sidewalk as I head

toward her car. The California plate on the front end reminds me of where she came from, but I'm still not convinced she's here to stay.

Kade and Amanda offer to help, so between the four of us, we unload Callie's suitcases and stack her few boxes in my old room, which sounds weird to call it that because it looks nothing like it used to, and I haven't slept here in years. But thinking of Callie sleeping here does weird things to my insides.

After a brief chat outside, Kade and Amanda take off, and Callie follows me to my Jeep, but my conscience won't let me leave yet. "Listen, I'm sorry for being a bit of an idiot tonight."

"Yes, you were. But thank you for apologizing." Her tone is teasing, but then she drops her gaze a moment. "Do you want to talk about it?"

"Why? I think admitting I was an idiot is enough."

"No, I mean this tension between us. You clearly resent me still."

I want to deny it, but it's true. But not for what she thinks. I'm mad that I'm still drawn to her as if no time has passed between us. That makes me wonder what we could have had. And I'm mad at myself for still feeling like I could fall for her all over again.

"Callie, let's leave the past in the past, okay?"

"Zane, I had to go and figure myself out. You get that, right?"

"Yeah, I do. I did then, too. But that didn't make it hurt any less." Telling her this is hard, but necessary, I think. Yet the unshed tears I see in her eyes make me second-guess my honesty.

She nods. "And I'm so sorry for that. But if I stayed, I would have made us both miserable."

"We'll never really know for sure, though, will we?" I sound a tad bitter, even to myself.

And it's like a standoff, me standing there, staring at her, and her staring back at me. I'm at a loss for words, and her silence tells me she is, too.

She tips her head back as she exhales. Moonlight highlights the silky smoothness of her neck before she drops her chin. "You're right. Let's leave the past in the past."

"Good. I'm glad you agree." I extend my hand. "Truce?"

"Truce." She slips her hand into mine—the most we've touched since she arrived, not counting her foot after the jelly-fish encounter. For a moment, I'm tempted to pull her to me, so I can bury my face in her neck, but I resist. The last thing we both need is to complicate this any further. Besides, I don't even know if she's interested in me like that anymore.

After she left eight years ago, I threw myself into my work, taking the lifeguard program to the next level once Theo handed me the reins. The first few months, I was numb. The next few months after that, I was angry. By the end of the first year, I shoved the past into a box that I never opened again.

Literally. Pictures, things I'd saved—all of it, shoved into a box and packed away so long ago I don't know where it is or if it still exists.

Like I said, the past needs to stay in the past.

For both our sakes, the best thing Callie and I can be for one another right now is colleagues. Perhaps friends over time. Nothing more.

But that may be easier said than done.

CHAPTER 12
Callie

O nce Zane helped bring my suitcases to his old room, he kissed his mother on the cheek and left without even saying goodbye.

I don't blame him. What he said to me was…hard, but in a way, I deserved it. I wish I knew then what I know now because I could have told Zane how scared and confused I was back then. I grew up with a father who wanted to control every aspect of my life. Although Zane is nothing like him, staying in Sarabella felt like I would be letting another man control my life. And the last thing I wanted was to wind up resenting Zane like I did my father.

So I moved away. Pursued one adventure after another until I realized I still wasn't satisfied. Then I discovered my passion for working with teens, helping them figure out who they are and what they want out of life.

Something I wish someone had done for me.

I understand this now, but it took me a few years and some therapy to figure myself out.

As I dump a handful of underwear and bras into a drawer, I hear a knock.

Sally stands in the open doorway, a hesitant smile on her face. "Sorry to interrupt."

I snort. "Not possible. Unpacking is worse than packing, I think."

"Need any help?"

"No, that's the last of it." I drop a stack of T-shirts and shorts into another drawer, then drop onto the queen-sized bed next to my empty suitcase. "Thank you again for the room."

"Not a problem. That's what it's here for. After Zane moved out, I turned it into a guest room. It's come in quite handy."

"You always were great at taking care of people in need. Including me."

Sally pushes away from the door frame and sits down next to me. "Of course. We loved you, Callie. You were—are like family."

Her words bring back my regrets. "I'm sorry I didn't keep in touch. I didn't know if I should."

"I understand. Zane was pretty hurt." Sally puts her arm across my shoulders and gives me a hug.

"Yeah, he told me." I tuck my chin, remembering the words he spoke.

"He did? I didn't think you two talked much after you moved."

"I meant tonight. When we went to my car to get my stuff."

She purses her lips as she thinks. "He forgets you were hurting, too."

I snap my head up. "How did you know?"

"Are you kidding? I could see it in your eyes every time you came over, how unhappy you were. I wasn't surprised when you decided to leave." Sally shifts on the bed to face me and takes her hands in mine. "And Zane did, too, Callie. I think he was more hurt by the fact that you didn't talk to him about your feelings."

My eyes are burning as I lift my shoulders. "I didn't know

how. Just seemed best if I left. Now I understand it was more out of fear. But that's another story."

She squeezes my hands. "I know, and anytime you want to talk, I'm happy to listen, okay?"

I brave a smile for her. "Thanks."

Sally rises to leave, but then pauses in the doorway, thoughtful, as if she's considering her words. "Zane will come around. Just give him time."

Amanda said the same thing, and these two women know him better than I do. I nod, hoping they're right because Sarabella feels like home. Eating dinner with Zane and his family felt familiar and comforting. I missed all of it more than I realized.

She waggles her fingers at me as she shuts the door.

I fall back on the bed with a groan. My phone chirps next to me. A text from Emily.

> Did you find a place to stay?

> > Yes, but you won't believe where…Zane's old bedroom.

> At Sally's?

> > Does Zane have more than one old room?

> Uh, sarcastic much?

> > Ha ha…as much as I can get away with.

The moving dots appear, then disappear, so I wait.

> You okay?

> > I'm good. No worries.

> Okay, see you in a few days.

> > Have fun!

As I'm about to drop my phone on the bed, it chirps again. Emily better not ask me to check on the house because I am going nowhere near that place. Perhaps ever again.

Except it's not from Emily. It's from Zane.

I'm sorry.

For what?

For leaving like I did.

I thought that was my MO. You thief.

Very funny. Still...

It's okay. We good?

Always. Night...

Night

Well, at least that's smoothed over. Still have the rest of what's sitting between us, but at least this is a start. And he did say 'always.' Maybe Sally's prediction about Zane coming around is already happening. I know we have other things to talk about, but small steps count. And I count this one as a better-than-average small step.

I lower my phone and stare at the ceiling, imagining Zane doing the same thing in this room for years. Somehow, it makes me feel closer to him. To share the same space and history he once did. One way or another, I have to show Zane that I'm invested not only in this program succeeding but also in rebuilding our friendship.

Beyond that...well, a girl can hope, right?

By the time I reach headquarters in the morning, Zane and Nick are already setting up in the area we cordoned off for today's drills. A few other trainees have already arrived—all girls —and they're huddled in deep conversations and giggles at the moment.

That leaves Isaac sitting off to the side at one of the pavilion tables by himself.

"Hey, Isaac. How's it going?"

He bobs his head up and down. "Good."

"Yeah? Enjoying the program?"

"Sure."

I slide onto the bench opposite him. "Good. Glad to hear it. Hey, do you have any suggestions so far? Anything you think might help the program? The kids in Cali are a little different."

He gives me a wide-eyed look at first, and I understand his surprise. Most teens are when I take this approach, which I do to build ownership in the program.

An invested teen stays interested and involved.

I almost sound like Zane, spouting one of his mottos.

Shifting into what is obviously an attempt to appear cool and detached, Isaac shrugs. "I don't know. It's only been one day…" His expression shifts, and it's like a metaphorical thought bubble appears over his head. "Will we be doing anything with partners?"

"We will next week. Do you like that idea?" I pose this question to give him a chance to express any concerns he might have, completely expecting him to say he didn't want to be partnered with Mark, which would be totally understandable.

Then he glances over at the group of girls standing near headquarters with a visible blush.

He drops his gaze to his hands on the table. "Yeah, sounds okay."

Evidently, Isaac is interested in one of the girls, of which I make a mental note. I'm tempted to ask more questions, but it's too soon.

"Good. Glad to hear it. If you get any other good ideas, be sure to let me know, okay?"

And that's when I get what I'd hoped for.

A smile.

It's small but nonetheless there. "Okay."

I rise from the seat. "I'll see you out there."

As I turn and step away from the table, I run smack into a wall of muscle. Zane's specifically.

"Oops. Sorry." I try to move back, but Zane still has a steadying hold on my waist, which he seems reluctant to release.

For a split second—if that—his gaze locks onto mine. Brief but potent.

He lets go and chuckles. "I'll give you better warning next time."

Next time?

Hmmm, sounds promising. I gesture toward Isaac. "I was just chatting with Isaac to see if he had any suggestions for the program."

Zane's frown is subtle at first, but his shift to a smile is admirable. Tells me he's processing my presence here. "I was just about to ask him for some help myself."

I don't know if Zane is playing along or was truly on his way to ask Isaac for help. Doesn't matter because Isaac's confidence just got a major boost, judging by the way his head popped up and his shoulders went back.

"I guess we're on the same page today." My meaning is subtle, but I'm pretty sure Zane will get my drift.

He gives me a tight smile. "Definitely." Then he returns his attention to Isaac. "I could use some help setting up an obstacle course. You interested?"

"Yeah, totally." Isaac jumps up and darts over to Zane's side.

Zane points to where several of the team are working to set up things. "Tell Nick I sent you over to help. I'll be right there."

I catch Isaac's attention and point to the group of girls. "Can you tell them to head out, too?"

"Uh, sure." His expression is hesitant at first, but I see a hint of confidence lurking behind his brown eyes.

As the group of teens jogs away, Zane turns to me. "What was that about?"

"I think Isaac has a crush on one of those girls. I was just giving him a reason to interact with them. You know, a confidence booster."

"I mean before that. You were talking to Isaac. I thought I was the one supposed to be connecting with Isaac."

"You are. I was simply building ownership."

"Ownership?" Zane takes his usual crossed-arms stance.

I start to do the same, but stop myself and move my hands to my hips. I don't want Zane to feel like I'm challenging him. "Page eighteen in the syllabus. Connecting a teen to the program through responsibility creates ownership, which keeps them interested, involved, and committed."

He seems to chew on what I said for a few seconds before lowering his arms. "I don't think I read that part yet, but I'll make a point of it."

Call me crazy, but I think I see a hint of admiration in his eyes. A zing of pleasure shoots through me as if I won the first round of a battle.

Another small step in the right direction.

My direction.

CHAPTER 13

Zane

After we finished with drills, Nick and the rest of the team surprised the kids with hot dogs up at the pavilion to celebrate our first week of training. I ducked into my office to finish reading Callie's syllabus, something I meant to do much sooner.

As I finish reading the section she mentioned this morning and the rest of what she calls 'mental health building and affirmation,' I sit back in my chair, more affected by her words than I thought possible. As I suspected, I saw and heard Callie's heart in all of it.

And not just the Callie I knew back then.

I have a better understanding and grasp of what she's overcome. My respect for her has doubled, at least. And I'm feeling like I'm due a slice of humble pie. I had no doubts Callie could create a good program, but now I realize I secretly doubted her ability to create an outstanding program, unlike anything I've seen.

Likely out of my typical need to be in control of everything —something I recognize in myself and have tried to get better about, especially when I ask Nick to step in at times.

But she exceeded 'good' by a long shot. I know I told Theo

that first day that I thought Callie's design was brilliant. Now I genuinely believe it. One hundred percent.

And I'll grudgingly admit, it's way better than anything I could have come up with.

Humble pie. One generous helping, please.

"Brought you a hot dog." Nick sets down a foot-long doused in ketchup, mustard, and onions in front of me.

The smell wafts up my nose and makes my mouth water. My stomach growls in response, so I oblige by taking a large bite.

"Thanks," I mumble through a mouthful of flavors exploding in my mouth. The pavilion café has the best dogs in town.

"I think the kids had a great time with the course we created. Especially the part in the water."

I swallow my bite. "Yeah, they did. Let's make sure we incorporate more water drills next week. I think they're ready for it."

Nick sits in one of the chairs in front of my desk. "Callie is really amazing."

My hand holding the promise of my next bite pauses in anticipation of where this is going. "Yeah, she is."

"So, I was wondering how you'd feel about me asking her out."

My gut clenches, letting me know lunch is over. I put the hot dog down. "Why are you asking me?"

Nick holds his hands up. "Well, you know…you two used to go out."

"That was eight years ago."

"I know, but I'm trying to respect your space, man."

His exasperation makes me chuckle. Yes, I'm enjoying his discomfort, but I also want to be reasonable. I can't put a claim on Callie. I never could.

"Do you think that's wise? To date someone you work with?"

"You and Callie did it."

"Yeah, and look what happened."

He dons a wry grin. "Good point. Guess I didn't think this through."

"Guess not. Glad you did now." Inside, I'm fist-pumping because I don't want to be that guy. You know, the one that acts all jealous when another guy shows interest in a girl he likes.

I mean, woman, and Callie is all woman from her sandy blonde hair to her long legs.

Plus, Nick's kind of a serial dater. I'm not keen on him adding Callie to his list.

Nick appears lost in thought.

"Still thinking, or are we done here?"

He snaps up from his seat. "Done. Thanks for the talk." He saunters out and grabs an apple from the fruit bowl sitting on the counter.

I shake my head and chuckle to myself. The guy may be a little light upstairs sometimes, but he's a stellar lifeguard and friend.

"Knock knock." Callie leans into the doorway.

I wave her in. "What's up?"

"I just got a text from Amanda that the T-shirts are ready. Mind if I head out now to get them?"

"Not at all." I check my watch. Shift changes in fifteen minutes. And I have an idea. "I'll go with you?"

She pulls her head back and draws her brows together. "With me?"

"Yeah. Like in the same car. We drive over together, and I give Amanda a check to pay for the shirts. Unless you were planning to eat the cost."

"No…I just planned to give you a receipt."

"This will be more efficient. Just give me a few minutes to take care of this." I gesture to the hot dog.

Callie shoots me a look that tells me she's suspicious. "Sure. No problem. Take your time." She walks away and sits down in the break area, and then starts scrolling on her phone.

Appetite restored, I wolf down the rest of my lunch, grab

my keys, and close the door to my office. But before we leave, I walk over to where Nick is signing out for the day. "Can you do me a favor?"

"Yeah, sure. Whatcha need?"

"I want to empty that storage room and make it an office for Callie. Feel up to helping me this weekend?"

Nick studies me for a moment. "Yeah, sure. Anything for Callie, right?" He raises his brows with his question, and his eyes tell me he's on to me.

Guess Nick isn't a dim bulb after all.

And yes, I'm having a second helping of humble pie.

WE'RE both silent on the ride to Amanda's shop, but it's not uncomfortable. I remember that from when we were dating. Callie loved to try new things and get crazy sometimes, but she also had this way of bringing peace to any situation. Especially me.

And I've missed that—a lot.

Once I park outside of Bloomed to Be Wilde, Callie hops out of my Jeep and starts up the walkway to the shop.

I grab the company checkbook, then scurry to catch up with her. "Hey, what's your hurry?"

She stops and turns around with one hand on her hip. "Were you and Nick talking about me?"

I do the proverbial skid to a halt with my hands in the air and mouth hanging open. "Whoa, where did that come from?"

"You walked over to Nick and said something before we left." So much for peaceful Callie. This one's on the warpath.

"What makes you think it was about you?"

"The way he looked at me after you turned around."

"Can't a guy look at you without you jumping to conclusions?"

"He wanted to ask me out, didn't he? And you told him not to."

"I did not." As I say the words, I realize I've been tricked and grimace.

She gives me a satisfied grin. "Thanks for confirming that for me. And I can deal with my love life just fine without you interfering." She spins around and climbs the steps to the flower shop.

I launch over the steps and grab her arm. "I only suggested dating someone you work with might be a bad idea. That's all. It had nothing to do with me."

"That's right. It has nothing to do with you."

You could cut a piece of paper with the edge in her voice. But now I'm getting riled. "It does when it affects how my guards operate. A distracted guard is—"

"An ineffective guard. Yes, yes, I remember your motto well. Didn't seem to deter you from coming after me back then." She suppresses a grin.

Is she enjoying this? The sparring?

Because I think I am…

"If memory serves me right, you're the one who started things when you kissed me."

"Your memory is flawed. I seem to recall you're the one who dove into the water after me."

The bells on the door jingling grab our attention. Amanda is standing in the doorway, shaking them to get our attention. "Do I need to call the police or book you two a room?"

Callie blushes. "Sorry, Amanda. Zane and I are just having a bit of a…"

I chime in. "Disagreement."

Amanda blurts a short laugh. "If you say so. I assume you're here to pick up the T-shirts?"

"Thanks for letting me know they're ready." Callie follows Amanda into the floral shop, past a table covered with an array of beach and summer items.

I stand off to the side, arms crossed and still bristling. That is until Amanda frowns, then mimics my crossed arms when Callie isn't looking. I shoot her a confused expression and hold my hands out, mouthing 'what'?

Callie unfolds the shirts to compare the sizes to her list. "These came out so great, Amanda. Thank you for getting them done for us."

"My pleasure. The names are so cute."

"The teens will love them. A great memento from the program."

As I write the check, Amanda and Callie start chatting about everything and nothing, which makes me kind of a third wheel.

"While you ladies chat, I think I'll head over to the coffee shop. Want anything?"

They both decline.

I give Amanda a questioning look. "Not even a piece of banana bread? I know how much you love it."

She pats her stomach. "A little too much. And it's bathing suit season."

"Okay, I'll tell Aiden he's lost his best customer for the summer."

Amanda swats my arm. "Don't you dare. I didn't say I wasn't eating it at all. Just cutting back."

I turn my attention to Callie. "Meet you at the Jeep in a few minutes?"

"You bet."

Amanda asks Callie a question about the latest episode of *Wave Watchers*, and that's my final cue to leave.

Over at The Last Bean, Aiden greets me with a friendly smile. At least someone is happy to see me, even if it's because I'm a customer. "Hey there, Zane. What can I get you?"

"Iced Americano with an extra shot." Figuring the ladies need a little more time to list all my faults, I sit at a table and catch up on emails.

Several minutes later, Aiden walks over with my coffee and slides into the seat opposite me.

"How's the summer program going?"

I slip my phone back into the side pocket of my shorts. "Great. How're those termites?"

"Gone, thankfully, but I'm not looking forward to the repairs."

"Let me know if you need help."

Another customer walks in, bringing Aiden to his feet. "Trust me, I will."

As he takes his place behind the counter again, my phone dings—a text from Callie, letting me know she's waiting by my Jeep.

I grab my coffee and head outside. Callie's leaning against the Jeep, a bag at her feet. I unlock the doors and slide in at the same time she does.

"Should I drop you off at Mom's?"

"I need to get my car." She sounds distant, so now I'm wondering what exactly she and Amanda talked about.

"Okay, I'll take us back. I have more work to do, anyway."

"Wait." Callie holds her hand out to stop me from starting the engine. "Can we talk for a minute?"

I drop my hand holding the keys and sit back in my seat with an exhale. "Okay, what's up?"

Concern riddles Callie's expression, which makes my insides knot up, especially since I don't have a clue what's got her upset.

She swivels her head to look at Amanda's shop before returning her gaze to me, eyes moist with unshed tears. "After I moved away, I tried to keep in touch with you, but you stopped replying to my texts. And then, last year, when you walked into Amanda's shop and saw me, you left without saying a word to me."

"Cal…"

She wipes her eyes. "I want to be here…working with you,

Zane, but if you still resent me for moving away, then I'm not sure how this is going to work."

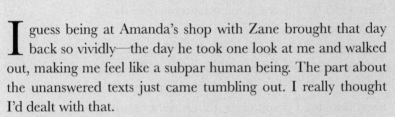

CHAPTER 14

Callie

I guess being at Amanda's shop with Zane brought that day back so vividly—the day he took one look at me and walked out, making me feel like a subpar human being. The part about the unanswered texts just came tumbling out. I really thought I'd dealt with that.

But in light of his honesty with me the other night, I felt like I should do the same. I understand Zane's thinking about leaving the past in the past—a typical guy solution to fix the situation—but clearly, the tension between us says otherwise.

Zane opens his mouth, then closes it. The muscle along his jaw pulses as he stares out the windshield.

"You were honest with me the other night, so I thought I should do the same." But part of me wishes I could rewind this day and start it over.

"I'm sorry, Callie." He turns to face me, and I can see by his expression that he's genuinely upset. "I didn't mean to hurt you. Seeing you…was unexpected. I didn't know what to say. As for the texts…" He shakes his head. "I just thought it would be easier."

I nod and tuck my chin. He was hurt. I was hurt. We were

both hurting. "Apology accepted. And thank you for hearing me out."

He turns his head toward his side window.

I rest my hand on his arm. "I mean it, Zane."

He whips his head around and stares at my hand on his arm. A battle is waging in those blue eyes of his, and I suspect I'm at the middle of it.

"Are you sure you've forgiven me for leaving?" I'm waiting for him to look at me because then I'll see for sure if he's still angry.

"The past is the past." His voice sounds rough, almost pained.

"That's not what I'm asking. If we're going to work together, there can't be any resentment hanging over us."

He nods. "I'm trying."

I lean back in my seat. "Well, I guess that's a start."

We stay silent on the drive back to headquarters, and I'm second-guessing myself the entire way there. Maybe I was an idiot, thinking I could make things right between us. As much as I'd love to stay in Sarabella and make a real go of it here, I can't stand the thought of us acting like a couple on the verge of a divorce.

Because that's kind of what it feels like. Not that I have any experience in that area. But I have watched a coldness settle between my parents over the years, and that is not something I want to emulate.

If Zane and I can't make this work…I may have to leave at the end of the summer.

The thought settles like a barb in my heart because the one thing I regret losing the most with Zane is our friendship.

Once we're back at the beach and head toward the pavilion, we have to weave our way through a crowd of people. Excited chatter surrounds us as we push our way into lifeguard head-quarters.

I seek out Nick, who's standing by the fridge with a bottle of water in his hand. "What's going on?"

Zane brushes up behind me, sending a shiver over my shoulders. And like a slow-motion vignette in a film, Nick walks over and hands the water to a man I never expected to see in Sarabella. Never. Ever.

"Hi, Callie." Jake walks over and pulls me toward him, and before I can react, he kisses me. "I missed you."

My shoulders almost touch my ears as I do this kind of hunching thing to lean away from him because he's still holding my upper arms. "Jake, what are you doing here?"

He's positively giddy with excitement. "Are you surprised?"

"You could say that." I glance over at Zane who's looking at Jake like a man-eating tiger, ready to pounce.

"I'm here for the rest of the summer." He runs his hands down my arms to hold my hands. Unlike Zane's warmth, Jake's makes me want to run for the ocean.

"Why?"

"Ratings are slipping, so I told the producer we should add a storyline about a youth program. Like the one you designed in real life. And he loved the idea. So here I am, to shadow you for the next few weeks and see how it all works." He finally releases me and holds his hands out with this big grin on his face that says we should all be as ecstatic about this as he is.

Then his gaze sweeps over everyone in the room to either confirm everyone feels the same or he's looking for attention. Or both.

I'm speechless. And I think every bit of saliva has hightailed it back to where it came from. Want to talk about your worst nightmare? I think I just discovered mine.

His attention later focuses on me again. "Isn't this great?"

Zane leans forward, hand extended. "Zane Albright, director of the lifeguard program."

I continue to stand there, dumbfounded.

Jake pumps Zane's hand with both of his. "Great to meet you, Zane. Hope you don't mind me barging in like this."

My tongue finally starts working. "Jake, you should have called and checked with us first."

He frowns and dons this look of incomprehension as he gestures to himself. "Callie-girl, it's me. I thought you'd be thrilled."

I glance around and take in a room full of lifeguards staring at me. Must be almost shift change, which means the shift out on the beach will soon know about Jake as well. Right now, I want to crawl into a hole like one of the sand crabs on the beach. My cheeks are burning beyond belief, and Zane's face just might be redder than mine. Any more of this, and steam will shoot from his ears.

Worst. Nightmare. Ever.

Zane moves from behind me and forces a toothy grin onto his face that reminds me of a shark. "Perhaps we should take this into my office."

I suck in a breath as if I just came back to life. "I think that's a great idea."

We file into Zane's office with a mumble of whispers behind us. Jake and I sit in the chairs in front of Zane's desk while he lowers himself into his chair with obvious reluctance.

Jake holds my hand. "It's so good to see you, Callie-girl."

What do I say to that? Because seeing Jake again is in no way *good* for me. I pull my hand away under the guise of pulling my hair into a ponytail. "This is quite a surprise, Jake."

I brave a glance at Zane, who's studying me, most likely trying to figure out what Jake means to me.

Jake bounces his dark eyes between us. "Hey, listen, I know this is unexpected—"

I snort. "Understatement of the year."

His smile slips as he sits back in his chair, appearing almost offended. "Look, if this is too intrusive, I'll go back to Cali and line myself up with one of the programs there."

Zane's brows draw together in a serious frown. "Why didn't you just do that to begin with?"

Great question. I'm glad one of us is thinking clearly.

Jake rests his arms on his knees as he answers Zane. "I thought about it, but Callie and I have a history together. She gets me. We work well together. And she's the best at what she does. I want that for our show."

Then he turns to me. "By the way, Steve said you're welcome back anytime." His demeanor shifts to appear modest, something I've seen enough times to recognize the ploy for what it is. "I, uh, told him we'd be crazy not to keep the door open for you, which he totally agreed with."

"And I told Steve I was done. I don't want to do the show anymore." It's all too much for me at the moment. "Go back to California, Jake. We're just getting the youth program up and running. You'll be too much of a distraction."

He tucks his chin for a moment, and I know he has something up his sleeve.

"You know, I brought that up with Mayor Stringer when I spoke to him about it, and he seemed to think we could downplay my presence here. Maybe make me one of your training staff so the kids get used to me being there."

And there it is—the ticking time bomb he waited to drop until he needed it.

My head feels like it's about to explode. I shoot a distressed plea for help at Zane.

His face turns so red again that he looks like he spent the day on the beach without sunscreen. "You spoke to Theo Stringer about this?"

Jake smiles and nods. "Yes, but I asked him not to say anything. I wanted it to be a surprise." His voice goes up an octave, and he grins at me like a kid at Christmas. "Big surprise, right Callie-girl?"

I'm ready to puke. "Oh, the biggest ever."

AFTER THE DUST SETTLES SOME, I can't get out of there fast enough. I need time to think and figure things out. As I walk to my car, Jake comes alongside me. "I've really missed you, Callie."

I fumble in my bag for my sunglasses. "I really wish you'd called first, Jake. This isn't ideal."

Before I can open my car door, Jake grabs hold of my forearms again. "What do you mean? It's perfect. You and I get to work together again."

"And I told you I was done with that life."

Jake didn't understand it then, and he clearly doesn't now.

"But we make a great team, Callie-girl."

I shrug out of his hold. "Stop calling me that."

When I was still starstruck to be the object of his attention, I made the mistake of telling Jake my father used to call me that. He latched onto it, convinced I would find it endearing, and has used it ever since.

"I thought you liked when I called you that?"

"No, Jake, I don't. In fact, I hate it. And while we're at it, stop kissing me. We're not a couple anymore. And besides, you're engaged! Or did you forget about your *fiancée* in this grand plan of yours?"

Jake appears genuinely stricken for a moment. "Debra dumped me last week."

Oh…that's what this is about. Like I said, every time one of his relationships fails, he comes running back to me.

"I'm sorry to hear that, but coming here and wreaking havoc with my life will not make that better. We're over. We have been for a while, in case you didn't notice." I yank my car door open and get in.

Jake grabs the door frame, holding it open. "I'm not here to start things up with you again, Callie-gir—Callie. I promise. But I need your help."

Closing my eyes, I tip my head back on the headrest and groan. "Dare I ask?"

"I wasn't joking when I said ratings have slipped. There's talk of canceling the show if we don't get viewers back."

"Then move on to something else. You must have a dozen offers waiting in the wings."

"You would think, but sadly no." He tucks his chin against his chest as he pinches the bridge of his nose. His voice mellows, which only happens on the rare occasion when he's being vulnerable. Or in a romantic scene on the show. "The competition is stiff. If I can get one more successful season out of *Wave Watchers* and leave on my own terms, the spin will be entirely different."

And just like that, I'm sucked into his agenda again. Maybe if I help Jake get his life back on track, he'll get out of mine. I clench my steering wheel and growl. "Fine, I'll talk to Zane and figure out the least disruptive way to do this."

His face lights up as he puts his hands together in front of him. "Thank you. I promise you won't regret it."

But I already am. And I fully intend to call Theo and give him a verbal thrashing. I'm sure Zane is on the phone with him now.

As I close my door, Jake jogs around to the passenger side and gets in.

I'm sure I look like one of those memes where the character's eyes are bugging out. "What are you doing?"

"I figured you could give me a ride to my hotel. I'm still waiting for the car rental to find me a convertible. Can't be in a place like this without the top down, you know?"

For the thousandth time, I wonder again what I ever saw in this man.

"Fine. Where are you staying?"

"This cute bed and breakfast called The Sandpiper Inn. Know the place?"

My teeth clench as I try not to yell at him. He must be the

one who booked their last room for the summer. Presumptuous idiot. "I've heard of it."

"Great. I really appreciate it." He rolls down his window to hang his arm out and leans his head back, eyes closed. Like a dog going for a ride with its owner. Except I have no intentions of taking care of this dog. "I don't know how you can stand not having a convertible, Cal."

Right now, I'm wishing I had one of those seat ejector buttons like they have in the Bond movies. I'd be pushing it like mad.

I muster up some sarcasm. "I suffer through it."

He pats my hand as I shift into reverse. "And you do it so well."

As I drive past the pavilion, I notice Zane standing just outside the door to headquarters, arms crossed in his usual stance. I'm guessing he witnessed my entire exchange with Jake.

The timing of this couldn't be any worse. It's like a dark comedy of disastrous events.

Zane and I didn't get to really finish our discussion about him forgiving me. Although, I'm not completely sure what else we had to say on that front. Feels more like we're at a stalemate.

Jake shows up just as we're getting the youth program off the ground, and I can only imagine how his presence is going to affect the teenagers. Mainly the girls because they're the demographic *Wave Watchers* appeals to most.

What else could possibly go wrong?

CHAPTER 15

Callie

I know it's a dream, but it's glorious.

Zane and I are laughing together and hanging out on the beach. The sun is setting as he takes my hand and leans in closer. But instead of kissing me, he opens his mouth and lets out a chirping sound, like a bird. And then another. And another...

I peek my eyes open to see the first hints of sunlight streaming around the blinds and reach for my phone. Then I groan and slap it down on the covers.

That chirping sound? A string of texts from Jake, asking what kind of attire he needs for Monday and where to go. Couldn't the guy just bring something from wardrobe?

But no, he wants all new stuff, so he blends in. Of course, he does. And then he's begging me to come with him to make sure he doesn't get anything out of line.

That's when I give up and throw aside my cozy covers and let go of my plans to have a relaxing day off.

When I reach The Sandpiper Inn, press trucks line the front walk, so I park off to the side. As I approach the entrance, a sea of eyes studies me. I never understood what Jake found appealing about the constant performance and being in the spotlight. But the guy seems to feed off of it.

As I'm about to reach for the heavy French door, Jake barrels out and into me. Camera shutters clicking and voices commanding film to roll flood my ears. Jake holds onto me, hamming things up with a kiss on my cheek. By this evening, video clips and articles will slam the internet and news channels.

Jake Ward Reunited with Old Wave Watchers Flame

I wrench away. "Can we go, please?"

"Sure." Jake waves as he follows me to my car.

Once inside, the noise is muffled, but I can tell the greedy news hounds will pounce on my car if we linger. I drive away as fast as I can.

"Thanks, Callie. I really appreciate your help."

I've been told at times that I'm too nice. Today, I almost believe it. I'd much rather be back at Sally's, enjoying a leisurely morning, but instead, I'm stuck shopping with my Hollywood ex-boyfriend. "I don't have all day, Jake, so let's just get what you need so I can drop you back off."

"And lunch."

"What?"

"I want to take you to lunch. To say thank you."

Oy vey, did he just wink at me? "Fine, whatever. Then you're on your own." I find a parking spot in front of the surf shop and pull in.

Right next to Zane's Jeep.

Serves me right for asking what else could possibly go wrong.

Jake's already out of the car, checking out the window display of swim gear and beach items. I audibly groan as I get out and follow him inside, determined to get in and get out as quickly as possible.

Am I foolish to hope Zane won't notice us?

I get my answer when I walk in. Toward the back of the shop, Zane's standing by a rack of board shorts as if frozen in place as he takes in first Jake, then me. Even from where I'm standing, I can see the tic in his jaw.

But then I remember the dream Jake so rudely interrupted with his texts. I haven't seen Zane laugh like that since I've been here. And something about the realization brings out my mischievous side.

My mission has now changed from helping get Jake what he needs and leaving as soon as possible to what I can do to make Zane laugh.

He nods his head, acknowledging my presence, and returns to browsing. I shoot over to the swimsuit rack, where Jake slides hangers as he checks each one out.

He lands on one that's blue with bright red, orange, and green parrots on it. "This one's cool." He holds it against himself.

I take it from him. "Absolutely not. Blend in, remember?"

"Right." He studies the racks and, thankfully, heads toward one with solid colors.

Catching Zane's attention, I hold the gaudy shorts up and put my finger in my mouth to pretend I'm gagging.

He smiles, then shakes his head while continuing to browse.

A smile is good, but I'm going for a laugh.

Jake finds several suits in solid colors and styles, then grabs a few shirts to mix and match. "I'll go try these on."

The fitting rooms—all two of them—sit at the back of the store just beyond a curved archway, giving an open view of the rest of the store. I stand against one side of the arch, waiting for Jake to emerge and give me a show. Because I know he will.

To my left, Zane's still poking around, but I can tell he's hovering to see what's going on.

Jake shoves the curtain back and struts with his arms out, dressed in a pair of red shorts and a white top that says lifeguard. "This works."

Zane looks like he's about to blow a gasket.

I make a shooing motion with my hand at Jake. "No way,

buddy. You're not a lifeguard in real life, remember? Those are for the real ones."

Jake dons his hurt puppy dog look. "But I thought—"

"You thought wrong. The shorts are fine. The shirt stays."

His shoulders slump, then he turns around and jerks the curtain closed again.

I turn toward Zane, roll my eyes up and pretend I'm trying to claw them out with my hands. He chuckles.

That's a start but still not good enough.

The sound of metal rings sliding on the bar alerts me to Jake's reappearance. He has on a pair of green swim shorts and a tan shirt that says 'beach bum' in bold, white letters on the front. But the word 'bum' is crossed out, and 'stud' is hand-written over it in black letters.

He grins at me. "This one's fun."

"Yeah, if you're a sixteen-year-old with too high of an opinion of himself."

When he pulls the curtain shut again, I look for Zane again. He's stopped browsing and has his arms crossed to watch the show. I pretend to pull my hair out and grit my teeth.

This time, his chuckle is almost a full laugh as he leans over.

Okay, I'm almost there.

Jake comes out of the dressing room again. This time the shorts are blue, and the orange shirt has 'I washed up like this' plastered across the entire front.

I grab three solid shirts from a rack nearby and hand them to him. "No words. Try these." I almost shove him back into the dressing room and yank the curtain closed.

When I turn around to look for Zane, he's leaning against the arched opening, arms still crossed.

I put my hands on either side of my face and do a silent scream face, like the famous painting.

Zane snorts as he breaks into a full laugh, covering his mouth with his hands while backing away.

Mission accomplished.

Jake pokes his head out. "Did you hear that?"

I stand in front of him to block his view. "Hear what? Did you try the shirts?"

"Not yet."

"Then get to it." I clap my hands twice for emphasis.

Jake looks me up and down. "You're bossy today."

"Yeah, well, deal with it." I yank the curtain shut.

I'm on a roll. I like this version of myself. I make men do what I want.

When I glance back toward the store, Zane's at the front, about to leave. He gives me a two-finger salute and grins.

I smile back at him. Things are definitely looking up.

CHAPTER 16

Callie

"This is a disaster."

Zane and I are standing side-by-side, taking in a situation with many moving—and broken—pieces.

A front moving in from the Gulf stalled over Sarabella just before we were about to start the training session. And now, a crowd of beachgoers stands huddled under the pavilion, waiting for their chance to see Jake Ward.

Therein lies the disaster.

As with all small towns, news gets around fast, so not only do we have the normal beachgoers for this time of year, but just about everyone else in town who's a *Wave Watchers* fan. And they're all lined up, waiting to speak with Jake and get autographs.

Nick had the good sense to herd the teens into headquarters with Jake, so they could get their turn with him first. And he gladly obliged every selfie and autograph request. That's Jake at his best, and I have to say, he was great with the youth, answering their questions and making them feel more comfortable with him. And excited over the idea that he'd be involved with the program, which I'm sure Zane inwardly cringed as hard as I did at that one.

And when Jake noticed the crowd waiting outside for him, he was the one who suggested going out and 'appeasing the fans' so as not to disrupt the kids.

Then the storm hit.

Zane unfolds his arms and sighs. "The storm should pass soon, and then we can get the teams to the cordoned area."

"Or should we just call it a day and send everyone home?" I know I'm fishing for a way out of this mess, but I can't help it. Still without a car, I had to pick Jake up this morning, which made us late because word got out he was at The Sandpiper. You can imagine that scenario.

Zane checks his watch. "At this rate, it'll be time to send them home before we get started."

I drop my face into my hands. "I'm so sorry I brought this on you, the kids, the program…Sarabella." Might as well list it all. It's all my fault we're in this mess.

His voice drips with sarcasm. "You mean you're the one responsible for all this?"

I swat his arm, which is more like a solid rock. "Stop. Don't make me feel worse."

This playfulness is nice. Feels like my antics on Saturday helped relieve some of the tension between us.

"I'm just trying to lighten the mood, Cal. This isn't your fault. Jake's a grown man who's responsible for himself."

"One would think." Now I'm the one standing with crossed arms.

He leans his head in closer. "Can I ask you a question?"

"Sure."

"What did you see in that guy?"

I meet his eyes and feel a rush as his blue orbs envelop me like a wave in the ocean. "He actually wasn't this bad when I met him. Then *Wave Watchers* became a hit, and he morphed into this."

"He seems to think you two are a couple."

Now, who's the one fishing?

"That's because he runs to me every time his latest relationship fails."

"And you take him back?" His tone is incredulous as if he believes I'm that dense.

"Good grief, no. But I had to work with him, so I did my best to just be a friend."

"But he kissed you."

"Yes, I'm very aware of that." I sigh. "I can't seem to get it through his head that we're just friends. If that. My life would be much simpler without him in it." I turn to look up at Zane. "And now you know one of the reasons I came back to Sarabella."

He gives me a soft smile. Or is that pity?

"Did you talk to Theo over the weekend?"

His expression darkens. "Yes, and he apologized for not filling us in—*again*. But it all happened so fast, and he never got a chance."

"Do you believe him?"

"Honestly, I'm not sure."

I can hear the disappointment in his voice. Something else is going on here. "Why? What else did he say?"

"That it will be great for Sarabella. That it will draw more tourists. That it will give him a big boost for the election in the fall."

"Theo said that?" My incredulous tone matches Zane's expression. Yet, I'm cringing again. I did present the youth program to Theo as good for Sarabella's image, but bringing Jake into the picture is taking things a bit far.

"Yeah, all stuff I never imagined hearing coming out of his mouth."

I sigh. "I need a drink."

"I have two bottles of water with electrolytes on ice. Care to join me?"

"I'd be delighted."

Zane is the first to enter headquarters. I follow behind and assume he's headed toward the fridge for those water bottles. Instead, shouts of 'surprise' blast through the room, making me jump.

Toward the back of the room, the teens line up with the trainers, excitement in their expressions.

I glance at Zane. "What's going on? It's not my birthday, is it?"

The teens laugh.

Zane chuckles. "No, just a little something Nick and I worked on over the weekend. The kids helped finish it up this morning."

The line of bodies parts, and that's when I notice the door to the storage closet is open. But instead of boxes and supplies filling the room, a desk and chair sit in the open area. A bookshelf waiting to be filled sits on one side of the small room, and an extra chair on the other.

"You did that this weekend?" While I was playing chauffeur to Jake, helping him find appropriate beach wear, this beautiful six-foot-two human being was thinking of me.

"Yeah. Figured you needed the space to do what you do best. And considering Jake's arrival, it can also serve as a hiding place."

"You planned this before Jake showed up?"

He nods. "That's what I was talking to Nick about before we left to pick up the shirts."

Now I feel like a total ingrate. "I'm sorry I jumped to conclusions."

"Already forgotten." He gives me a meaningful look that reminds me of the last thing he said that day.

I'm trying.

"Thank you, Zane. That means a lot." I wander into my new office to check it out, still a little overwhelmed by the gesture. This feels more permanent, like he wants me to stay.

The noise of the crowd outside grows louder as the main

door opens. Jake rushes in and pulls the door shut behind him, turning the lock as well. "I need a break."

He spots us standing in my new office and heads our way.

As I turn to face the oncoming onslaught of Jake Ward, I feel Zane shift to stand just off to my side, right behind my shoulder. And then something unexpected happens.

He wraps his hand around mine and dips his head so that his lips brush my ear. "Do you trust me?"

The sensations running down my neck and back steal my voice, making my reply sound more like a breath. "Yes."

"Then follow my lead." Zane moves next to me so that's it obvious that we're holding hands.

It's like watching a scene in a movie shift into slow motion. The closer Jake gets, the more his smile lessens as his gaze focuses on mine and Zane's hands, clasped and fingers intertwined. But I can hardly focus on Jake because of the onslaught of memories from the past and the physical reminder between us of what it felt like to be in love with Zane.

To be *loved* by Zane…

Jake stops in the doorway, a baffled expression on his face that I can totally relate to at the moment. He wags a finger back and forth at us. "Are you two an item?"

"Yeah, we are. You know how that old flame works." Zane sounds composed, sure of himself.

I dart a glance at him, then back at Jake, and smile. Well, try to anyway. "It just kind of happened." The truth of my words hits me after I say them. But I'm not sure Jake is buying it. "I meant to tell you over the weekend."

He turns his head to the side just so, in that way he does when he questions a director. "I don't believe it."

I wrap my free hand around our clasped hands and hold the mingled mass against my midsection. "It's true. I told you about Zane." Despite the flood of panic making my heart thump loudly in my ears, I attempt to look at Zane like a woman in love. "Seems the flame never went out."

"That's right." Zane meets my gaze and devours me with his blue eyes in a way that I almost believe could be real.

But then Jake calls our bluff. "Prove it. Give her a kiss, Zaney-boy."

I see the cringe in Zane's expression. Is it the abhorrent nickname or the demand to perform and kiss me?

Oh no…to kiss me…

My lips are already tingling at the suggestion, and I'm wondering how on earth we're going to get out of this one. But before I can think any further, Zane spins me toward him and lowers his head.

As our lips touch, I'm sucked into the duality of past and present colliding all at once—the memory of kissing him years ago and kissing him now. My eyes flutter shut, and I lean into Zane, noting the feel of his hands on my back.

And, of course, I kiss him back.

For believability.

That's all it can be, right?

Zane lightens the kiss, then brushes his lips just under my jawline as he makes his way to my ear. I'm on the verge of turning into a trembling mess as I reach for the desk nearby.

Then Zane whispers, "Great job."

And there's my confirmation that it's all fake.

I stop the cascade of wonder pelting every part of my being and hear the crash of my heart at my feet.

Zane rests his arm across my shoulders. "Proof enough, Jakey-boy?"

I don't see Jake's reaction because I can't bring myself to lift my face, but I hear it in his heavy sigh before he speaks. The sound of defeat. "Yeah, no problem. I'll leave you two lovebirds alone."

When I look up, it's only to see Jake's back as he walks by a small sea of youthful faces still in awe of the great Jake Ward in their presence. But I see the insecure boy named Ward Jacobson, who left his small town for Hollywood in search of greatness.

And I am speechless, yet again.

Appearing embarrassed—or is that regret?—Zane clears his throat. "I think the storm passed. I'll get the kids outside. We can at least do some drills or team tags."

"Yeah, sure. I'll be right out." I'm just not sure I can walk yet.

"No hurry." He shuts the door as he exits, leaving me alone in my new office. So casual, as if the kiss didn't affect him at all.

I lean against my desk, head hanging down and my heart a hot mess.

That may have been a show for Jake's benefit, but it seems I was telling the truth about Zane and me.

Our flame has never gone out.

CHAPTER 17
Zane

T hat kiss…*that kiss…that kiss…*
My brain keeps repeating this over and over. *That kiss…*

Blew.

My.

Mind.

Not something that can be faked. At least not on my end.

Callie? I don't know. I want to believe it affected her as much as it did me, but she seemed so…so full of regret. Even when she joined us on the beach, she seemed withdrawn. Or sad. Did I make a bad call? Does she still have feelings for Jake?

I drop my head into my hands, too distracted to deal with the paperwork sitting on my desk. I never should have done that. I recognized the risk, but I was willing to take it to help Callie.

To help get Jake out of her life.

But at what cost?

Just when we were finding our way back to being friends…I may have blown it.

And all that work Nick and I did to make the storage room an office for her? Totally eclipsed by Mr. Jake Ward, star of *Wave*

Watchers, and too self-centered to see the chaos his presence is wreaking on the program already.

A knock on my door breaks my stream of regret and self-flagellation. "Yeah?"

The door opens, and my chest constricts to see Callie. "Can we talk?"

"Sure." I gesture to a chair, which Callie slides into with a sigh. Before she can speak, I jump to the punch. "Listen, Cal, I'm sorry about…uh…"

"Kissing me?" Her brows shoot up with her question.

"I thought I was helping, but now I'm wondering if I did more harm than good." Despite my apology, I'm watching the play of emotions on her face for any sign that she felt something like I did. I can't deny the feelings are there. For me, at least. And the way she responded, I'd hoped…thought she might still feel something, too.

"What was it you said earlier? Already forgotten?" The corners of her mouth tic up the tiniest bit.

Our kiss was forgettable…

I gotta admit, that stings, but I guess it's better than a total meltdown of the friendship we've rebuilt between us so far. "Okay, then, what can I help you with?"

"I'm concerned about Isaac."

"Did something else happen?"

"No, but he didn't seem himself today. Did you notice?"

Do I admit that I kept reliving our kiss and blanked out at times? "No, I guess I missed it."

Her eyes shift upward as if she's searching her memory. "He didn't raise his hand once during the drill tests, and he seemed kind of…down."

"I'll be working with his team during tomorrow's practice. Maybe I can get him to open up."

"That would be great." She finally smiles, which somehow makes me feel redeemed from my earlier blunder.

"No problem." I wait to see if she has anything else to say

because she's still sitting there staring at me. "Anything else on your mind?"

"Yeah." She blinks and ducks her chin for a moment. "Thank you for the office. I really appreciate you doing that."

Now I get to return her smile. "Thank Nick, too. He came in on his day off and helped."

"I will." She rises from the chair but stops in the doorway. "I told your mom I'd make my California specialty tonight. Care to join us?"

"What's your specialty?"

"It's an endive salad with avocado, bacon, tomatoes, and cilantro. The aged balsamic vinegar really makes it, though."

Just the description has my mouth watering. "I think I can make it."

"Good. I'll make sure to set the table for one more."

And then she's gone, back into the wild of the break room and thanking Nick for his part in setting up her office. Nick grins and glances my way with a nod of appreciation.

I attempt to scan the paperwork on my desk, but my mind is still engaged in what just passed between Callie and me. We felt like friends again.

More connected.

As for that kiss…she might forget it, but I know I never will.

WHEN I ARRIVE AT MY PARENTS' home, I knock. Mainly out of respect and because it's not my home anymore. But even after seven years, it still feels weird.

The door swings open, and Callie fills that gap with her smile, a flowery sun dress that makes her hazel eyes look greener, and her hair pulled up with soft tendrils cupping her face.

Breathtaking. My hand itches to tuck back the strand tangling with her eyelashes, but fortunately, I have a pie in my hands. "I brought dessert."

And I sound like a doofus, like a teenage boy in front of his high school crush. The thought makes me think of Isaac, so maybe I can draw on this weirdness when I have that talk with him.

When Callie takes the pie from me, her hands brush over mine almost intentionally. Then she smiles. "Dinner's almost ready."

She stands back so I can come in, which again feels strange to be welcomed into my parents' house by my former girlfriend.

Who lives here now.

Again, totally weird.

I shut the door as Callie dashes off toward the kitchen. My mother and father are sitting in the living room, which is bizarre as well. Since when does my mother stay out of her kitchen?

And she must read my mind as she holds up her hands and widens her eyes. "Callie wanted to make the whole dinner, so I've been relaxing with your father."

I drop onto the couch with a grunt.

My father gives me a commiserating glance. "One of those days?"

If he only knew. "You could say that."

My mother pops Dad on the arm with a snort. "You say that every day."

"If you hauled around potted plants and bags of mulch all day, you'd say the same."

Mom kisses him on his sunburned nose. "I know."

Callie hollers from the kitchen. "Dinner's ready!"

"That was nice of Callie to invite you tonight." There's a clear question in my mother's expression, but I have no intention of indulging her.

So I play innocent. "Yeah, can't wait to try her California specialty."

Mom frowns for a split second but then lets it go. Thank goodness. The last thing I need is my mother trying to play some kind of matchmaker between Callie and me.

But it does bring up a thought I need to talk to Callie about. Now that we've made Jake think we're an item, we may have to keep up the act until the guy leaves.

Dinner is a surprise, to say the least. Callie picked up some serious cooking skills in California. Even my mother's impressed, raving over the combination of ingredients in the salad Callie says she created on a whim one day. And her baked teriyaki salmon with brown rice and capers caused my father to make what my mother calls 'yummy' sounds.

The evening feels so…domestic. Comfortable. Easy.

I offer to help clear the table and help Callie with the pie I brought while my parents sit in the living room talking.

Callie hands me a stack of dessert plates from the cabinet.

I set them down by the pie and pull forks out of a drawer. "Listen, I've been thinking about our ki—what happened today."

Her mirthful expression tells me she noticed my redirect. "Oh, you mean that thing I've forgotten about?"

Busted. "More along the lines of Jake. Now that he thinks you and I are…" I wag a handful of forks between us.

"An item?" She's totally enjoying my discomfort.

"Right."

"We have to keep up with the charade?"

I exhale. "Right again."

She slices the pie and puts pieces on plates. "I was thinking about that, too."

Again, I'm waiting for her to say more, but she just keeps prepping plates of apple pie. Then she licks her thumb.

My gaze drops to her lips when she does this, and she notices. I clear my throat. "I wasn't sure what you wanted to do. Do you want to tell Jake the truth?"

"Definitely not. For the first time since he got here, he hasn't blown up my phone with constant texts." A mischievous glint appears in her eyes. "Any chance we can keep up the ruse until he leaves?"

I can be as casual about this as she is. I lift one shoulder. "Sure, I guess we can figure out how to do that."

She takes a bite of the pie, makes an *mmm* sound as her eyes close. "Delicious."

Yes, she is. I look away. "It should be. I picked it up from Bake My Day. Emily says hello, by the way."

"I think she misses me living with them."

"Why? Aren't they still newlyweds?"

"It's not that. It's the whole house repair thing because of the termite damage. They're having trouble agreeing on what needs to be done."

I snag a bit of pie from one of the plates. Apples, cinnamon, and flaky crust take turns overwhelming my taste buds. "I told Aiden I'd help him out. I'll reach out and see what he needs."

"That's a great idea. Be a peacekeeper."

"A what?"

"You know, a peacekeeper. Help keep them working together in peace."

"Ah, I see." I lean against the counter, unable to resist a little flirting. Let's call it practice for dealing with Jake. "Is that what we'll be doing to keep the peace with Jake?"

Now she's licking a bit of apple from the corner of her mouth but misses.

So I figure I can help her with that, too. I swipe the crumb away and pop my finger into my mouth.

Callie blinks at me, and her irises expand. "Yes, but without the kissing."

"Kissing?" My mother somehow walked into the kitchen without us hearing her.

Callie's face reddens, and I'm sure the heat around my neck looks the same.

I shake my head. "Something that happened at work today."

With a knowing smile, Mom takes two of the plates. "You two must have a lot of fun at work."

Then she walks out, leaving Callie and me in a sudden burst of laughter.

It's easy…and comfortable in a surprising way. We grab our plates and join my parents in the living room. I study Callie as she interacts with my parents. It's like a heavenly spotlight is shining on her, and I can see nothing else.

Nothing but Callie.

And me? I'm sitting here, wishing our little arrangement included kissing.

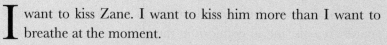

CHAPTER 18

Callie

I want to kiss Zane. I want to kiss him more than I want to breathe at the moment.

Why? Let me tell you what happened.

It's Friday, we're on the beach, working with the teens, and suddenly, the lifeguard whistles start going off from tower four, which sits between the training area and the shoreline. Everyone froze at the sound, including the teens, which, as I reflect back, was impressive. They recognized the warning.

We all stood there, watching and waiting. Then the whistle went off again, along with the walkie-talkies.

That's when Nick took off toward the beach, with Zane following hard and fast after telling me to take over. The other trainers and I herded the teens toward the beach, so they could witness a lifesaving event in action.

Four terrified parents. Two kids. And one rip current.

Rip currents are one of the most common causes of drownings. Even seasoned football players have perished in them. My heart was beating hard against the hand I held against my chest. I don't think I've ever heard the beach so muted this time of day. All of us were silent and terrified as we watched the two children struggle in the current.

The two guards on duty swam hard toward them, followed by Zane and Nick. From the corner of my eye, I saw Jake start to move forward, but Graham, our behemoth of a lifeguard, casually put his arm out to stop him. Jake shot him a questioning look as Graham gave him a curt shake of his head.

Thankfully, Jake relented and started explaining to the kids about rip currents. I'm not sure they listened, though, because the scene in front of us was unfolding and intense.

With Nick right behind him, Zane caught up with the other guards as they surrounded the two children and worked their way parallel to the shore to swim out of the current.

Then I saw Zane shift the youngest child toward him to start mouth-to-mouth. Something we only do in the water if it's to save the victim's life. One of the mothers let out a wail, which set me into action. I motioned to one of the other female lifeguards to assist me in comforting the parents, but also to keep them from running into the water and risking their lives and other lifeguards' as well.

Once Zane hit shallow water, he ran to the sand with the child and dropped to his knees, continuing to resuscitate her. I guided the parents over, and as we reached Zane, the little one broke into a loud shriek. He lifted, then held the child to his chest as if she was the most precious possession in the world before handing her over to her mother, who was bawling hysterically.

And now I'm staring at Zane, overwhelmed by what I just witnessed, and all I can think about is how much I want to kiss him as this mother sobs her gratitude.

"My baby! Thank you! Thank you so much."

Nick carries the other child, who's fine except for the terrified expression still lingering on his face, to the other parents.

I approach the mom clutching her crying daughter. "Let's get her up to the pavilion so we can examine her." The distant sound of a siren reaches us, confirming the EMTs will arrive shortly.

Zane's bent over, hands on his knees, catching his breath. Nick pats him on the back as he walks by and leads the parents up the beach.

I get Graham's attention. "Take the teens to the cordoned area and tell the other guards to talk them through what happened." I catch his arm as he's about to go into action. "And be sure they're allowed to express any fear."

He nods and starts giving orders.

Several bystanders applaud as we move and regroup, but my focus is Zane. I can't get to him fast enough. Once I know the teens and guards are heading to their places, I walk over to Zane. When he straightens, I cup his face with my hands...and kiss him.

Because he saved that little girl. Because he risked his life to do it. Because, even knowing this is what we do on a daily basis, I'm so overwhelmed by his selfless act that this is the only thing I can think to do.

I feel his heart pounding under my hand on his chest, and he tastes salty. Though brief, our kiss is intense with emotion.

Zane lifts his head. Eyes that match the ocean meet mine. He wipes away the water drops that fall from his hair to my cheek. "I thought you said no kissing."

"I make exceptions for heroic acts."

He grins. "I'll keep that in mind."

"You okay?"

"Just winded." Though still rapid, his breathing slows.

"We better get up there. I told the other guards to walk the teens through what happened."

"Good. I want to make sure that little girl is okay."

Zane makes a slow jog up the beach, which will allow his muscles to recover, but I know from experience that it's still a push.

I follow a few feet behind, drinking him in and wondering how I can keep up the pretense of our fake relationship to keep Jake out of my hair.

Because it's anything *but* fake for me now.

As we reach the pavilion, the EMTs are on the scene, examining both children.

Zane comes to a stop next to Nick. "How's it going?"

"So far, so good, but they'll want to take them in for a more thorough check." Nick's crop of dark hair is still dripping, so I dash into headquarters to grab towels for him and Zane.

Jake is sitting at a table, staring out into space.

"Jake? Are you okay?" I walk over to the cabinet that's loaded with towels and supplies.

"Yeah, just needed a moment to regroup." He shakes his head. "I didn't know what it was like."

Towels in hand, I pause in front of him. "You mean the rescue?"

"Yeah, what they did...I'm so blown away." He jumps up from his chair, his eyes darting back and forth as he forms words. "I mean, I know this is the kind of stuff you do, but that," he gestures toward the beach, "that was incredible."

"All in a day's work." I head to the door so I can take the towels out to the guys, but Jake blocks me.

"Train me."

"What?"

He pats his chest. "Teach me to be a real lifeguard."

"Why, Jake? You already have the fantasy." I pat him on the shoulder. "Stick to what you know. It's way less stressful."

I try to go around him, but he jumps in my way again.

"No, I mean it, Callie. I want to train to do the real thing."

"What about your acting career?"

"Don't you see? This will make my performance better on the show. I can even do all my own stunt work. You know, like Tom Cruise."

I roll my eyes. "So that's what this is about? The show? Give me a break."

Before I can push past Jake, the door opens, and Nick and Zane file in. I hand them each a towel. "Jake wants to be trained as a lifeguard."

Zane uses the towel to help conceal his laugh and makes it sound like a cough. "Does he, now?"

Jake holds his hands together in front of him in a plea. "Please. I mean it. I'll do whatever is necessary. I'll even pay for it or donate money to support the program."

"I'll do it," Nick blurts.

I spin my head to look at Nick just as Zane does the same.

Zane shakes his head. "This isn't a game."

"I'll do it on my own time." Nick stares at Zane, waiting for a reaction.

I jump in. "I think this might be a good idea."

Nick grins and points at me. "See?"

Zane gives me an incredulous look. "Have you been in the sun too long today?"

"Give us a sec, guys." I tug Zane to the side.

Zane lets me lead him to the other side of the room. "I can't believe you're supporting this."

I hold a finger to his lips. "Just hear me out. If we let Nick do this, we can get Jake out of the way for the rest of the program. It's a win-win situation. Jake gets what he wants, and we get to focus on the youth program without the constant distraction."

A slow grin spreads across his face. "I like the way you think, Cal."

"I know." Still grinning over Zane's praise, I walk back over to where Jake and Nick are conversing. "Okay, here's the deal. Nick, you train and work with Jake while we're working with the youth program. That way, we still have the same schedule as we do now. I'll—" Zane raises a brow at me. "Zane will find a replacement for Nick to work with the kids. Sound good?"

All three nod in agreement.

Jake hugs me. "Thank you. You won't regret it." He zips out the door.

Nick tosses his towel in the hamper basket. "Don't worry. I'll work him hard."

Zane hangs his towel around his neck and holds onto the ends. "Make him puke."

"You got it." Nick heads out the door.

I turn to face Zane, hands on my hips. "Make him puke?"

"Yeah, that way, he gets a real feel for what it's like. This isn't a game."

"You already said that."

"Well, I'm saying it again. Your boyfriend there needs to understand this is serious."

"Boyfriend? Jake is not my boyfriend."

"Does he know that?" Zane sounds downright cranky now. He heads toward his office.

"He gave me a hug to say thank you. That's all."

Zane shuts his door, and that's the end of the conversation. I'm left standing in the middle of an empty room, wondering how I'm the one getting flak when I just solved our biggest issue.

Then the main door opens, and the youth and trainers file in, chatting excitedly about what happened on the beach. I assume they're talking about the rescue until I see Graham walk in with Isaac and Mark in tow, one with a bloody nose and the other with an eye that's swelling shut fast.

I groan. "What on earth happened now?"

CHAPTER 19

Zane

I bounce my gaze between the two boys sitting in the chairs in front of my desk. On the left, Mark is holding a bag of ice wrapped in a hand towel against his eye. Isaac has a wad of paper towels held against the tampon stuck up his nose.

Undoubtedly a day of extremes, to say the least. From the rescue earlier to this...and I—we still have the parents to deal with.

Standing behind the boys, Callie shifts her weight from one foot to the other, arms crossed and a frown on her face that I find endearing somehow. Guess it's the way her nose tightens up and her lips pucker.

I drag my focus back to the bruised and bloody mess in front of my desk. "This isn't the first time you two have come to blows. What's going on?"

Both boys look at each other, then at me but remain silent.

Leaning back in my chair, I put my hands behind my head. "You two either start talking or start walking. There's no tolerance for this kind of thing in the program."

I catch Callie's subtle eye roll. When we were dating, she would rib me about my mottos and slogans. Seems her humor at my expense is still present.

Isaac clears his throat of drainage to speak. "I was trying to talk to Alyssa, and he interrupted."

Mark jerks his body around to face Isaac. "You were hitting up my girl."

"She's not a possession. Sheesh." Isaac shakes his head as he turns away from Mark.

Callie steps between them, putting a hand on each of their shoulders, which forces them to look up at her. "Enough. You two are smarter than this. You joined the program to be part of something important. Are you seriously going to let a girl distract you from that?"

I'm a little surprised at Callie's approach, considering she's a huge distraction for me these days, but I have to say, I admire her neutrality in the situation. "Callie's right. A distracted guard is an ineffective guard. You have to keep your head clear and in the game because there will always be distractions. Especially on the beach. Focus is key."

Callie's attempt to hide her smile behind her hand does nothing to conceal the humor dancing in her eyes.

A knock on the door precedes Nick popping his head in. "Parents are here."

I nod at Nick. "We'll be right out." I return my attention to the boys. "I'm giving you both one more chance. If this happens again, you're both out. Understood?"

"Yes, sir." Mark gets to his feet.

Callie opens the door. "I'll walk Mark out to his parents and give them an update."

"Great. Thanks." After the door closes, I prop my arms on my desk. "Isaac, who's picking you up today?"

"My mom." Isaac's voice carries a subtle hint of dread.

I tap my fingers on the desk, unsure of what to say next. "Your Uncle Theo really wants you to do well in the program."

"I know. And just for the record, I didn't start it. Mark did. He always has it in for me." The frustration in Isaac's voice is palpable as he defends himself.

"Why do you think that?"

"Because he does. Alyssa isn't interested in him, and it makes him nuts that she likes me and not him."

"Was this going on at school, too?"

Isaac just nods.

I can still remember being a sixteen-year-old boy with raging hormones and having a thing for the most popular girl in school. Ironically, I can even relate to it now with Callie back in the picture. Except this isn't high school anymore, and the stakes go way beyond the schoolyard.

But right now, Isaac is my concern. I know it's not my job to parent him, but I feel like I need to do something to help the kid.

"You know, I wasn't much older than you when I first met your Uncle Theo right here on this beach."

"Yeah, so?"

I can tell I'm not winning points for my storytelling, so I'll get to my point. "He helped me see what really mattered in life. You said you enjoyed helping people, right?"

"Yeah, so?"

With tremendous effort, I try to hide my amusement at Isaac's repetition. "So, is fighting with Mark helping anyone?"

He drops his eyes to the bloody paper towel in his hand. "No."

"Then what can you do to help the situation, Isaac? Without using your fists?"

Isaac just shrugs.

"Why don't you give it some thought tonight and then come see me tomorrow with any ideas you come up with. I'm happy to help, okay?"

He nods. "Sure. Can I go now?"

"Yeah, I'll walk you out. I'm sure your mom will want to know what happened."

"My nose isn't bleeding any more. Can we just skip that part? She's got enough to deal with these days."

"Sorry, can't do that. But I promise I won't make a big deal out of it. How's that?"

"Fine." He draws the word out with a frustrated sigh.

"Come on. How bad can it be?"

Isaac rolls his eyes again. "You have no idea."

I'M BACK in my office, still feeling a tad guilty for how things went with Isaac's mother. She didn't want to talk about Isaac at all. Just said she'd deal with it. But I could see the steam about to combust from her ears as she walked away with Isaac in tow by the arm.

The kid glanced back once as if to say, 'I told you so.' Maybe I can get a call in to Theo and see if he has any idea what Isaac's home life is like. I haven't talked to Theo since our call about Jake Ward, which still sits like spoiled milk in my gut, but I'll have to put that aside for Isaac's benefit.

I'm about to reach for my phone when Callie walks in and drops into a seat. "I'm honestly glad this day is almost done."

"How'd it go with Mark's parents?"

"His dad picked him up. When I first told him about the altercation, he asked Mark to explain. As soon as Mark mentioned a girl was involved, he turned all macho attaboy. Forgive me for saying this, but I wanted to smack him upside the head."

I chuckle. "I can understand your desire to do that."

She sits back in her seat with a harrumph and crosses her arms. "It's like I'm back in the middle of the twentieth century."

"Sarabella is a small town."

"It's not too small for manners."

I try not to laugh but fail.

She drops her arms and gives me an indignant stare. "I can't believe you're laughing at me."

"It's kind of hard not to when you look," I wave my hand up and down at her, "like that."

Her disdain fades, and a wicked gleam lights her gorgeous eyes. "You think I'm being cute, don't you?"

Oh, I'm in it deep this time. I raise my hands in surrender. "I said nothing of the sort."

"You didn't have to."

We stare at each other for at least ten seconds, which feels more like minutes. And we may be saying nothing with our mouths, but our eyes are having a detailed exchange.

And I like it. A lot. More than I'm ready to admit.

Callie breaks eye contact first. "Since I'm done for the day, I think I'll take a walk."

"Mind if I tag along?"

Callie's eyes round to match her mouth. "Uh, sure. If you want to."

"Unless you prefer to be on your own. I thought we could bounce around some ideas about the second half of the program. I have some thoughts now that we've gotten our feet wet, so to speak."

"That's fine. I'll go get my sunglasses."

"I'll meet you outside. I just need to put a call in to Theo."

She pauses mid-rise out of her chair. "About Isaac?"

I nod.

"We can talk about that, too, then." She closes the door behind her when she leaves.

Theo's cell goes straight to voicemail, so I'm guessing he's busy or in a meeting. I leave a brief message, asking him to call me back when he gets a chance. And honestly, I'm not disappointed he didn't answer because I'm itching to talk to Callie about some thoughts I've had about modifying her program design in one area.

That and I'm finding myself becoming addicted to our banter like we were back then, but even better. She's more confident and comfortable with herself, as am I. I grab my sunglasses off my desk and shoot out the door.

Callie's standing where the sand meets the cement of the pavilion with her back to me, hands on her hips as she scans the beach. The breeze plays with her hair, revealing the curve of her neck in a game of peek-a-boo.

She must sense my presence because she turns around and smiles before I even say anything. "Ready?"

I resist the urge to touch her shoulder or to just hold her hand. "Let's go."

We take our time, walking in silence to the shoreline, then turn right to head north up the beach. With the onset of late afternoon, many of the beachgoers are packing up to head home. And as the sun begins its descent, more walkers will start showing up.

But now—this is my favorite time of the day on the beach. This transition from day to evening. The water reflects the deepening blue of the sky as it prepares for the sunset.

Callie bends over to pick something up from the sand and then holds it out to me—a small sand dollar that's almost complete. "Sand dollar for your thoughts?"

My fingers brush hers as I take the gift, but what I really want is to linger there, holding her hand, feeling her warmth. "Nice find."

"The sand dollars are different on the West Coast. They're thicker. Sturdier."

"So I've heard."

"You should come out there sometime and see for yourself."

I don't miss how she says this, as if she'll be there if I do. Do I take that as confirmation that she plans to go back? "Do you miss it? The Pacific?"

She brushes back the errant strands of hair blowing into her face. "Sometimes. But I like the change of pace. And Sarabella has changed a lot."

"You think so?"

Her expression turns thoughtful. "Yeah, it's growing up."

I purse my lips. "Never thought of a town that way."

We continue to walk along the water's edge as waves lap the shore. Seagulls chime in with their own opinions about the day while sandpipers dash about in front of us, scurrying to stay ahead.

"That's because you've grown with it."

Now I'm intrigued. What specifically does she see in me that's changed? "Have I?"

Callie swivels her head to look at me. "Yes, you have. We both have. It's been eight years. How could we not?" She finishes with a soft laugh.

I tuck my chin. "Right."

Silence falls between us as we walk. The sound of the ocean lapping on the shore in a gentle rhythm fills the gap. To our left, two young children chatter about the sandcastle they're building. A gentle, warm breeze caresses my skin.

It's peaceful, but the tension in my chest is building. I'm not done exploring Callie's thoughts about staying in Sarabella. "Do you miss it?"

"What? The Pacific coast? LA?"

"Yes, all of the above."

She pauses, then shrugs. "Sometimes, I guess. It's hard to say. I haven't really been back that long. Still feels like I'm on vacation."

"I can understand that." I pause, digging for the courage to ask my next question. "Do you think you'll go back? Or would you ever consider staying in Sarabella?"

She stops walking and turns to face me. Blonde strands whip around her face as the breeze has grown stronger. She pushes her sunglasses up to the top of her head, pulling her hair back and revealing her eyes. Imploring and…hopeful.

"Are you asking me to stay, Zane?"

Her question sucks the air out of my lungs. I want to tell her yes, but that's a risk I'm not ready to take. At least not yet. What if I open myself up to Callie like that again, and she decides she doesn't want to stay?

I can't do flings. Never have. Probably why I've dated very little since Callie left eight years ago. When I give my heart away, it's a done deal.

But I don't know where my heart is in all this yet. I'm not even sure I have anything left to give.

CHAPTER 20
Callie

With the sun moving behind us, Zane is backlit like a glowing Adonis. The sun brings out the gold in his hair, and, though I can only see my reflection in his sunglasses, I can tell he's conflicted.

And still hasn't answered my question.

But I want— No...I need to know what's on his heart, something he was never good at when we dated. But I meant it when I said he's changed—grown up. I see hints of his thoughts and feelings simmering below the surface. If I can get him to trust me again...maybe share what he's feeling right now...

About me.

About us.

If there can even be an us, which, with each day, I find myself wanting more and more. An us that's meant to last forever.

Because I'm done running after things that leave me dissatisfied in the long run. Sure, my run in LA has been great. I wouldn't be the person I am now if I hadn't ventured out to explore and expand my horizons. But now I want more.

I want the six foot two, blue-eyed hunk of man standing in

front of me, who has been my best friend, colleague, and for a brief while, the man I loved.

And…still do.

But maybe he doesn't—can't feel that way about me anymore. Maybe it's too late.

"You know what? Don't answer that. Clearly, that's not a question you can deal with right now." I'm trying not to feel hurt as I march down the beach, fighting the tears burning my eyes. The crushing weight in my heart whispers my deepest fear that I may have lost my chance with Zane.

Forever.

"Callie."

I hear him calling my name above the chatter of seagulls and children playing in the sand, but all I can do is keep walking because I do want to stay in Sarabella. But not if Zane doesn't want me here.

"Callie!" Zane grasps my arm from behind and spins me around. His sunglasses sit on top of his head now, giving me a clear view of the turmoil in his eyes, like a storm churning in the middle of the Atlantic. "I told you, I'm trying."

I make the mistake of blinking, which sends rivulets of tears down my cheeks. And my lips tremble. I've always been an ugly crier, which I hate. Why can't I be like those actresses on set who manage to keep a beautifully poised face as tears flow down their perfect skin?

"I know." That's it. That's all I got. Ugly face and all.

He cups my face with his hands, hands full of warmth and strength, and sweeps my tears away with his thumbs. His eyes dart back and forth, searching mine. "Then give me time."

I nod as I tuck my chin, attempting to conceal my emotional state. Right now, I feel like a blithering idiot.

But Zane won't let me hide. He tugs my chin up with his knuckle. "Don't give up on me."

My smile is tremulous at best. "Not possible."

A slow smile spreads across his face, then he draws me to

him and holds me. As I lay my head against his chest, he kisses my temple. The soft beat of his heart comforts me.

"Aren't you two cute?" Jake's voice splits us apart faster than the matching poles of two magnets.

"Jake, what are you doing here?" So much for our tender moment. I'm sure my annoyance is showing, too.

Jake holds his hands up. "Just saying hello. Nick's orders. Daily jogs down the beach to finish my daily training, so you can thank him for the interruption."

Then he just stands there, staring at us as if he's waiting to be let in on some inside joke.

I make a shooing motion with my hands. "Then I guess you better get back to it."

Jake does a casual salute. "Yes, ma'am." He shifts his focus to Zane. "Is she always this bossy?"

Expression stern, Zane leans back as he crosses his arms. "Always has been."

I'm standing right next to Zane, so you'd think he'd be more on the ball about lash-back. I shove my elbow into his side without even looking away from Jake and find Zane's responding *oomph* very satisfying.

But then he just laughs and commiserates with Jake. "And pushy."

Jake shares his mirth before continuing his jog down the beach again.

Both of them laughing at my expense. How did this happen?

I spin around to face Zane. "You totally deserved that."

He straightens, rubbing his side. "Totally worth it."

With a snicker, I flounce back the way we came. The man can be tender one moment and insufferable the next. As I turn up the beach toward the pavilion, I dare a glance over my shoulder to see where Zane is but see no sign of him.

Probably taking his time coming back. I hope he thinks long and hard about my elbow punch.

When I reach headquarters, Zane's leaning against the wall by the door, sporting a smug grin. Sweat drips down the sides of his forehead. It may be near sunset now, but the temperature still hovers close to ninety, and the humidity is ever-present. I have to admire Zane for the energy he spent to pull off beating me back.

"What took you so long, Cal?"

I want to be mad at him, but I love this playful side of him. "I'm in no hurry."

As I reach for the door, he leans toward me. "Glad to hear that."

Hope blooms in my heart again because I know he's referencing our exchange on the beach before Jake interrupted us. Like he's telling me that he's giving me another chance.

But I'm going to need help. Time to call in the big guns.

MISSION NUMBER ONE: Make myself irresistible.

Mission number two: Drive Zane crazy with my irresistibility.

Mission number three: Convince Zane I'm staying in Sarabella.

I know. It sounds juvenile, but Zane opened a door, and I plan to walk through it. Maybe it's more like a window, but I can crawl through. The point is, I have an opportunity to win Zane back, and I am going to take full advantage of it.

How? Well, I'm not entirely sure, but I'll figure it out. Starting today.

Because I want to stay and be with him more than anything. So I'll do just about anything to make that third mission a reality.

I haven't had a lot of experience with attracting men on purpose. Most of the time, I just don't think about it because

I'm too busy with work or personal interests. But I know someone I think can help.

It's my day off, and Emily is meeting me at The Turtle Tide for lunch, where I intend to pick her brain for details about how she nabbed Aiden. I even secured an umbrella table outside for a little more privacy, too. And just to show how serious I am, I brought a notebook and pen with me and jotted down my three missions as I waited for Emily to arrive.

True to form, Emily arrives ten minutes late and greets me with a warm hug. "I'm so glad you called. We haven't done lunch in ages. Not since you moved out."

"I know. But I have to confess. I have an ulterior motive."

Emily pauses mid-motion in putting her purse on one of the empty chairs at our table. "Should I be worried?"

I wave my hand at her in reassurance. "No, I just need some dating advice."

She drops her purse with a squeal of excitement. And this is why I chose an outdoor table. I know my best friend.

She claps her hands with excitement. "Who are you dating? Is it Nick? I saw him at the coffee shop the other day. I can't believe that man isn't taken yet."

"No, it's not Nick."

Emily pops out her bottom lip in a pout, which I make a mental note of because she's so cute. I could try that one on Zane.

"Bummer."

"No biggie."

Her pout turns to disgust. "Please don't tell me you want to get back together with Jake."

"Oh, good grief, no!"

Emily got the full story of shopping with Jake, which included me whining about the man's egocentric taste in clothing. However, I left out the part about Zane being there and my antics making him laugh.

"Thank goodness, because I would have had to leave. So,

who do you have your eye on?" She leans forward, her face a perfect picture of anticipation.

I clear my throat and wiggle in my seat as I straighten my skirt. "It's, uh, Zane."

Her excited expression morphs into one of concern. "Zane? Are you sure?"

I gotta say, I'm feeling a bit deflated by her reaction. "Yes, why?"

She throws her hands up as she leans back in her chair. "I don't know. Just seems...risky."

"I know. You're right, but I think Zane's cracked open the door again to us."

Emily studies me for a moment. "Are you sure? I mean, you two are working together again, which was part of the issue when you were dating."

"I know, but this time, things are different."

"How?" Her reply is quick, and her face deadpan.

I fiddle with my silverware. "I know who I am now. I'm much more confident."

"You sure about that?" She gives a pointed look at my hand, which I jerk back into my lap.

I lift my chin in defiance. "Yes. Completely."

"What was it you said back then? Something about being in Zane's shadow." Emily is doing her best to appear as if she's searching her memory, when I know full well she remembers clearly my reasoning for leaving.

"It's been eight years, Emily. And in that time, I've designed a nationally recognized youth program and consulted on a major television show. I think I've made my own shadow prominent enough."

She giggles. "I was just checking your convictions." She lets out another squeal, but more contained this time. "I was so hoping."

My mouth about hits my napkin on the table. "Really?"

"Yeah, you two are meant to be." Her voice takes on a

dreamy quality, as if we're talking about some Disney princess movie. Or the latest rom-com.

I sigh. "I'm not sure Zane believes that."

"Why? Wait… Did you two talk about getting back together?" Her eyes are plate-sized now.

"Kind of."

Another squeal. A loud one. Now people inside are looking at us through the window.

"Take it down a notch, Em. Remember how small this town is?"

"Right. Okay, so what's your strategy? That's your ulterior motive, I assume." Her eyes drop to my notebook. "And why you brought pen and paper."

My whiny side spews out. "I'm kind of clueless about what to do."

"That's because you've never had to work for it, Miss Blonde Bombshell."

"Hey, I told you in high school, I'd take your red tresses any day."

"Only to make me feel better."

"But it was true." I give her a small smile. "Still is."

Her smile spreads to her ears. "Great. I'll make sure I buy a box of red hair dye for the next time you come over."

My turn for the deadpan look.

"Okay, moving on. What have you written down so far?"

I pop open my notebook and show it to her.

"Three missions. That's a start." She darts her eyes around as if she's looking for help.

I think I'm doomed to fail. A long groan escapes my mouth, and I drop my head onto the table just as our server approaches.

Emily holds her hand up. "No specials. Just two large sweet teas and the biggest plate of nachos you can make. We're going to be here a while."

CHAPTER 21

Zane

"What exactly did you ask her?" Mandy is my closest friend who's a girl, so naturally, I've come to her for help. I dropped in to pay her a visit and find a gift for my mother's upcoming birthday party.

"I asked if she'd ever consider staying in Sarabella." I mostly mumble, but I'm guessing by the way she's trying not to laugh that she heard me loud and clear. "What? Why is this so funny to you?"

"Because you really stepped into it this time." She comes from behind the counter and gives me a hug. "But I'm proud of you for being brave enough to ask."

See? At least she gets it. It did take courage. Like I told Callie. I'm trying. "What should I do next?"

"That depends."

"On what?"

"On when you decide to forgive Callie for leaving eight years ago." She pats my chest. "It's a heart issue. You have to deal with the hard stuff at some point."

"But I have. At least, I thought I had until I saw her in your shop last year."

Mandy widens her eyes and points at me. "Which you then left without saying a word to her."

Nothing like getting scolded by one of your best friends. "I've already apologized to Callie for that."

"Then see? You're already on the right track."

I shake my head. "Why is this so hard?"

Mandy tilts her head. "Maybe this is more about trusting her again? Does that resonate?"

I chuckle. "Resonate? Since when do you use words like resonate?"

She smacks me on the arm. "Since I started taking an online psychology class."

"A what? Why?"

She lifts one shoulder. "I'm trying to expand my horizons."

"Okay."

Her expression turns sheepish. "And understand what makes people want to buy things so I can optimize my store."

"Wow. Who's being manipulative now?"

"That's not manipulation. It's called being an entrepreneur." She lifts her nose in the air as she says this.

"Okay, Miss Snooty Face, use some of the psychology on me and help me figure out how to trust Callie again."

Mandy walks over to a display of succulents and holds one of the smaller ones up. Bright green paint with little red hearts cover the ceramic pot. Without a doubt, Kade's niece, Eliana's work.

"See this little plant? It doesn't know what the future holds. All it knows is that it needs water a couple times a week to stay plump. Does it worry about growing? I don't think so."

"Seriously? You're talking about a plant as if it's sentient."

Mandy dons an offended expression I'm pretty sure is for my benefit. Then she glances at the plant in her hand and holds a finger over her mouth. "Shhhh, it might hear you."

I roll my eyes. "Now I wish I never came."

Mandy grins. "My point is, this plant simply does what it's programmed to do. As long as it has enough water and sunlight, it will grow bigger."

"And your point is?"

She puts the plant back on the display table. "Keep building on your friendship with Callie, and the trust will come."

Why does an image of Kevin Costner suddenly pop into my head? "Mandy, I think you've spent too much time alone with your plants."

"Kade says the same thing."

I give her a lopsided grin. "He really gets you, doesn't he?"

My gut clenches, and my chest feels warm as her expression reveals just how much she loves Kade.

I want that. I want Callie to look like that when she thinks about me.

And more importantly, I want to think about her that easily, without past baggage.

"Yeah, he does. He's pretty great, actually."

"I'm really happy for you two." I croak out the words.

"Thanks. And I know you and Callie will be the same way."

"Hmm. You really think so?"

She nods. "I do. You two are kind of meant to be, you know?"

And this is where the bottom falls out for me. "No, I don't. But I'm hoping."

AFTER I LEAVE MANDY, I put the gift I found in the back of my Jeep and walk over to my mother's shop. This time of day, she's probably putting out new inventory or rearranging the old to keep busy. Mid-afternoons tend to be slow on Mango Lane.

As I enter the shop, I hear a familiar voice conversing with my mother toward the back of the store.

"Do you think it really works on me?" Callie's voice sounds unsure.

"Spin around one more time." My mother sounds like she's on the verge of laughing. "No, you're right. Try this one. I think the color might suit you better."

As I approach the back area, the curtain to one of the dressing rooms pulls shut. I'm guessing that's Callie in there.

My mother turns around and breaks into a smile. "Zane! What a pleasant surprise."

"I was in the neighborhood and thought I'd drop in."

"Let me guess. You popped into Amanda's store to buy me a birthday present."

I stop in my tracks. "Do you have the entire neighborhood bugged, Mother?"

"No, I'm just that good." She giggles as she draws out the last word.

The sound of metal rings on a bar snaps my attention to the dressing rooms.

Callie pokes her head out. "Hi, there."

I wave. "Hello, yourself. Fancy meeting you here."

"Hmmm." She gives my mother a pointed look before disappearing again behind the curtain.

My mother does this little hop. "Oh, right!" She lunges at me like a woman with a mission, then grabs my arm and tugs me toward the front. "I'm so busy right now, hon. Why don't you come by for dinner tonight, and we'll have a chat."

"Mom, what's going on?" I bring us to a stop, which isn't hard, considering my mother's a good six inches shorter than I am.

"Nothing. Nothing at all." Her face is flushed, and I know it's not from menopause. She's definitely hiding something.

A quick glance around the shop confirms we're the only ones here, and I see no boxes of inventory sitting around. "You don't seem that busy. And it's just Callie. Seriously, what's going on?"

She nudges me closer to the door. "Nothing. I'm just helping Callie pick out an outfit for…for an event. She's feeling a little nervous about it. You know how that is."

An event? Does she mean a date? We just had that conversation on the beach a few days ago, and now she has a date? I resist the growl sitting in my throat. "Fine. I'll come by later."

"Good." She opens the door. "I'll see you later. Bye!"

The door shuts, leaving me standing on the sidewalk with a dumbfounded expression I see in my reflection in the glass. I must look like the biggest fool on the peninsula, and I'm beginning to feel like one, too.

Mandy made a lot of sense when she talked about trusting Callie. But if she's decided to date other people, I don't see a clear path to that. Maybe she just wants me in the friend zone, which won't be easy. But Mandy did recommend I focus on our friendship first.

I head back to my Jeep, so lost in thought that I don't notice my phone vibrate in my pocket. But when I get in my Jeep and check, I see five missed calls and two texts from Nick.

> Trying to reach you.

> Need you at headquarters, ASAP!

I start to text a reply, then decide a call is better.

Nick picks up right away. "Finally. Been trying to reach you."

"I see that. What's going on?"

"Theo's here, and he's livid. Wants to see you right away."

"Why didn't he just call me?"

"I asked him that. He said this needed to be done in person."

"Okay, fine. I'll be there in five minutes." I end the call and start my engine.

Theo must be worked up about Isaac. That's the only thing

I can think of that would get him so wound up. Guess I'll find out.

But as I drive to headquarters, the only person I can think of is Callie, and who her mystery date could be. Just the thought tightens my chest and makes me furious. Something I don't like to admit, but Theo isn't the only one riled up.

CHAPTER 22
Callie

W hen I hear Sally come back, I poke my head out of the curtain. "Is he gone?"

"Yes, hon. Don't worry." Sally waves at the door as if brushing away a fly.

"Did you tell him why I'm here?"

"No, of course not. I just told him you needed an outfit for an event. I left my birthday out of it because I didn't want to give him any ideas." She lets out a conspiratorial giggle.

I came in search of an eye-popping dress for Sally's birthday party celebration, not intending to say anything about my purpose for it. But…it kind of slipped out, and Sally went ballistic when she found out I'm trying to win Zane over.

And I trust Sally not to say anything to Zane—well, mostly —but what if things don't work out, and she winds up disappointed? I already have Emily involved. Too involved, if you ask me. She texted me most of the evening yesterday with ideas and memes of people falling in love. I finally had to tell her to stop.

With a deep breath, I walk out of the dressing room, wearing a flowing halter top dress, tie-dyed in rich shades of crimson. A cinch ties at my chest, creating an open circle before tying around my neck. It's a little more low-cut than I would normally wear, but I'm pretty sure Zane will like it.

Sally's eyes and mouth round in unison. "Oh my, I had a feeling that would be *the dress*."

I step in front of the large mirror and hold the sides of the dress as I turn. The softness and color of the fabric give an almost velvet-like appearance. "I think I'm in love."

Sally gasps and holds a hand to her mouth.

I spin back around to her and put my hand on her arm. "I mean with the dress."

I'm not ready to tell her I'm still in love with her son. Again, I have no desire to be a dream crusher.

She blurts out a nervous laugh. "Sorry. Guess I'm getting ahead of myself."

Honesty seems the best course here. "I just don't want to get your hopes up. Zane may want nothing to do with me. Romantically, I mean."

Sally takes my hands in hers. "Trust me, hon. He does. He just doesn't want to admit it yet."

I glance down. "He isn't ready to forgive me."

"For what? Going after your dream? If he doesn't understand that, then he's the one with the problem." Sally sounds so fierce, especially considering he's her son. But Sally's always been one to love on the person in front of her, no matter who it is. I see so much of her heart in Zane, and I envy that. Not that my mother isn't great. She is, in her own way, but Dad had a way of overriding her nurturing with his regimented attitude.

I'm getting antsy, feeling like I've overstepped some kind of family boundary. "Listen, I shouldn't be telling you all this. Zane's your son. He's a great guy, and he told me he's trying."

"Callie, you are part of our family, no matter what happens between you and Zane. I have no control over him, but if he can't see how much you love him, then he's looking in the wrong direction."

Sally's words bring a surge of panic. "Am I that obvious?"

"Maybe only to me. Remember, I saw what you two shared eight years ago. And I still see it. But don't worry. I won't tell anyone." She pulls me into a brief hug. "And the dress is on me."

"No, I want to pay for it."

"Nope. I have a lot of birthday and Christmas presents to make up for. Consider this one of them."

I'm so overwhelmed by her love for me and this gesture that I wrap her in another hug. "Thank you, Sally. Not just for the dress but also for being so kind. You're amazing."

Her laugh rumbles out as we part. "Thank you, hon. I try my best. Now you get changed, and I'll package up your new dress. I can't wait to see you in it on that dance floor."

My stomach flutters and a thrill runs up my spine as I think about wearing the dress and dancing with Zane. Emily is going to flip when I show it to her. I think she'll agree this will go a long way in accomplishing my mission.

The party is just a week away, so I have time to figure out other ways to show Zane I'm planning to stay in Sarabella and that I want to be a part of his life.

Permanently.

I DIDN'T PLAN to go into headquarters today, but after I left Sally's shop, I decided to drop in and hang some of the framed photos from various California beaches I worked at and a couple from the set of *Wave Watchers*, one of which is a group photo of the cast.

Yes, Jake's smack dab in the middle, and I'm standing there next to him. I tried to stay on the back row of that one, being as tall as I am (some actors are way shorter than I realized), but that day, Jake was in between relationships and was determined to wiggle his way back into my heart. Before I could navigate my way out, the photographer said to smile, and I was stuck.

But I still love the picture as a reminder of my time on the show. The experience alone is gold in my mind, even if Debra is blatantly ogling Jake in the photo.

How did I miss that before?

With an armload of pictures, I make my way toward the pavilion but slow my steps when I notice Zane and Theo walk out the door. Somehow, their parting looks stiff and uncomfortable. Zane stands there, rubbing the back of his neck as he watches Theo leave.

I quicken my step to reach him. "You okay?"

He drops his hand. "Just fine and dandy."

I glance in the direction Theo left. "He didn't look thrilled. Is he not happy with how the program is going?"

"No, he's not. Isaac's mother called and complained about what happened between Mark and Isaac last week, and she's not letting him come back."

"What? Why not? You told her we dealt with the situation."

"I know, but she doesn't feel like he's safe here."

My stomach knots and feels like I've been gut-punched. The thought of a mom feeling this way hits me hard. I've always taken pride in my program and the safety measures I developed in the water and on the beach, but teenagers have minds and wills of their own. And sometimes they make bad choices.

"Let me talk to her. I can reassure her we've dealt with the situation and told both boys that if it happens again, they have to leave the program."

"I told her that already. She didn't find it reassuring at all."

"Then I'll personally guarantee Isaac's safety and promise her there will be no more issues."

Zane holds his hand out. "Cal, you can't make promises like that."

I put my hand in his and hold on. I know it's a bold move,

but I want him to realize he's not alone in this. That we're a team. "We're a team, Zane. We'll figure something out."

His nostrils flare as his gaze drops to our clasped hands, then he drops his hand. "I need to go for a walk. Tell Nick I'll be back in time to relieve him for my shift."

"Want me to go with you? I just came in to hang some pictures in my new office. I can do it when I get back." I'm hoping my positivity will help lighten the mood.

But his expression remains turbulent. Like the clouds in the distance, building up to an afternoon storm. "Thanks, but no. I need to think."

He strides away toward the beach.

I let out a long breath of frustration. That's one thing that hasn't changed about him. Zane still thinks he has to solve all his problems on his own.

The growing weight of the pictures in my arms reminds me of my mission this afternoon. Plus, I need to convey what Zane said to Nick. First, I go inside and deposit the photos on my desk, and then I return to the common area in search of him.

I find him sitting at Zane's desk, studying the program manual I created. "Hey, Zane's taking a walk. He'll be back in time to relieve you."

Nick lifts his head. "Thanks. Guess he's pretty steamed."

"Apparently. He didn't say much. Only that Isaac's mom isn't letting him come back."

He runs a hand over his short crop of dark hair, giving him that telltale bad boy look I've seen so many times on set with some of the lifeguard actors. They work at it while Nick just does it naturally. "Theo sounded pretty mad. I could hear them through the door when I was working out."

"I offered to talk to Isaac's mom and reassure her, but Zane didn't think that was a good idea."

"He probably doesn't want to rock the boat any more than it already is. Theo threatened to shut the program down. Says he doesn't need the liability right now."

Now I'm starting to see red. "Zane didn't tell me that."

Nick grimaces. "Maybe I shouldn't have told you either."

I lean against the door jamb. "Too late. Cat's out of the bag, but I won't tell if you don't."

A grin spreads across Nick's face. "Deal."

With a push away from my perch, I start to leave and then turn back. "Hey, how's it going with Jake?"

"Good. He's a pretty fast learner."

Sounds like typical Jake. "Just be careful. Sometimes he gets ahead of himself."

"Good to know."

Once I locate a hammer and some nails in the cabinet, I get to work hanging my pictures. I'm so engrossed in what I'm doing that I don't notice that Zane is back until he slams the door to his office and makes the wall we share shake, dislodging the picture I just hung. A crash of glass follows.

As I'm grumbling to myself and picking up pieces of glass, a shuffling sound alerts me that someone is standing in my doorway. I glance over and see a pair of bare feet. "I wouldn't come in here if I were you."

"I'll behave." Zane's voice rumbles over my head.

I rise to my feet. "I mean the glass."

Despite my warning, he walks in, crouches, and picks up the photo and broken frame. "Sorry. I'll replace the frame." He studies the picture before handing it to me. "You and Jake."

Is he making a statement or asking me something? The only hint I have is the tic in his jaw. "Ancient history."

"Then why are you hanging it up?"

"Because we just finished shooting the first season and found out the network renewed the show for two more. We *all* were ecstatic." I emphasize 'all,' hoping Zane will understand this picture has nothing to do with a relationship between Jake and me, which was nonexistent at this point.

He nods, but his mouth remains a straight line. And there's that pulsing in his jaw again. But then I see a flash of interest behind his eyes, and his expression softens. "Maybe you can tell me about it sometime. What exactly you did on the show."

I smile. "I'd love to."

One side of his mouth tics up. "I better get out there."

Zane shuffles out of my office and through the main door.

I'm not entirely sure what went through his mind there, but I'll count it as a win. And hope I can keep counting more.

CHAPTER 23

Zane

I know it's a colossal risk, but I don't see any other way. Isaac's mother won't return my calls, and I'm not one to let go of a loose thread even if there's a risk of unraveling the entire sweater. Not that I have much use for sweaters.

Besides, Isaac's too important to let go. Even if Theo thinks that would be for the best.

When I suggested what I'm about to attempt, Theo shut me down. I don't understand his position, especially since he was so emphatic at the beginning about starting the program because his nephew needed it. But I don't know what family dynamics are at work here.

My first knock went unanswered, so I knock again but still no response. I turn around and start back down the steps when the door opens.

"What do you want?" Isaac's mother stares me down like I'm some kind of intruder.

And maybe I am, but, like I said, this thread needs to be pulled a little. "Mrs. Richmond, I'm sorry to bother you—"

"Then don't. I already told Theo this was a bad idea."

"But Isaac is great at it. Have you asked him how he feels

about it?" I hold my hands out to implore her to think this through. Somehow, I have to find a way to reach her.

And that's when I notice the curtain move on the front window that looks like it's seen better days. Isaac's eyes grow wide, and he drops the fabric when I look straight at him.

"Doesn't matter what he thinks. I'm his mother."

"Of course. I'm just trying to help your son. He seems a bit lost." Might as well be straightforward. I have nothing to lose here.

This seems to affect her. Her expression softens, and her eyes turn glassy. "That's his father's fault. If he hadn't walked out on us…I have to work, so it hasn't been easy. Driving him back and forth has been a challenge."

I take a step closer. "I understand. How about this? If you let Isaac come back to the program, I'll come pick him up every day and bring him home."

"I can't ask you to do that."

"You're not. I'm offering. And I promise to look out for Isaac, Mrs. Richmond. He's a great kid, and he deserves a chance."

Her smile is hesitant at first, but it's there. "All right. I guess we can give it a try. But if anything happens, we're done. Understood?" She lowers her chin and widens her eyes as she points at me.

"Understood."

She steps back in the doorway and lifts her chin to call out, "Isaac!"

I notice the curtain move again in my peripheral vision. The sound of feet hitting the floor grows louder until Isaac shows up behind her.

"Come here, son." His mother waves him forward. "Zane has agreed to pick you up and bring you home every day."

His eyes light up. "That's great!"

"But there are conditions." Mrs. Richmond's brows nearly meet her hairline. "You will make sure your room is clean, and when you get home, you do your chores. Otherwise, no more lifeguard program. Is that clear?"

I have to give the woman credit for working the situation to her advantage. She is a working mom, after all.

Isaac bobs his head. "Crystal."

"Good. Now thank Zane for being so generous with his time."

He flashes me a wide grin. "Thanks, Zane."

"No problem. I'll see you in the morning. Bright and early, okay? We have to be on time."

"I'll be waiting for you outside."

"Good deal." I wave goodbye and head back to my Jeep with a sense of satisfaction and a reminder of those ideas I wanted to run by Callie. Now I'm even more convinced we should expand the program to run year-round with an eye to help kids like Isaac.

And I'll admit, I like the idea of Callie staying in Sarabella to help. Maybe even spearhead it herself. She's more than proven herself capable.

Now, if I can find a way to get Jake out of the picture—yes, pun intended—and get my head in the right place, Callie and I might have a chance at something real this time.

THE NEXT MORNING, Isaac is true to his word. He's standing outside with his backpack and jumps into my Jeep as soon as I park in the driveway. And before I back out, I make sure he's fulfilled his promise to his mother, too.

When we walk into headquarters, Callie rewards us with a big grin. "Isaac, I'm so glad you're back."

Then she gives me a questioning look.

I call Graham's name to get his attention. "Grab the cones and take Isaac out to help set up the drills."

"Sure thing." Graham waves Isaac over and starts loading his arms with the bright orange cones.

I step into my office and wave Callie in.

She shoots a conspiratorial glance toward them, then turns back to me. "How did you make that happen?"

"I went to Isaac's house and had a little chat with his mother." I gotta say, I'm loving the impressed look on Callie's face. I'm like one of those wild parrots that flit around, chattering and preening themselves like they rule the world.

"What did you say to convince her?"

"I told her I would pick Isaac up every day and bring him home. And I took a page from your playbook—told her I'd look out for him."

"Well done, Mr. Albright." She pauses, hesitates like she's not sure how to say what's on her mind.

"Just spill it, Cal." I wanted my comment about the playbook to be a compliment to her because she was right. I should make that clear. "You were right about reassuring Isaac's mother. Good call."

She shakes her head. "It's not that. And by the way, glad that worked." She hesitates again. "Why didn't you tell me that Theo threatened to shut the program down?"

Oh, that. "Because I didn't want to worry you."

"But this is my program, too, Zane. If we're going to work together as a team, you can't keep things like this from me. I don't care if it's hard stuff. We're a team, right?"

"Right. I'm sorry. I guess I didn't think of it that way."

"That's part of the problem. Always has been. You never saw me as your partner. More like your assistant. And that's not how this works. Not then and not now."

The emotion in her voice about does me in. Is that what she felt all those years ago, that I didn't consider her—value her as a partner?

I take her hands in mine. "Cal, is that why you left?"

She keeps her eyes diverted. "Partly."

I feel like the biggest heel on earth. "Was I that hard-headed?"

This time she meets my gaze. "Sometimes."

"Why didn't you talk to me about it?"

"I tried, but you would shut me down, which was easy back then. I was so used to butting heads with my father that it seemed easier to walk away. But there were other reasons... mostly to do with my father." She lets out a nervous laugh.

I've prided myself on being someone who jumps in to help when I see a need, goes above and beyond to bring justice to wrongful situations, and is perceptive to the needs of those around me. But clearly, I failed Callie all those years ago. And that crushes me.

How could I have been so blind? And what can I do to make things right?

"Cal, I..." I run a hand over my mouth as I struggle to find the words, but nothing seems adequate. "I know I can't fix things to do with your dad, but I promise to do better about treating you like my partner and not my assistant."

Her smile rewards my effort. "That's a brilliant promise."

I give her hands a light squeeze. "Glad you approve."

CHAPTER 24
Callie

We're doing drills with the youth in the water today, and they're having a blast. But I can't stop stealing glances at Nick working with Jake in the cordoned area. Nick set up cones like a relay race and has Jake running the course repeatedly.

I look over again. Nick shakes his head and gestures for Jake, who looks like a wrung-out rat at this point, to start over. Nick gives the signal, and Jake launches again, except he somehow trips and lands flat on his face in the sand.

Like Nick, I burst out in laughter.

"What's so funny?" Zane's standing next to me, observing the trainers and the youth as they do drills.

I lean my head toward him. "Jake just did a face-plant in the sand."

He glances over my head, searching the training area to get a look. "Did he make him puke yet?"

I laugh again. "Push too hard, and Jake might sue us."

"Just what we need." Zane blows his whistle, calling the teens to gather in front of him. Mark and Isaac stand at opposite ends, avoiding each other, which is a relief. No confrontations today. And the girl they're both interested in is staying clear of them both. I don't blame her. Who needs that kind of drama?

In my experience, forcing teenagers to be friends rarely works out. Teaching them to respond to one another with respect has much better results. At least we have peace in the ranks for now, which is great for all of us. I can't stand the idea of the program being canceled, and, like Zane, I'm baffled by Theo's position on this. But tempers have a way of speaking more fear than truth.

"All right, everyone. You had a stellar week. Take a swim and cool off before heading back up to the pavilion. We have a surprise waiting for you up there." Zane gives his whistle two short blasts to signal the end of the day.

The surprise? An ice cream truck we hired for the teens to have whatever and however much they want, within reason. Even teenagers love ice cream.

And lifeguards and actors, too, it appears. Nick and Jake are standing in line with the kids by the time I get up there.

"You two are the biggest kids I've seen on the beach yet," I tease as I join them.

Nick grins. "And yet here you are in line with us. That makes you one, too."

I smile back at him. "I never said I wasn't one."

When our turn comes, Jake orders a Choco Taco. Even outside of California, his affinity with taco-style foods makes an appearance. He also orders a firecracker, which suits him perfectly.

Nick only orders an ice cream sandwich. And that's it.

"Really? That's all you're getting?"

He pats his gut. "I have to watch my girlish figure." Then he winks at me, which Jake notices and frowns.

I order a snow cone. Not because I want one, but because I'm feeling nostalgic. I remember eating them on the beach with Zane after a long day of training in the lifeguard program. Back then—don't I sound old?—ice cream trucks made regular rounds in Sarabella. I know they're still around, but I don't see them as often.

When Zane saunters over, I conceal my icy treat by staying behind Nick and Jake. Why? Because I want to see what Zane gets without influencing him. I'm not close enough to hear what he orders, but when he turns around...

Yep, you guessed right. A snow cone. As he joins us, I lift mine and take a bite, staring right at him. Delight skitters across his eyes as he meets my gaze and grins. Then he brings his cone up to his mouth without looking away.

That's when I see that delight shift to desire, and I know he's remembering the same thing I am.

Our first kiss. A hot summer day on the beach. Two young lifeguards. Two icy snow cones, melting and drippy. Well, you can imagine how we wound up helping each other clean up the mess on our faces.

My heart is pounding so loud. I'm sure Jake and Nick will notice us, but they're both engrossed in exchanging stories about their childhood ice cream favorites, which is a relief. I'm not sure how long we keep staring at each other, but a loud shout from behind us breaks the moment.

"Back off, Mark!"

Zane spins around, throwing his unfinished cone into the nearby trash can as he strides over to where Isaac and Mark stand in a face-off. And poor Alyssa, near tears, stands off to the side, her ice cream cone dripping down her hand.

I follow suit, tossing mine into the trash, and approach her while Zane deals with the boys. "Alyssa, let's get you some napkins so we can clean that up."

She follows me back toward the truck, where I grab a few napkins from the window counter. As I wipe her hand, she sniffles. "I'm sorry. I was just trying to get them to be friends."

I stop wiping her hand and meet her teary gaze. "That's a noble gesture. What made you want to do that?"

"They used to be best friends. We all were. Until Isaac and I realized we liked each other. Now we never hang out anymore."

I purse my lips and nod my head. "That's really hard."

Her lips tremble and contort as her tears turn into a sob, and I'm instantly connected to another ugly crier. I draw her in for a hug, not caring if I get her ice cream all over my swimsuit and shorts. "It's okay, Alyssa. You did nothing wrong, sweetie. I think it's wonderful that you tried to get them to be friends again."

As we part, she wipes at her face with her clean hand. "You do?"

"Yes, of course. You're concerned about your friends, and you want to help them make peace. That's commendable."

Her tears stop as she sniffs and nods. "Thank you."

"Why don't you go clean up in the restroom and then order a new ice cream? I think the heat has finished off this one."

She giggles softly with me. "Okay."

After Alyssa enters the women's restroom, I turn around. Zane is sitting on a picnic bench, arms resting on the table in front of him. Mark and Isaac sit across from him but on opposite ends of their shared bench. Mark has his arms crossed with his back to Issac, who has a similar pose.

But it's Zane's expression that has me enamored as he speaks. The care and compassion I witness in his expression melt my heart faster than the heat that melted Alyssa's ice cream cone.

The man is gorgeous inside and out. Actually, it's what's inside of him that makes him so dang cute and sexy. I can't look away.

"Wow, you really love him, don't you?" Jake's question snaps me out of my trance.

"What?" I snort and wave him off. "I'm just concerned about the boys. Zane seems to have it under control, though."

"That's more than concern, Callie. As much as I hate to admit it, I saw it that day you two kissed in your office, too."

I feel a blush rise as he stares at me, and I feel this need to fess up. "That wasn't a real kiss, Jake. Zane just did it to help me…"

"Get the message across that you're not interested in me?" His crooked smile doesn't hide the hint of pain I see in his eyes. "Trust me. I know acting when I see it, and that was no act."

"I'm sorry." I blink, trying not to tear up.

"No, I'm the one who's sorry for not getting the message sooner. It's okay. No harm, no foul."

"Then you're okay?"

He looks up as if in thought. "I will be. I'm learning a lot here, so I'm still ahead of the game, you know?"

Smiling, I nod at Jake, proud of the man he's becoming. There's hope for the guy yet. He gives me a hug before joining Nick and the other trainers standing near the ice cream truck.

I sense Zane's presence before I see him. The scent of sunscreen and juniper fills my nose as he rests his hands on my waist and lowers his lips near my ear. A chill skitters down my spine.

"Do I need to fight for you?"

"I don't know. Do you want to?" I turn around to face him, not caring who sees our closeness because the tone in his voice tells me he *does* want to fight for me.

For us.

"I thought that was clear by now."

"No, but it's getting clearer right now." I want to kiss Zane more than I want to breathe at the moment. And judging by the shimmer in his eyes, he feels the same.

But under the pavilion with twenty teens and four trainers watching, not to mention all the other beachgoers mingling around, it's not the right time.

Zane's keenly aware of this, too, as he clears his throat and releases his hold on my waist. "Any chance you're free tonight?"

"No, sorry." I almost laugh at his confused expression. "Your mother's birthday party is tonight, remember?"

He tilts his head back with a groan. "I forgot." He frowns. "Wait. Mom said you were buying a dress for an event. Was it for that?"

I give him a side-eye, flirty look. "Did you think I had a date?"

He glances down. "I did, actually."

I'm not gonna lie. The thought of Zane seeing red over me sends a thrill right down to my toes. "Bet that made you a little crazy."

Something borderline fierce flares behind his eyes, and his voice deepens almost to a growl. "Maybe."

I am *so* loving our flirtation, and the temptation to keep it going is undeniable, but I think I'll let him off the hook. "And if the dress is for your benefit?"

"Then I can't wait to see you tonight."

CHAPTER 25

Zane

C allie turned down my offer to pick her up for the party tonight because she doesn't want to make our budding relationship public knowledge yet. Somehow, I think most people know. And if they don't know by now, they will soon.

Because tonight I plan to dominate the dance floor with her. As long as she'll have me, anyway. Been a long time since I've danced with anyone. Callie was the last one, come to think of it.

A sign stating The Turtle Tide is closed for a private event sits outside the entrance. My mother's known the owner of the place since it opened ten years ago, and she and my father are regular customers. But when I walk in, the first person I see is Jake Ward. Let's just say, that doesn't float well in my gut. I'd hoped for a break from that guy.

I search the place for my parents and stride to where my mother is setting up appetizers on a long table on one side of the room.

Pure delight lights her face when she sees me. "Zane!" She wraps me in a hug as if I were still eight years old, even though I outweigh her by a good fifty pounds or more.

Once she releases me, I hand her my gift. An envelope with

a card and a coupon for a full day of pampering at Ocean Breeze Day Spa.

Her eyes light up as she studies the seal. "Should I open it?"

"It's your birthday, Mom. You get to do whatever you want." I chuckle at the battle I see waging in her expression. She purses her lips as she rips the envelope open and makes an *aww* sound when she reads the card, then gasps when she sees what's inside.

She throws her arms around me again. "Thank you, hon! I love it."

"Happy birthday. You deserve it." I kiss her cheek.

She cups my face. "You're such a sweetheart. Now, go get yourself a soda or whatever. The bar's open."

Her hands are still on my cheeks, so I hold onto her wrists so she can't escape. "I will. But first, tell me how Jake Ward wound up coming to your birthday party, please."

Her eyes widen to match the water crackers on the table, and I think I see stars flash around in there. "He came into my shop to look around, and I recognized him right away from his show. I thought, what better fun than to have a famous TV star at my birthday party?"

I groan inwardly as I release her. "Sure. Okay. Just keep him to yourself."

She swats my chest. "Zane, I thought you two were good friends. He raved about you and the program."

"I wouldn't call it friendship."

"Then let's call it a working relationship that could benefit the youth program."

"Have you been talking to Mrs. Stringer again?"

"Bettina may have mentioned something."

It takes everything within me not to roll my eyes. "The youth lifeguard program isn't some political tool, Mother."

"I never said it was, but as an entrepreneur, I understand the dynamics of building mutually beneficial relationships. This could be one of them." She pats my chest, then heads toward the kitchen.

Shaking my head, I turn back toward the front to check out who else has arrived and recognize most of the shop owners from Mango Lane. Amanda and Kade are chatting with Emily and Aiden on the other side of the room, so I head their way to join them. But then Callie walks in and brings everything in my world to a complete and utter stop.

She's gorgeous.

Those are the only words my brain can produce at the moment because the sight of her has stolen the air from my lungs. She swept up her hair in a soft array of blonde waves, revealing the curves of her neck and that dress…

Remind me to thank my mother.

On second thought, don't. I can only imagine how the woman who gave birth to me would gush and start planning a wedding in her mind, which doesn't sound appalling.

Actually, it sounds plausible.

Even right.

My chest warms as our eyes connect, and suddenly, I can't imagine my life without her. I know now, if she were to ask me that same question she did on the beach, I would answer with, 'Yes, I want you to stay.'

Because I do. More than anything.

Callie's smile grows as she walks across the room to where I'm standing. Like a gawking teenager, I'm sure. My gaze drinks in how that dress hugs her curves and dances around her calves, which are just as shapely in the heels she's wearing. The red color accents her tan to perfection, and the neckline makes my heart speed up. As she comes closer, the scent of gardenias and something musky finishes off my senses. I am so in trouble.

"Hi, there." My voice sounds gruff, so I clear my throat. "Hi."

She steps close enough that I can feel the warmth of her body. "Hi, yourself."

With her heels, she's only a couple of inches shorter than me now, which gives me easy access to that spot just below her ear, which I'm about to take full advantage of.

I lean in. "You look amazing."

Her soft gasp tickles my ear when my lips brush her skin. "So do you."

The band hasn't started playing yet. Otherwise, I'd whisk her into my arms and hold her the rest of the evening. Somehow, I'll have to make do with just being near her until they start.

But then Jake walks up and ogles Callie, and I clench my fists at my sides.

"Wow, Callie. You look hot. And I don't mean sunburned."

A low growl rumbles in my throat.

Callie wiggles her fingers into my fist. "Can it, Jake."

Jake chuckles. "I'm just kidding." He meets my gaze and falters. "Inside joke. From one of the episodes of *Wave Watchers*."

"Hmm, funny." But my tone is anything but humorous.

Jake glances at the bar behind him. "I think I'll go get a drink."

"Good call," I growl out my affirmation.

As Jake walks away, Callie presses her face against my shoulder and giggles. "You can be such an alpha sometimes."

"Alpha?"

"You know, an alpha male." She raises delicate brows to make her point.

"A Hollywood reference?"

"A character reference. Like in the show, Jake's character is the alpha. He's the hot, sexy leader that women love."

Love? The word resonates in an unexpected place deep inside. "The only woman I'm interested in being an alpha to is you, Cal."

CHAPTER 26
Callie

D id I just leave reality and step into a romance novel? Because that's what this feels like.

Zane's alpha comment left me breathless, and his blue eyes are devouring me as I think about how much I want him to kiss me.

Soft music plays in the background.

Zane reaches for my hand. "Care to dance?"

I still can't speak, so I nod.

He keeps holding my hand as he leads me to an open spot on the floor, then pulls me into his arms, giving me a heady whiff of cedarwood and musk.

Being this close to him brings back so many memories. But I'm not interested in those tonight. I want this to be the beginning of something new between us. Which only makes sense. We're different people now—a little older and wiser. I know I've changed a lot, and though Zane may not see it, he has, too.

But one thing hasn't changed. This chemistry between us.

He increases the pressure of his hand on the small of my back and touches the side of his face to mine. "I've wanted to hold you like this since that first day on the beach."

I giggle in his ear at the memory. "You mean that day with the Beach Bunny?"

He grunts. "Don't remind me."

"She certainly seemed grateful."

He leans his head back. "Is that really what you want to talk about right now?"

I know he's joking, but the glimmer in his eyes tells me he's more interested in what's happening between us.

And so am I. "No."

One side of his mouth rises before he returns to his earlier position. His lips brush my ear again as he speaks, "The last time I danced was with you."

Now it's my turn to lean back. "Seriously?"

He lets out an embarrassed laugh. "Yes, seriously."

"I find that hard to believe." I give him the side-eye.

"It's true."

More couples have moved onto the dance floor, including Kade and Amanda, who are grinning at us. I give her a subtle wave.

"So, not a lot of dates, I'm guessing."

"No."

"Why not?"

He looks up for a moment, as if he's trying to figure that out himself. His hair brushes against my hands clasped behind his neck. "Just not interested. I'm not a player. "

I can't resist running my fingers under the bottom of his hair. "Glad to hear it."

Zane takes our little game up a notch when he moves his thumb back and forth on my back in a subtle caress.

"What about you? LA's a big city. You probably had a full menu of choices."

I try not to laugh at his subtle attempt to ask if I dated a lot. "Of food, yes. Of men, less than you'd imagine. And I didn't really have a lot of time to date. Work kept me busy, and I liked it that way."

"Even when you worked on *Wave Watchers?*"

"That kept me even busier."

"Except for Jake."

"Except for Jake…but is that really what you want to talk about right now?"

He chuckles. "Touché."

As we continue to dance, Zane's eyes drop to my lips as he leans in. I'm honestly floored that he wants to kiss me right in the middle of the dance floor.

But just as our lips are about to touch, the music stops, and Zane's father's voice booms over the microphone. "Time to sing to the birthday girl!"

I think Zane emits a low growl as he releases me. "To be continued?"

Feeling bold, I kiss his cheek. "To be continued."

I WIND up chatting with Kade and Amanda while Zane and Jacob help Sally pass out pieces of her birthday cake. Even though it's her birthday party, the woman insists on making sure everyone else is having a great time.

"I think I've eaten my weight in shrimp." Amanda holds her hand on her stomach and groans. "They're just so good. I don't recall shrimp tasting this good in New York."

Kade laughs and shakes his head. "Based upon what you've told me, you probably couldn't afford to eat shrimp there."

Amanda eyes another pink prawn on her plate and dips it into a mound of cocktail sauce before popping it into her mouth. Thankfully, she chews and swallows before replying, "Very true."

Zane walks up to us, holding three plates of chocolate cake with white icing. "Cake?"

We each take one, but Zane's gaze lingers on me before he walks away again.

"Wow," Amanda says with her mouth around a forkful. I look back and forth between them. "What? Did I miss something?"

Kade has a goofy smile on his face. "I don't think I've ever seen Zane look like that."

Amanda swallows. "That's because you weren't around the first time these two hit it off. Zane walked around looking like that all the time."

Now I'm genuinely curious. "Like what exactly?"

Amanda and Kade look at each other first before shifting their focus to me. Amanda speaks first. "Like he's completely and—"

"Totally smitten." Kade shakes his head in mild disbelief.

"By you." Amanda points her fork at me. "And you kind of look the same way."

Heat spreads up my face, but what did I expect would happen? We've pretty much announced to the entire town tonight that we're together. "Thanks for the blunt honesty, guys."

Amanda rests her hand on my arm. "I thought you'd be happy about that?"

I don't know why I'm feeling so emotional suddenly, but my eyes are burning, and my voice is choked. "I am. More than you know."

Amanda tilts her head. "Having a hard time believing it's real?"

I hesitate, then nod. "Maybe." I search the room for Zane and find him hugging his mother. The man is the full package of love, compassion, and faithfulness. He didn't have to tell me why he didn't date a lot because I already know.

He never got over me, and now I realize I never truly got over him. Jake was just a placeholder I thought could work out. Now I can say without hesitation that I'm thankful for the day I saw Zane in Amanda's shop because it made me realize how much I missed him.

And I'm so glad. Glad that we have this second chance. Glad that we still share the same passion for our work. Glad that we still have a future to explore together.

Amanda lays her head on Kade's shoulder. "Hmm, how cool would a double wedding be?"

Kade chokes on his bite of cake, and I bet I look as surprised as he does.

"Let's not get ahead of ourselves, shall we?" That's when I notice Amanda is giggling behind her hand and has a wicked gleam in her eye. "Are you sure you and Zane aren't related by blood?"

Now she's full-on laughing. "Who do you think I learned it from?"

She sobers and points to something behind me.

Or someone.

As I turn around, Zane catches my hands and leads me back to the dance floor. I glance over my shoulder and blow Amanda a sisterly kiss because that's what she feels like to me now. She grins and gives me a vigorous wave.

And I can easily picture the whole thing. A double wedding. A life with Zane and his family. A youth lifeguard program we continue to build together.

Finally, all the pieces seem to be falling into place.

CHAPTER 27

Zane

H olding Callie as we dance makes me want to forget everything else.

No concerns about Theo and his threat to shut down the program.

No worries about Jake trying to weasel his way back into Callie's heart.

Not even about Isaac and his mother…although that one does earn some concern. The last time I dropped Isaac off, I asked him about the front window. He mentioned that every time it rains, water leaks in. I already asked Kade if he had time for a little construction project, and he said he'd bring the tools.

But right now, this moment is all about Callie and me. We danced most of the evening, ate more food than would fit on a plate, and conversed with most of the folks from downtown Sarabella during the evening.

Except for Theo. He and his wife didn't make an appearance, but I'm determined not to let that worm of worry make its way into my head and ruin my evening.

But what I want more than anything at the moment is some time alone with Callie.

We need to talk.

I need to know what we're heading toward because tonight has been amazing. It's like we're falling in love all over again.

She's standing by the dessert table at the moment, talking with Emily.

As I approach, Emily stops her animated chat and glances at me. Then she juts her chin in my direction, alerting Callie to my presence. Their topic of conversation has shut down, and I suspect it may have been about me.

Callie pops a brownie bite into her mouth as she turns around and continues to chew with a smile.

"Emily, mind if I steal her away for a minute?"

Emily beams at me. "Of course. And you can keep her. I think I'm going to find Aiden and tell him I'm ready to go home. I'm so tired all of a sudden."

Callie gives her a hug and says goodbye before focusing her attention on me. "Are you here to ask me for another dance?"

"More like a walk."

"A walk?"

"On the beach. Care to join me?"

"With the mosquitos, you mean?"

I check my watch. "Sunset is in twenty minutes. I'll make sure we're back before they start feasting."

"Okay." She links her hand through my arm as we head out the back French doors of the restaurant.

Once we cross the patio, Callie slips off her heels and loops the straps over her fingers to carry them. The Turtle Tide sits at the north end of Mango Key Beach, which is closer to the waterline, making our walk to the ocean short.

We head south down the shoreline, silent except for the gentle slosh of waves on the sand and the sound of palm fronds rustling in a steady breeze. The night is humid, of course, so I'm glad I chose a linen button-down for the evening.

As we leave the residual lighting from the restaurant, the evening envelops us. The sun has moved closer to the horizon, so we stop to watch its final descent. Before the last of the sun's light is about to wink out, Callie wraps her arms around my waist and lays her head against my chest.

My hands rest against the skin on her back as I hold her, and I know the tremble I feel isn't because she's cold. "What are we doing, Callie?"

Her laugh is soft and deep against my chest. "Reigniting an old flame?"

"Our flame never went out."

She lifts her head to look at me. "I agree."

As she cups my cheek with her hand, I turn to press my lips into her palm and hold them there for a few seconds. When I return my gaze to hers, question marks ride across her eyes as she searches my face. "That day on the beach...I was trying to ask you to stay."

Something sparks in her eyes. "I know."

"I do, you know. Want you to stay."

"Then ask me." She's flirting with me again.

I can't resist kissing her anymore. I lower my head, pressing my lips to hers as I inhale her peachy scent that's mixed with the ocean and feel this sense of rightness in my world. I'm on the beach I love with the woman I'm in love with.

And I do love Callie. So much it scares me. I realize now I never got over her eight years ago. If she leaves again, I don't think I'd recover. But that's part of what I need to know—is she here to stay this time?

But all those thoughts dissipate when I hear her sigh, which ignites my passion. My need for her hits me so hard I deepen our kiss as if I'm trying to devour her. All the emotions and longing I locked away eight years ago break loose through this kiss until she pushes back to catch her breath.

She touches her forehead against mine. "Wow."

I can feel her heart pounding against my hands on her back, and I'm sure she can feel mine under her hands on my chest despite my shirt. My voice sounds rough, even to my own ears. "Please stay."

She cups my face in her hands. "That's been my plan…my hope all along."

I kiss her again, softer this time because I want to convey what I'm feeling but am unable to say. Yet.

That I love this woman with every fiber of my being, and I have no intentions of ever letting her go.

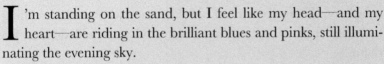

CHAPTER 28
Callie

I'm standing on the sand, but I feel like my head—and my heart—are riding in the brilliant blues and pinks, still illuminating the evening sky.

Zane wants me to stay.

He wants me, and I want him.

I love him—I never stopped loving him. And I suspect he feels the same about me. We may not be saying it to each other at this moment, but I feel it. I know he'll say it when he's ready—I'm in no rush.

We kiss again, but this time, the kiss is tender and sweet. Almost like we've made the decision to be together, and we're signing an agreement.

The sky is darkening, and the first buzz of a mosquito zips past my ear. "We'd better head back before we get eaten alive."

Zane holds my hand the entire walk back to the restaurant. Once we reach the patio, I hold his shoulder to slip my heels back on. He keeps his hand on the small of my back to steady me, which I find symbolic of our relationship. I tend to keep my head in the clouds at times, and Zane keeps me grounded.

I like to think I bring some adventure and unpredictability—no, spontaneity to his structure-driven world. We always have made a great team, and we still do. I can't wait to tell Emily what happened after she left and make a mental note to check up on her.

Zane tugs me back mid-step back to the party. "Wait a second. There's something I want to talk to you about."

"Okay, but make it quick. The mosquitos had a meeting, and they decided you're the sweeter catch tonight."

He chuckles. "I think they made the wrong choice."

I grin, loving this comfortable banter we've started.

"It's about the youth program."

Now he has my full attention. "What about it? Did something else happen?"

"No, nothing like that. It's just…I've been thinking. What if we made it year-round? We could do after-school and weekend programs. There are a lot of kids like Isaac who need something to tether them to what's important, and we could do that for them."

Just when I think I couldn't love this man any more, my feelings for him double. "I think that's a great idea, Zane. I love it!"

"Then you're on board for this?"

"Of course!" I'm pretty sure my feet just left the sand, and I'm soaring among the emerging moon and stars.

Zane crushes me against him. "Thank you, Cal. We make a great team."

My heart feels like it's about to burst, and not because Zane is holding me so tightly. This is everything I wanted.

And more.

"I'm sorry I had to bail last night." Emily sits across from me at her kitchen table, looking a little green. I dropped in unannounced because I couldn't wait to tell her about what happened, but now I'm wondering if I should have called first.

Plus, I'm having a difficult time finding the words or where to start. Last night was so…magical. On the beach, under the stars, with the sound of the ocean accompanying us. Almost as if that was our song.

I almost can't believe it…Zane and I have finally found our way back to each other.

"You look like you're still not feeling well. Should I go?"

"No, I'm fine. You know how my stomach acts up some- times." Emily leans on the table. "What's Zane up to today?"

"He and Kade are working at Isaac's place. There's a leaky window that needs fixing."

"Aww, that's so sweet."

"Yeah, it is." I smile.

Emily rubs her face, then holds her head. "So, what else happened last night after we left?"

Now I'm grinning so hard my cheeks hurt.

"You look like the Cheshire Cat in *Alice in Wonderland*." She jerks her head up and gasps.

I nod to confirm her conclusion. "Zane and I are together."

She bounces up and down in her chair as she claps her hands. "Please tell me there was kissing. Lots of kissing."

Her exuberance makes me laugh. "Yes, lots of kissing and lots of dancing."

She jumps up from her chair and dashes around the table to hug me. "That makes me so happy."

"Me too!" I sigh. "I think I'm having a hard time believing it's real."

"I can understand that. I felt the same at my wedding." She giggles. "Aiden thought I was having second thoughts because I looked like I'd checked out or something."

"Seriously? You never told me that."

"It wasn't important." She sits in the chair next to me. "So…did he say he's in love with you?"

"No, but I'm pretty sure it was implied. He asked me to stay."

Emily claps her hands like a toddler. "This is getting so good!"

I blurt out the rest in a rush. "And he wants to expand the youth program to be year-round and wants me to help him."

She hugs me. "You two are so good together."

As she lets me go, her expression shifts to panic. She jumps up, runs toward the bathroom, and slams the door. The sound of retching filters through the door, then the flush of the toilet. The door opens, and Emily totters out.

"Are you okay? Did something you ate last night disagree with you?" I open the fridge in search of some Ginger Ale, which she always keeps stocked in the fridge for her sensitive stomach. I open a can and hand it to her.

After a sip of soda, she shakes her head and sits back down. "No. I think I'm pregnant."

I suck in a loud breath. "Really?"

She nods and gives me a weak smile. "I'm three weeks late."

"Does Aiden know?" Still stunned, I slide back into my chair.

"Yeah, he's having a hard time keeping it to himself."

"Uh oh. You told me."

"I just threw up in front of you. I didn't have a choice."

I giggle. "You could have just said yes when I asked about eating something that disagreed with you."

She dons a sneaky smile. "But that wouldn't have been as fun."

"I'm so happy for you, Em." I reach out to hold her hand. "And I promise I won't tell anyone."

"Thanks." She takes another sip of her soda. "Callie?"

"Yeah?" I slide my hand back.

"If I asked you to stay, would you?" She gives me a sickly, tired grin that tells me she's joking. Mostly…

I tilt my head and smile as I reach for her hand again. "Of course. As long as you don't throw up on me."

CHAPTER 29

Zane

When I pull into Isaac's driveway, I take another look at our handiwork. Kade and I had to remove the window, then reframe and reset it. Thankfully, the window itself looked in decent shape. Otherwise, we would have had to buy a new one, which I know Mrs. Richmond couldn't afford.

Isaac hops into the passenger side. "Hey."

"Hey. How was the rest of your weekend?"

"Good. Chill." He fist bumps with me.

Before I back out of the drive, he bends over and pulls something out of his backpack. I recognize the wood from the two-by-fours we used—one of the leftover scraps he said he wanted to keep. I assumed he wanted to make something out of them but never imagined he'd carve something out of the wood.

My name. And each letter has an image related to life-guarding or the beach carved into it. He even stained it.

He hands it to me. "My way of saying thank you for the window."

I hold it in my hands like a priceless treasure. "You made this?" I know it's a stupid question—obviously, he did, but I'm floored. The kid has game.

He makes this grunting laugh sound. "Yeah, worked on it all day yesterday."

"I didn't know you knew how to carve. Who taught you?"

He shrugs and lowers his head. "My dad."

"Isaac, this is amazing." I turn the carving around to take in all the details.

"I started one for Kade, too. Just didn't have time to finish it yet."

I place his gift in my center console so I can drive. "I'm sure he'll love it."

An interesting mix of pride and humbleness expands in my chest on the ride to headquarters. Pride in Isaac because of how much he's grown and matured in a few short weeks. Humbleness to be part of it and to receive such a gift.

I've grown so accustomed to our morning and afternoon rides together that I can't imagine not doing it anymore in a couple of weeks.

After I park my Jeep and cut the engine, I drape my wrists over the steering wheel. "Listen, Callie and I are thinking about expanding the program to go year-round. You know, weekends or afternoons. Something that would work around a school schedule. Would you be interested in being part of that?"

"You mean, like, more training?"

"Yeah, but if you'd like to be a permanent part of the program, we could make you an assistant in the summer. Then once you graduate, you could join us full-time. Or part-time if you're planning to go to college. But only if you want a career as a lifeguard. You interested?"

"Heck yeah, bro." He grins at me before hopping out of the Jeep.

I sit there a minute, cataloging the moment. Isaac's used that term with the friends he hangs with in the program but never with me. This is breakthrough territory—more confirmation that the youth program has more potential for a positive impact on the youth community in Sarabella and beyond.

Callie will love this. I can't wait to tell her when I see her today.

ೕᔋ

Isaac and I are a few minutes late arriving at headquarters, so the place is already buzzing with activity. Graham and Nick are gathering items we'll need for the day's training events. And several of the teens are sitting at the tables, hanging out and chatting as they wait for the day to start.

My chest expands at the sight. This is everything I could have hoped for and more. And I'm beyond pumped for the potential to come for the program.

Not seeing Callie in the main area, I head toward her office. She's sitting at her desk, studying a document. As much as I want to tell her about my conversation with Isaac, first things first.

She smiles at me as I enter. "Hi, there."

I shut the door, then pull her up from her seat and into my arms. And when she starts to say something, I silence her with a kiss. Like I said, first things first.

She giggles. "I could get used to that."

I brush her lips with mine. "Me too. Plus, something great just happened."

"Do tell.".

Her smile and that look in her eyes almost make me forget what I intended to share with her. "On our way in, I asked Isaac if he wanted to become a more permanent part of the youth program. I told him about our plans to expand to year-round and told him we could make him an assistant in the summers until he graduates. He loved the idea. Isn't that great?"

Her eyes widen. "I hadn't thought of apprenticeships."

I tilt my head. "I hadn't thought of that word for it, but you're right. That's essentially what it would be."

She nods her excitement. "A great way to grow the overall program, too."

I love this. How in sync we are. This is what I wanted eight years ago, but now Callie and I have the maturity to do this well.

Before I can say anything else, a loud knock comes on the door. I grab the handle and open it a few inches. "What's up?"

Nick's brows tic up, and his tone has a warning element to it. "You both need to hear this."

Callie follows me out to the main area.

All eyes are on Jake, who's standing near the front end of the room, true to form like an actor on a stage. "Now that everyone's here, I can share some spectacular news. I've talked to my director, and he's agreed to come to Sarabella to shoot a special episode of *Wave Watchers*."

The room erupts with cheers and squeals from the teens. The guards, however, are sending me questioning looks that are asking why they weren't filled in.

But I can't deal with that right now. I'm so hot around the neck my head feels like a rocket about to launch. "Jake, can we have a chat?"

He swings his gaze back and forth across the room as if assessing his audience before he connects with mine. "Yeah, sure."

I open the door to my office and wait for him to go in, then wait for Callie to enter as well. After I shut the door, I get ready to let loose, but Callie beats me to the punch.

"What are you doing, Jake?" Hands on her hips and head jutted forward, she reminds me more of a drill sergeant about to tear apart one of her soldiers.

Jake flashes his teeth and holds his hands up. "What? I thought you'd love this. I've taken care of all the arrangements, so there's nothing else you need to do."

"But you should have discussed it with us first." Callie glances at me, and I nod my agreement.

His smile fades. "I wanted it to be a surprise."

My turn to speak. "In case you didn't notice, Jake, it's not your place to make those kind of decisions. This is our program. Anything you want to do, any ideas you have, you run them by Callie and me first."

Callie shoots me an appreciative smile. "Jake, you can't film the kids without parental consent."

"Already in the works. The show's legal counsel is prepping the forms and whatever else we need to do this right."

"The right thing would have been to talk to us first. Zane and I need to talk about this before we move forward."

Confusion blankets Jake's face. "Everything's already in motion. I really thought you two would be pumped about this." He gestures toward the door. "The kids are so excited. If you cancel this now, they'll be disappointed."

I run a hand over my mouth. What I'd really like to do is clock the guy. "I'm more concerned about their safety, Jake. Like I've said before, this isn't a game." Plus, I have no idea how Theo is going to react to this. "We also need to speak to Mayor Stringer."

Now Jake looks more like a kid caught stealing a candy bar. "I already took the liberty of talking to Theo. Hope you don't mind. And he's totally on board." He ends with a reassuring tone as if he thinks this makes everything okay.

He says Theo's name like they're old friends now. I clench my fists at my sides. "You can leave now, Jake."

Jake stares at me a moment, then looks at Callie. "Sure. You two talk."

Once the door closes, I slump into my chair. "Okay, now I get it."

Callie frowns at me. "Get what?"

I lean forward, gesturing toward the spot where Jake was standing. "Jake's full spectrum of self-absorption."

Her concerned expression slips into a sad smile. "Welcome to my life."

I shake my head. "No, thank you."

She snorts, then laughs. "Too late."

The reality of our situation crashes back in. "I don't believe this."

Callie lets out a breathy sigh. "Jake always acts first and asks for forgiveness later."

"He's going to destroy everything we're working toward, Callie."

She drops her gaze. "We'll figure something out, right?"

I nod, then rake my hands through my hair, fighting the urge to break something. Or pound my desk with my fists. Anything to release this boiling heat inside of me.

"We better get out there and do damage control." Callie hesitates at the door. "You coming?"

"Yeah, be there in a minute." I fall back in my seat as I exhale against the tightness in my chest. Just minutes ago, my world seemed to spin on a perfect axis. Now it's off-kilter by a hurricane I never saw coming.

And I don't have a clue what to do about it.

CHAPTER 30
Callie

I'm concerned about Zane. And this thing with Jake? It's a ticking time bomb, and I'm starting to feel responsible for the havoc it's wreaking. I'm the one who thought Nick's idea to train Jake was a good one. But now, I think it just opened a bigger can of worms than we know what to do with.

"Okay, take a break. Get some water. We're going to have some fun on the volleyball courts next."

The irony of this situation strikes me. Sand Volleyball is one of the sports I incorporated into the program for team building. So much of the program revolves around this concept. Like an organism with many parts.

And Zane has done a stellar job embracing that mentality and how to apply it more broadly, which doesn't surprise me. He's already done a great job building a strong team in the lifeguard program.

But this spins everything out of his control, and I know how much he hates that. This will push him way out of his comfort zone.

Nick comes to a stop by me as the rest of the guards and youth make their way to the volleyball area. "Hey, Callie, you okay?"

I give my brain a mental shake and refocus. "Yeah, why?"

"You just seem off. And it didn't look like you and Zane knew about Jake's set-up."

I fiddle with my whistle. "We didn't, but we'll handle it."

Nick swipes away the sweat beading on his brow. "I'm glad Zane has you to help him navigate this. He seems way happier with you around."

I'm blushing *and* smiling this time. "Thanks. I'm glad I'm around."

"By the way, Zane doesn't even watch the show."

I laugh. Is Nick saying what I think he is? "You do?"

"Oh yeah, big fan. It's lifeguards, right? Although I will say meeting Jake in person for the first time left me a little lackluster. But he's changed a bit since I've been working with him."

Could have fooled me. That earlier scenario was classic Jake Ward. "Glad to hear it. He needs some good non-Hollywood influences in his life."

Nick quirks his head to the side. "I do what I can."

With that, he jogs off to join the others.

I refocus my attention on the youth as they bounce the volleyball back and forth with ease. Zane has seemed distracted all morning, so I feel the need to check on him.

Positioned on the sidelines of one of the sand courts, Zane keeps a steady stream of encouragement and score updates flowing to the teens.

I trudge through the powdery sand and stop next to him. "You okay?"

Arms crossed in his usual stance, he keeps his face forward. "I'm not thrilled about Theo's endorsement of Jake's plan."

I left my sunglasses on my desk, so I shield my eyes so I can see him better. "I figured. Are you planning to call and talk to him about it?"

He slides his eyes to the side to look at me. "Yes, but I'm not convinced he'll listen to me."

"Let's talk to him together. Maybe I can help."

"Yeah, sure." He sounds more like he's appeasing me than interested in my help.

I know Zane's upset, but I feel the need to justify myself. "Theo might listen to me since I have a history with Jake."

"Don't remind me." He blows his whistle when the ball goes out of bounds. "Out of bounds! Ball to the other team!"

Seriously? This again. Zane—wall. Me—head bashing.

"I'm taking a water break." I walk away and head toward the pavilion. My part of the training is technically done, so I could stay in my office and sulk, which sounds more appealing than dealing with Zane's stubbornness at the moment. Hopefully, he'll open up and talk to me once he's processed this situation more.

I sit down at my desk to check my email and find a message from the show's legal team containing the form letter we're to distribute to the teens for parental approval, but also one from Steve, the director.

Callie,

I had a long chat with Jake and the producers of the show. They're thrilled with Jake's ideas and feel confident this will result in the show's renewal.

Jake was adamant about needing you back on the set, stating your input for integrating the youth lifeguard program concept into the show concept would be crucial to its success. And we'd like you to be part of the casting for that new addition. We really want to get this right.

So, yes, you guessed it. That means a pay hike for you. You know how we work in this industry. See our attached offer. I hope you'll accept. Always loved having you on the set as part of our team.

Best regards,

Steve

(P.S. Between you and me, I'd ask for more money and a show credit for you and your true-to-life program. They're champing at the bit to get you back.

. . .

I OPEN THE ATTACHMENT, which is fairly brief, and after a quick scan, sit back in my seat. They more than doubled my previous number, and Steve thinks I should ask for more? To say I'm stunned would be a major understatement.

As intrigued as I am by the offer—especially the casting part—I want a full partnership package with all the benefits of a lifetime.

And the only one I want that with is Zane, even when he's being grumpy.

I smile to myself as I hit reply. No point delaying a response.

Thanks, Steve, but I'll pass. I'm right where I need/want to be. Appreciate the offer, though. And…good luck with Jake.

I hit send and close my mail app. That's one thing taken care of.

Next on my mental list? Figure out how to minimize Jake's interference with the youth program.

CHAPTER 31

Zane

After I drop Isaac off at home, I head back to headquarters to finish up my day. Callie never returned from the pavilion earlier, so I'm guessing she's holed up in her office. Or gone for the day, which makes my chest tight at the thought of not seeing her until the morning.

I wanted to talk to her about it more, but it wasn't the time or the place. Guess I could have done a better job explaining that, but I was too caught up in my head about what to say when I call Theo.

I don't know how to deal with the man who was a mentor to me early in my career yet hardly resembles that guy now. Until recently, we've been on the same page for this program—a page he originally created. And when he handed it over to me, I built upon that, kind of like fleshing out an outline into a fully expanded paper that's still being written.

But now? I feel like he's gone off on a whole new tangent that has nothing in common with what he started. That's not the Theo I knew and respected.

When I step inside headquarters, the place is quiet. Shift change happened thirty minutes ago, so the guards from first shift have already left. I dump a stack of cones still sitting on the floor into the bin as Nick walks out of my office.

Nick saunters over as I grab a bottle of water from the fridge. "I left the schedule for next month on your desk. Let me know if you need anything changed."

"Thanks. Did Callie leave yet?" I glance toward her office, but the door's closed.

"I don't know. I didn't see her when I came in."

"Okay, thanks."

As he starts to leave, I call him back. "I meant to ask how things are going with Jake's training."

"Good. He's a pretty fast learner. Plus, he was already in good shape."

I nod. "Do you think he's being upfront about all this?"

Nick draws his brows together. "I think so. Why?"

"Just wondering what his angle is. Going to Theo about doing the show here and never discussing it with us before he told the kids—makes me suspicious."

"Yeah, you and Callie seemed as surprised as the rest of us. Probably just the actor in him. He is a bit of a show-off sometimes, but I guess it comes with the territory, you know?"

"I guess."

Nick glances over his shoulder toward Callie's office. "Callie did seem upset earlier."

I tuck my chin, knowing full well my foul mood earlier contributed to that. "Yeah, some of that may be on me."

"You two okay? I mean, it's pretty obvious you're a thing." He grins. "She's good for you, Zane. Let her in." With that, he pats my back. "Speaking of women, I better get going, or I won't have time to clean up before my date."

"Second one this week. Same girl?"

He grins at me but says nothing.

I shake my head. "Find the right one and stick with her, Nick. You'll be happier in the long run."

"I will when I'm ready." He gives me a two-finger salute. "Keep it real."

Nick leaves just as Callie opens her office door and turns out the light.

"Hey, Cal."

"Hey, yourself." She seems hesitant.

Nick's right. I need to let her in on what's going on with me. "Listen, I owe you an apology."

"I'm listening." I can tell she's still a little salty about earlier today.

When she meets my gaze, my heart starts to race. I want to kiss her like crazy, but I need to know what's going on in that beautiful head of hers.

"I'm sorry I shut you out earlier. This thing with Theo has me a bit unmoored."

"I can tell. And I understand." Her smile reassures me we're good.

"When I texted Theo, he said he had time to talk this afternoon. I'm about to call him. Still want to sit in?"

"Definitely."

"Thanks. Let's go in my office and get this over with."

She catches my arm. "I'm sure he has an explanation."

"Yeah, but I'm not sure I'm going to like it."

"Give him a chance." She slides her hand into mine and lifts imploring eyes that make me want to be every bit of the man she deserves.

Her encouragement feeds that place that's felt dry as sand since I found out Jake had Theo in on his plans. I know I probably smell like a gym after being on the beach all day, but I draw her closer as I lower my head. "I've wanted to kiss you all day."

"You could have fooled me." Now she's teasing me, which she knows by now I can't resist.

So, I do the only thing I can. I steal a quick kiss. For fortitude. "Okay, now I think I can deal with Theo."

"Zane, I understand both of your concerns, but this is a good arrangement."

I have my phone on speaker, so Callie and I both can hear Theo.

"My chief concern is that none of this was run by Callie and me first. We found out the same time the kids did."

Theo's sigh filters over the connection. "That's unfortunate. Jake said he wanted to be the one to tell you both about it. I'm guessing he got caught up in the excitement."

Callie leans closer to the phone. "That's part of Jake's problem, Theo. He doesn't think things through. I know he has good intentions, but he doesn't think of anyone but himself. Most of the time, anyway."

"Then I'm counting on you two to monitor him." Voices in the background come through.

Somehow, I have to make Theo understand what's in jeopardy here. "Theo, you were ready to cancel the entire program after the altercation between Isaac and Mark. What changed?"

Theo seems to hesitate. "Optics. This is a good thing. For the program, for Sarabella, for all of us."

My gut twists at what he's not saying. His political career. Something I never expected him to put above the well-being of the kids. "I know you want this program to work. We want the same thing. Cal and I are even discussing ways to expand the program." I glance at Callie to make sure she's okay with what I'm saying.

She gives me a thumbs up.

"But to do something this big so early in the development could put the entire program at risk."

"Jake reassured me the show's legal team would cover this."

Callie leans in to speak again. "They are. I've already received an email with the permission forms for the teen's parents, but I agree with Zane. There are still risks here."

More voices in the background come through. "Look, I have to step into a meeting right now. But rest assured that I've listened to both of you and noted your concerns. Keep me up to date, and we'll address any issues as they come up."

The call ends, leaving me feeling sick. And judging by the expression on Callie's face, she's in the same boat.

I shake my head. "He didn't even acknowledge our plans to expand the program. He's totally made this all about the publicity."

Her face a mask of compassion, Callie reaches across the desk to hold my hand. "We'll make sure things go as smoothly as possible. I've been around this stuff long enough to know what to look out for."

I cover her hand with mine and relent with a smile. This feels good, working together like this. Callie's right. Together, we'll make sure there are no hiccups and no more surprises. "Want to go for a swim?"

"You know what, I'm beat." She draws her hand back as she rises from her seat. "Your mother said she might make her famous baked spaghetti tonight. That and a hot shower sound like heaven at the moment."

"Yeah, she texted me earlier, insisting I join you all for dinner."

She leans across the desk and kisses me. "Then I'll see you later?"

I want nothing more than to pull her back and continue that kiss, but I'm feeling the day myself. And knowing I'll get to see her later is enough for now.

"Count on it."

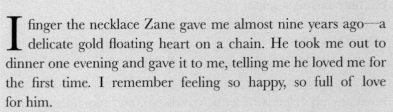

CHAPTER 32
Callie

I finger the necklace Zane gave me almost nine years ago—a delicate gold floating heart on a chain. He took me out to dinner one evening and gave it to me, telling me he loved me for the first time. I remember feeling so happy, so full of love for him.

At that moment, our future together seemed so full of promise. So sure…

Though I stopped wearing it, I kept it all these years. I thought I just wanted to keep it as a memento, but I should have realized that, like this chain holds the gold heart, Zane holds mine.

I pinch the clasp open and secure the necklace around my neck, wondering how long it will take Zane to notice. As I leave my room, the aroma of garlic bread, tomato sauce, and Parmesan make my mouth water and fill with saliva.

My stomach growls and reminds me I never ate when I got back to the house. After a shower, I lay down on my bed to catch up on some emails on my phone, and then the next thing I knew, I was waking up. I didn't even hear Emily's texts asking me how things went. I promised to catch her up tomorrow.

In the hallway, Zane's laughter draws me to the kitchen, where he's helping his mother with dinner.

Sally notices me first. "Callie, you're just in time. Did you have a good nap?"

How did she know I fell asleep when I didn't even know until I woke up?

She tilts her head and smiles. Like she knows exactly what I'm thinking. "I knew right away when you walked in the door that I needed to delay dinner for an hour."

Zane shakes his head at me. "You should know by now that my mother knows everything."

When he glances at me, I smile, waiting to see if he notices the necklace, but he doesn't linger long enough since his mother has him making a salad.

I move to the other side of the island where Zane's working. "Can I help?"

"Yeah." He hands me a carrot. "Peel that, then use the peeler to make carrot strips over the top." He gestures to a large bowl already filled with lettuce, radishes, and tomatoes but still doesn't notice.

Obviously, the salad-making is distracting him, and I'm thinking that might be a good thing, considering his mother is stirring a pot of sauce just a few feet away. Not exactly an ideal setting for something intimate.

Per his instructions, I start peeling. "When did you become so domesticated?"

"I live alone, and a man's gotta eat," he grouses, but his tone is playful.

With a wooden spoon still in her hand, Sally leans back from her pot. "And his mother taught him how to cook."

Zane skillfully chops a red onion into smaller chunks, then lifts the cutting board and sweeps it over the salad using the back of the knife.

"I'm impressed." And I truly am. I've tried that before, only to have the blade catch. Never thought of using the back of the knife.

For the next twenty minutes, we continue to prep dinner, set the table, and place all the food on the table to eat family style. And that's what this feels like—family. My heart must be bulging out of my chest because it feels too big for my frame.

Jacob walks in from the garage to wash his hands in the kitchen sink, which sends Sally into action, swatting his backside with the kitchen towel, telling him to go use the bathroom sink so she can drain the pasta.

Zane's already busy filling glasses with iced tea and even adds slices of lemon for garnish. And the banter is fun and ongoing, full of joy and life as we share this beautifully prepared meal.

I want this to be my norm. To have dinner with Zane's parents regularly. To hang out and play games together after we're done eating. To do dishes and clean-up the kitchen together while his parents relax on the back patio.

Like we're doing now.

"Get a towel out of that drawer and dry those." Zane points and gives directions like he does at headquarters.

"Yes, sir." I grab a towel that has Kiss the Cook on it and hold it up for Zane to see.

He chuckles and shakes his head. "I'd really rather not kiss my mother at the moment."

I act coy and saunter closer to him. "Why, Mr. Albright, I did help make the salad."

When he looks at me, attraction flickers in his eyes. "That counts."

He yanks the towel from me to dry his hands, then tugs me against him.

My lips tingle in anticipation of meeting his...so close...but then he stops.

A soft hiss comes from his mouth instead as his fingers brush the heart pendant on the necklace, sending my actual heart into overdrive. "You still have it."

His reaction makes the delay worth the wait. "Does that surprise you?"

His gaze snaps to mine. "You have no idea." His voice is rough, and then he kisses me as if I've given him something precious.

When he breaks the kiss, his breathing is as rapid as mine. "I remember the evening I gave that to you."

I kiss the corner of his mouth. "You told me you loved me."

"Callie." He growls my name.

And I'm undone. "Me too."

Zane wraps his arms around me, pressing his hands against my back like he can't get enough of me. And I, him. I'm lost in the moment and don't want it to end.

The sound of the patio door opening reminds us where we are. We break apart and attempt to appear as if we're still cleaning the kitchen, which was mostly done already.

Sally walks in with Jacob trailing behind her. "Well done, kids. But you're not kids, are you." She gives us a knowing look.

I cover my mouth and try not to laugh. Zane tries to look busy by folding the dish towel that started it all.

"I hope it was a good kiss." Jacob flashes us a silly grin.

And now we're all bent over laughing at his unexpected contribution to the situation, which bypasses the awkwardness completely.

Zane yawns. "I'm going home. Unlike you, I didn't take a nap, and if I don't leave now, I'll be crashing on the couch since there's a beautiful woman in my old room."

"I'll walk you out." I slip my hand into his as he says goodbye to his parents.

We're both loathe to end the evening when we reach his Jeep. Every time I try to walk back to the house, Zane grabs my hand and spins me back to him for another kiss.

It's glorious, and I don't want it to end.

The last time Zane does this, he just holds me against him. I wrap my arms around him and press my ear against his chest so I can hear his heartbeat.

"I don't want this to end, Cal." His voice rumbles through his chest into my ear.

I lift my head so I can see his face. Why is he saying this? Does he have doubts about us? "I don't either."

"Are you sure?" His blue eyes seem full of doubt.

"Yes, completely."

Relief washes the doubt away as he cups my face with his hands. "Cal, I have never stopped loving you. Took me a minute to realize it, but it's true."

Tears spring to my eyes as he speaks the desire of my heart. I don't care if I ugly cry. This man can see it and still appreciate me.

Because he loves me.

And I need him to know how much I love him, too. "Good. Because I want a life with you, Zane Albright. More than anything."

He searches my face with eyes so blue and full of his love. "Does that mean you love me, too?"

Guess I left that part out. "Isn't it obvious?"

"Just making sure we're on the same page." He brushes my nose with his, promising another kiss.

"We are, and I do. Love you, that is." I can barely get the words out as his lips brush mine.

With a final kiss, we part. He drives off, and I float to my room, full of hope that this time, we've figured out how to do things right.

CHAPTER 33
Callie

"They all brought their consent forms in. Half of them have sticky notes from the parents, asking how they can help." I drop the stack of forms onto Zane's desk. "Could Theo be right about all this?"

Zane gives me a skeptical look as he grabs the stack. "Let's not jump to conclusions so fast, okay?"

I sit on the edge of his desk. "Why not? It's fun."

"And dangerous."

I lift one shoulder. "Maybe I like danger."

"Callie." He growls my name again, like he did at his parents.

I can't help myself, but I love it when he does that, so I give him a playful push whenever I can. It just doesn't get old. You know what I mean?

"All right." I laugh and drop into a chair in front of his desk. "Steve, the director, just let me know the filming crew arrives tomorrow. They need a day to scout the area and plan, then a day to set up. He also said they should be ready to start on Monday. I told him we have to keep our schedule for the mornings, just like we discussed, but afternoons are fair game. Oh, and he asked if they could take some shots of our training sessions as filler. I told him that was fine as long as they stay out of the way and don't distract the kids. Sound good?"

Zane leans back in his seat and crosses his arms. "Sounds great. Good job."

"Why, thank you." I preen a bit in my chair.

This last week has been amazing. I feel as if Zane and I have stepped into a whole new level of partnership. A real partnership. We've spent every evening together, either at headquarters, walking the beach, at his parents' house, or going out to dinner, all the while discussing ideas for expanding the youth program…and other things. Like the future. Our dreams. Things we want to do and experience together.

"I told Theo I'd keep him updated. He called after I took Isaac home."

I don't miss the marginal cringe in the set of his jaw. "How's that going?"

He drops his gaze to his desk. "It's fine, I guess."

I reach out and put my hand on his. "Awkward?"

"Yes." He lifts my hand to his mouth and kisses my fingers, sending sparks up my arm.

"Like you're talking to someone else?"

"Kind of."

"Makes you wish things could be like they used to?"

"I guess. Cal, what are you doing?"

I giggle. "Just trying to help you work through this."

He grins at me. "You're outrageous."

"I try." A little more preening.

"Try what?" Jake leans in, his hands braced on the doorjamb.

Now I'm all business and professional because it's Jake, and per usual, his timing stinks. "Nothing. What's up, Jake?"

"Just wanted to check in and make sure we're good to go."

I point to the stack of forms on Zane's desk. "Consent forms are done. Crew's on the way. Filming starts Monday." I give him the short summary because my patience is trending on the short side with Jake today.

And he seems surprised. "Oh, then you already know the plan for the weekend."

"The scouting and set-up? Yes, Steve already filled us in." I dart a glance at Zane, who's tapping his pen on the desk. Jake may not see his agitation, but I do. As much as I don't want our time with the youth to end, I'll be glad when Jake's back in LA.

"Well, then, I guess I'll see you guys on Monday. Unless you want to watch us plan the shoots this weekend? I told Nick he's more than welcome to come watch. You should join us, Callie. Like old times."

"No, thanks. I have plans with Zane." Anytime Jake says 'old times,' that's my cue to run in the opposite direction because he's fishing to see if I'm available. I turn toward Zane long enough for him to see me roll my eyes. I can tell he's pursing his lips together to keep from laughing.

"Okay, no problem. See you on set Monday." Jake does that double-clicking noise with his mouth like he used to do on set all the time. It got to where anytime I heard a sound resembling that, I'd look for him so I could hide. He drove me—and the entire set, for that matter—nuts when he did it.

Once he's gone, I sigh and drop my head. My hair falls around my face, and I linger for a moment in my isolation. I can tell I'm going to dread Monday.

"That guy is a piece of work." Zane is still watching him make the rounds with the next shift of guards coming in.

Jake's probably telling them all about his plans this weekend.

"Yes. A very insecure piece of work, I'm afraid."

"And a braggart." Zane lifts my hand to his lips again and kisses my fingers below the knuckles. "You're kinder than me."

"No. I just have better things to do with my time than worry about Jake Ward."

"Such as?"

I glance up for effect. "Like where you're taking me out to dinner tonight."

Zane jerks in his seat. "Oh, that reminds me. I need to get going." He shoves the consent forms into a folder and puts it into a basket on his desk with all the other documentation we've had to study in preparation for this shoot.

"I…have an appointment to keep." He checks his pockets for his keys and grabs his phone.

"What kind of an appointment?"

"Just something I need to take care of."

"Want me to come with you?"

"Uh, no need. I can handle it on my own. Call you later?"

"Sure." I frown as he dashes out of his office and out the main door.

He better not be defaulting to independent Zane, who thinks he can do everything himself again. We just found a good rhythm to this 'us' thing, and I don't want him to blow it.

CHAPTER 34

Zane

I'm at Kade's metalworks studio, looking at his ring sketches because I want the perfect ring for Callie, and Kade is the best metalsmith around.

Am I moving too fast? Probably.

Do I care? More than you know.

Am I planning to ask Callie to marry me? You betcha.

I'm not letting her get away again. And had we stayed together, who knows how many wedding anniversaries we would have behind us by now?

So this is about making up for lost time. Eight years' worth.

I've even started researching places for our honeymoon. I'll leave the wedding plans to Callie and my mother, who will be thrilled.

Kade flips to another page in his sketchbook. "What about this one? I incorporated the lifeguard cross into the sides."

It's subtle, but it's there. "Mmm, I think I want something more personal."

He flips to another page, and I know right away. I jab my finger at the page. "That's it. That's the one."

The setting looks like a heart that wraps around a diamond in the center…and reminds me of the necklace I gave her.

Kade grins. "That's my favorite, too." He flips the book closed, but not before I catch a glimpse of something ring-like but with leaves.

"What was that?"

When I try to flip the sketchbook open again, he slams his hand down on the cover.

"Nothing. Just some other projects I'm working on." He's trying very hard not to smile.

"That was for Mandy, wasn't it?"

"Maybe."

I don't relent with my stare.

"All right, yes, I'm working on a ring design for Mandy."

"That's great, man." We shake hands and bro hug. "When are you planning to ask her?"

"Not sure yet. You?"

"I'm still trying to figure that part out." I want to do this right, make the moment something she'll never forget.

Kade leans against his workbench. "Beach?"

"That's the obvious choice. But I don't know. I want it to be unique. Something she'll remember."

"Remembering isn't the problem. It's how it stands up to all the other proposals out there."

Say what? Now I'm worried I won't get this right. "So, how much time do you need to put this together?"

"A couple of weeks at the most. Once I find the right diamond, the design will go together fast."

I pat him on the shoulder. "That's great. Thank you."

"No problem."

Kade follows me to the door. "I hear you're about to have some excitement on the beach."

"The *Wave Watchers* thing? Yeah, I guess word is getting around."

"At least twice. Mandy said that's all people talk about when they come into her shop."

Great. Just what we need. More people on the beach will

mean more eyes needed. I may have to revamp the schedule Nick made after all.

Kade's brows draw together. "You don't look happy about this."

I shake my head. "I'm not. At all." Too many loose threads that I have no control over. The whole thing makes me nervous.

"I'm not a lifeguard, but if you need help with something, let me know."

I appreciate Kade's offer more than he knows. "Will do. Thanks, man."

As I leave, my phone vibrates in my pocket. A text from Callie.

> Am I going to see you tonight? (Waiting with bated breath for your reply.)

> Bated breath? In that case, no.

> Ha ha, very funny. Bate, not bait.

> I know. But it was funny.

> So what's your plan? I may have a better offer waiting in the wings, you know.

> Emily?

The three dots show that she's typing. I want every minute I can get with Callie, but after what I just did at Kade's studio, I'm still buzzing with anticipation and could easily spill the proverbial beans.

> No, the script for the episode. Courier just delivered it to headquarters.

> I'm on my way.

"Well, it seems tame enough." I close the last page and flip it over. The title, 'Day of Destiny,' sits in the middle of the page, larger than life. "It's not as long as I expected either."

Callie flashes a grin at me that makes the already residual heat I'm feeling ramp up a notch. "It's not a book. Scripts are much shorter."

"And yet they manage to pack in so much."

"That's the beauty of having sets and visuals that do all the work, along with actors that take the script and create believable characters."

"Impressive." I prop my arms on the table in the common areas where we opted to sit to discuss the script and eat the dinner I picked up on the way. And I have to say, I really like this. Feels more like we're on an even keel, working as a team, like our new norm.

"It's fascinating to watch the actors take creative license and develop nuances for their characters. Even Jake does a good job at it."

"How so?" I think this is the first time we've delved into her time working on a television show in Hollywood.

She pauses to think. "So, you know how the character Jake plays always wants a cheeseburger after a major rescue?"

"Um, no. I've never watched the show."

"Never? Not even one episode?" She looks at me as if I've sprouted an extra head and two more arms.

"No, I'm not into shows like that."

"But it's about lifeguards." She splays her hand on the table between us as she looks up at me in disbelief.

"I figured it was all staged. You know, not realistic."

Callie pulls her hands into her lap as she falls back in her seat. "That's why they brought me on to consult, so that the storylines and scenes would be as realistic as possible."

"As possible, being the keywords."

"Hey, I was good at my job." She crosses her arms and dons an offended expression.

I laugh before I have the sense to stop myself. Now she looks even more offended.

"I'm sorry. My bad. I guess I should stream a few episodes so I can appreciate your professional input."

"You should. It's a decent show." Now, she just sounds petulant.

"Tell me about what you did on the show."

She sits forward and rests her hands on the table, sending her floral scent in my direction. "Mostly gave input on the scripts as far as the right terminology, situations, and how they played out. Proper equipment, settings, and rescue details. You know, the real stuff we deal with."

"And they'd follow your input?"

"As much as they could. Sometimes, they had to adjust because the writers didn't know how something would really play out. Or what they wrote didn't translate on camera as well as they hoped. Then they'd adjust and ask me for input."

"Wow, sounds intense."

"Sometimes. Other times, it could be boring beyond belief. Like waiting around for delayed equipment to arrive or an actor who overslept to show up."

"Jake?"

"Every time." As she rolls her eyes, they nearly double in size, which makes me laugh.

"What's so funny?"

"You. I still can't picture you with him. You two have nothing in common."

"No kidding. I think I was just star-struck early on. Then I got wise." She picks up her soda to take another sip.

All I can focus on is the way her lips encircle her straw. Lucky straw. And now I'm annoyed at the table separating us. "You are the most interesting, amazing, and intriguing woman I've ever met."

She lowers her cup to the table. "That compliment almost makes up for not taking me out to dinner."

"Hey, I thought you liked my surprise dinner." I point to the containers covering the table.

Her smile is dazzling. "I did. I'm just kidding." Her entire demeanor turns shy. "Thank you. That's high praise from your lips."

I point to my mouth. "These lips?"

"Yes." She tilts her head as if to question why I'm taking our conversation in this direction.

My chair scrapes the floor when I move closer to her. I can't resist starting our banter again. "These lips that have been itching to kiss you since I got back?"

Her smile widens. "Yes, I believe so."

"These lips that are about to kiss yours?"

She leans in so close that I feel her breath and warmth, and I can almost taste the salt from her steak fries. "Tell your lips to stop talking."

The heat between us ignites, and we're lip-locked in a kiss that shakes me to my core. I almost wish I had that ring right now. Maybe I'm overcomplicating proposing. The most important thing Callie needs to know is how I feel about her.

I break the kiss and rest my forehead against hers as I cup her face. Her eyes are hooded, but I know she's as affected by our kiss as I am.

"Theo did one thing right. He brought you back to Sarabella."

Her eyes flash open to meet mine. "Good thing he replied to my email."

Her admission jars me back to reality. "What? Wait...I thought Theo sought you out."

She pulls back. "No, I emailed him my outline and offered to come and help start the program here."

"He didn't tell me that. I thought Theo contacted you first."

"Does it matter?" She searches my face with those gorgeous hazel eyes.

I consider her question for a moment. "Just makes me love you more."

Her face practically glows. "Good answer."

CHAPTER 35
Callie

Three days of shooting has the entire team on edge. Even Nick, who has a talent for going with the flow, seems off today. He never grouses, yet today, he's been an endless stream of complaints.

And then there's Zane. The constant stops, starts, interruptions, and shifts in direction has his grumpy flag flying high. I knew this endeavor would mess with the planner in him, but even I feel pushed to my limits at times.

The teens are the priority, though, and all the fuss and craziness of watching a television show filming has turned into the highlight of their week. And, of course, they love Jake. The man turned on the charm both on and off camera, which sent the girls into squeals and the boys into groans. Although, I think several of them are just as enamored as their female counterparts but don't want to admit it.

The director has reassured us they'll finish by early next week, which will leave us with some peace and normalcy for the last few days of the program.

Then Zane and I can formalize and plan a year-round program to present to Theo. I can't imagine him saying anything but yes to the idea. Especially if we speak his political language and show how good this will be for Sarabella—and his reputation—if he's the one to sign off on it. I know Zane won't be thrilled with that aspect, but if that's what it takes, right?

Nick, Graham, and the other guards have the teens doing water drills in the shallows. The film crew prepping the shoot for today resembles a colony of ants scurrying around with their loads of equipment—a challenging feat when sand is involved.

Zane has made tower one a pseudo office so he can keep a close eye on everything. That's where I'm headed now to give him an update. We—and by we, I mean Steve and I—agreed that I should be the go-between for Zane's sake and his. Think *Clash of the Titans* on steroids. Although I'm not sure who exactly are the monsters and the gods in this production, I'm pretty sure I know which one Jake considers himself.

Even I'm getting grumpy now.

I make my way up the steps like I'm trudging through quick-sand. Steve said they have a new scene to add, thanks to Jake, and, lucky me, I get to tell Zane about yet another change.

He takes one look at me and drops his head for a moment. "What now?"

"New scene. Apparently, Jake had some inspiration last night and rewrote it."

"What does that even mean?" His expression tells me everything I need to know. He's about had enough of the whole thing.

I hold up my hands. "I have no idea, but we're about to find out. They like Nick and Isaac because they seem to have a good vibe. Plus, Nick has tattoos. The director's words, not mine."

"Fine. I'll pull them from drills." He lifts the walkie-talkie sitting near him to his mouth and gives instructions, but as he finishes, his brows go down, and blue eyes darken. "What the…?"

I spin around to check out what has Zane so throttled. A small speed boat and two jet skis arrive about fifty feet from shore. "Oh, no."

Zane launches out of the tower and onto the sand without touching the steps. I take off after him, not only concerned about what these additions mean, but also about keeping Zane from losing his cool entirely.

I manage to catch up but just barely, as Zane comes to a stop near Steve and points toward the boat and jet skis. "Are those part of the scene change?"

Before Steve can reply, Jake jumps in. "Yeah, isn't it great? More drama."

"We don't need more drama, Jake." Zane's height and size dwarfs Jake a bit, especially in his agitated state.

Jake scoffs. "That's what makes the show, Zane. What I like to call dramatic tension."

Oh no, Jake brought out his 'I know more than you' persona. I witnessed him do this on the set *so* many times, and it never ends well.

Hoping to deflect even more drama, I take a step forward to insert myself into the equation. "Not at the expense of safety, Jake. The consent forms said nothing about motorized vehicles."

"I know. I checked with legal, and they said the wording is good enough."

Zane's eyes bug out. "Good enough? Good *enough*?"

"*Not* good enough, Jake," I interject before Zane explodes.

Nick joins us, with Isaac close behind. "So, what's the plan?"

Zane and Jake are having a staring contest. Steve is distracted by the various crew members demanding his attention to implement the various parts of the scene. Isaac has already wandered toward the water to check out the jet skis— every teenager's secret dream.

And I'm thrust into this surreal situation of opposing sides. "Run down the scene with us, Jake."

Zane looks at me as if I'm nuts even to consider this.

"Let's not make assumptions. Remember your motto?" I give him a pointed look.

He crosses his arms and tucks his chin. "Fine." Then he

points to where Isaac's checking out one of the jet skis. "But if it involves one of our youth on one of those, that's a definite no."

Jake holds his hands up. "Of course not. We'd never do that. This is your typical rescue scene."

As if he understands typical.

Jake continues, "I'm in the boat with one of the guards and youth, aka Nick and Isaac. We're doing some basic stuff. You know, surveying the water because there's been a shark sighting. When suddenly these two jet skiers come on the scene, riding like crazy out of control." He gesticulates for emphasis. "They collide—but not in reality, of course—and they're potentially injured, which means blood, which attracts the shark, which means we go into action and save the day. That's it. In a nutshell."

Jake stands there with his hands on his hips, waiting for our reaction.

"I still don't like it." Zane, at least, seems calmer.

"Neither do I." I probably look like Zane's doppelgänger with my arms crossed next to him.

He gives me an appreciative glance while Nick continues to observe our exchange.

Steve finally tunes into the situation. "Look, we have it under control. Jake's had some experience with this kind of boat before, but the instructor will give him a run down to make sure he has it down. We'll put a life preserver on the kid, of course. The jet skis are where the real action happens, and that won't be anywhere near the boat."

Isaac walks up. "This is so rad." His face is flushed from his excitement and the heat.

Nick clears his throat. "Seems harmless enough. I'll make sure Isaac stays safe."

Zane and I connect in a silent interplay of consideration. I love how he and I do this and know what we're each thinking. I lift one brow to let him know I'm following his lead on this one. He gives me a curt nod to say okay.

Then he stares Jake down again. "If anything goes wrong, it's on your head, and this shoot ends."

With an overly confident smile, Jake pats him on the bicep. "Nothing's going to go wrong. I promise."

Zane says nothing. Just glares at the spot where Jake touched his arm before redirecting it at Jake.

Jake's grin slips a few notches before he claps and turns around. "All right. Let's get to work, people!"

"I THINK Isaac may have found his true calling." I recognize that Hollywood bedazzlement—I remember feeling it myself the first few months I consulted on the set, imagining myself as more than just a bystander. Then, the full reality of it all settled in—the time and talent required.

I knew then it wasn't for me, but I won't deny daydreaming about it for a while.

Standing next to me by the tower railing, Zane nods. "Looks that way, doesn't it?"

Isaac has a smitten look. Of course, he's only sixteen, but if the lure of acting were a mosquito, I'd say he'd been bitten by the way he's bouncing on the balls of his feet and has his hands clasped and ready to do the run-through.

Our vantage point from the tower gives us more of an elevated view of the scene. The practice runs went well, which relieved a lot of tension for us both. And now they're about to shoot the real deal.

"Nick looks like he's having a good time, too." I point in his direction where he's sitting in the back of the boat with his arms splayed out and sunlight glinting off his sunglasses.

"As long as he keeps an eye on Isaac, he can have all the fun he wants." Zane lifts his binoculars to his face. "Jake looks frustrated with the guy standing with him by the controls."

He hands the binoculars to me.

"Yeah, typical Jake. He thinks he knows more than he does." But the crew knows that, too, and they've learned how to handle Jake. But I don't recognize this guy. He may be the local they rented the equipment from.

I hand the binoculars back. Zane lifts them to his face again with one hand while his other clutches his whistle. He's in his prep stance, ready to jump into action.

If I were superstitious, I'd cross my fingers right about now. Filming starts, and the jet skis go into action. Jake maneuvers the boat, just like he has in the run-throughs, and the scene plays out seamlessly.

Zane and I both breathe audible sighs of relief, then look at each other and smile.

I still have my eye on the boat as Zane says, "Glad that's finished."

And that's when things go horribly wrong.

Just as Isaac stands up in the boat, Jake throws the engine into full throttle and turns the boat sharply at the same time. It's like watching a movie shift into slow motion as Isaac pinwheels backward. Nick jerks around and grabs his life jacket with one hand. And then they're both tossed off the boat into the water.

Zane's blowing his whistle in loud blasts as he launches off the tower, rescue tube in hand. Several other guards launch into action with their tubes as well. Zane must have had this backup plan in place ahead of time, just in case.

I fly down to the water's edge and then wait while four seasoned guards make it to the boat in record speed, outswimming the stunt team. Thank goodness Isaac has a life jacket on, but it's Nick I'm most concerned about. Pain twists his expression as he treads water with only one hand near Isaac.

The one thing Jake did right was to cut the engine as soon as he knew something had gone wrong. The residual wake totters the boat back and forth while Jake stands watching with his hands on his head. He knows he screwed up.

I almost feel sorry for him as I imagine what he's feeling,

which would be worse if Isaac or Nick had hit the engine blades. Maybe this time, Jake will learn how damaging his impulsiveness can be.

Two guards swim with Isaac to the shallows and then wade the rest of the way to shore. As Isaac nears, I walk over. "Are you okay? Anything hurting?"

"No, I'm fine. Nick's the one who got hurt." Dread and concern sit in his face in a battle for dominance.

The on-set medic checks his pupils and asks if he hit his head at all as he prods to make sure Isaac is unhurt.

I give Isaac's shoulder a reassuring squeeze as Zane and Graham swim up, bringing Nick floating on his back between them. When they hit shallow water, they help him to his feet. He grunts with the effort, clutching his right arm against his body. The medic meets them at the shoreline and examines Nick.

After several minutes of this, Zane lags back as Graham and the medic help Nick up the beach. "He's in a lot of pain. We're taking him to the ER to get him checked, but I'm guessing he tore his rotator cuff."

The weight of that settles in. A torn cuff could mean surgery. Weeks, even months, of physical therapy at the very least. Nick won't be on duty for a while, which I know will hit him hard.

I make a split decision. "I'll go with you."

"No, stay here." His voice is gruff, and his words short. He's angrier than an aggravated wasp, and I don't blame him. Zane drops his chin momentarily, like he's trying to regain control. "One of us needs to be here to talk to the parents and explain what happened. I think that should be you."

I know our emotions are riding high, and I know he's not technically angry with me. But I can't help but wonder if he blames me for this disaster. I am the reason Jake showed up here in the first place. "Sure. Of course."

"And can you take Isaac home for me? I have no idea how long we'll be at the hospital."

"No problem."

He starts to turn around, then stops and turns back. A sneer twists his lips as he spews again. "And make sure that Jake doesn't show his face around here again. We're done."

The knot in my throat makes speech impossible, so I simply nod. My stomach is churning as I walk with Isaac toward where the rest of the teens and guards are watching from the training area. Thankfully, the guards kept them corralled while this disaster played out.

We finish the day with some normalcy as the boat and jet skis ride out the way they came. The filming crew packs up and trudges up the beach with their loads of equipment. On his way out, Steve stops to reassure me that Nick's medical expenses would be covered. One way or another, they'll step in if Jake doesn't.

Speaking of whom, not a sign of the guy, so I'm guessing he's already gotten the message to make himself scarce.

Now the beach is clear. No more crew members scurrying around. No equipment cluttering the sand. No actors, stunt people, or directors.

It's almost as if none of it ever happened.

If only it could be that easy.

CHAPTER 36

Zane

News traveled faster than a waterspout yesterday about what happened, and my phone started blowing up shortly after. Concerned parents, townsfolk, news mongers…I explained to each one that we handled the incident and that the film crew would not be returning.

Theo left a message, but I haven't had a chance to call him back yet. After spending the rest of the afternoon at the hospital with Nick, then taking him home and making sure he had everything he needed for the night, I barreled into my own place, ready to drop. I had to turn my phone off just so I could get some sleep, which wound up fitful at best.

Then, this morning, things started all over again. Several parents texted or called to let me know their teenager wouldn't be there today. Some are deciding whether or not to pull their kid out of the program permanently.

This is my worst nightmare.

I have little doubt that Theo will shut down the youth program before it even gets started. Probably not worth planning a year-round program at this point, either.

And I need to talk to Callie in the worst way.

When I pull into the drive, Isaac isn't waiting for me like he usually does. His mother is. And she doesn't look happy to see me.

This is so not good.

Clearly, she's decided to keep Isaac home and didn't go in to work so she could tell me in person. I climb out of my Jeep, wishing I could crawl under it and hide.

"Morning, Mrs. Richmond."

She shakes her head, and her eyes flash with a mama bear fierceness, which I recognize from my own mother. "Mr. Albright."

"Let me say again how sorry I am about what happened yesterday."

She nods. "Isaac and Callie explained what happened. Needless to say, this family will never be fans of Jake Ward."

A small sense of relief floods me, knowing Callie must have waited around to talk to Isaac's mom. "I understand, ma'am. I feel much the same."

She blinks and drops her gaze. "Though I know this isn't your fault, you did make me a promise."

"Yes, I did. And I intend to keep it. Keep Isaac safe—all the youth safe. That's why I ended the filming. The rest of the program will finish as usual." That is, if we have any youth coming. I'd so hoped Isaac would be one of them.

She studies me for a moment. I assume to consider her words. "I'm keeping Isaac home with me today so we can have some time together. But I'm telling you now, I don't know if he'll be back at all."

I swallow down the knot that's formed in my throat. "I understand that, too, but I want you to know that Isaac is an amazing young man. Did he tell you about our plans to expand the program to be year-round and that I've asked him to be a part of that?"

"Yes, he did."

"He's the only one I've shared that with because he has the

right heart and mind for it. And he's good at it." I want her to be proud of her son and know that I see his potential.

She nods and gives me a faint smile that tells me I've succeeded. "I'll keep that in mind."

I glance at the window Kade and I helped repair to see Isaac watching us. He waves, but the disappointment on his face is clear from where I'm standing.

"Tell Isaac we'll miss him today, but I hope you two have a special day together. And please think about letting him come back for the rest of the program. We can work things out from there."

Mrs. Richmond hesitates at first, then gives a curt nod, which I'm grateful for. I understand her position. She's a single mom with a lot on her shoulders, and she wants the very best for her son.

That's the part that hits me the hardest. Isaac and kids like him need this program to help them build a future they can be proud of. I don't want to see him miss out on anything.

With that, I climb back into my Jeep and drive off. And all the way to headquarters, my only thoughts are of how to save the program.

But I'm not even sure that's possible anymore.

HEADQUARTERS IS BUZZING with activity when I arrive. The first shift of the day is prepping to go out, and the trainers are standing around, waiting for more teens to show up. So far, only four have—the eighteen-year-olds of the group who are college-bound in the fall.

As I head to my office, Callie leaves hers and follows me in, shutting the door behind us. "Where's Isaac?"

I drop into my chair, which gives a loud squeak of protest, mirroring my own thoughts about how things are going down so far. "Not coming back."

With a sigh, she lowers herself into one of the other chairs like a deflated balloon. "Mrs. Richmond told me she'd think about it yesterday."

"I encouraged her to do the same. Thank you for doing that, by the way. I didn't expect you to hang around until she got home from work."

"I wanted to make sure Isaac was okay and reassure her we've dealt with the situation."

"Yeah, she's no fan of Jake Ward."

Callie's expression tightens. "Neither am I."

I don't want to ask, but I need to know. "Has he tried to talk to you?"

"No, but I'm sure he will at some point." She exhales. "Have you spoken to Theo yet?"

"Next on my to-do list. I spent most of the evening on my phone and have several calls yet to return." I run my hands down my face, wearier than if I'd spent the entire day out on the beach doing drills in the hottest part of the afternoon.

"Several of the parents reached out to me last night, too. They don't want to give up on the program, but they're concerned. They're not sure what to do."

"This is unfamiliar territory for all of us." I drop my hands on the desk with a loud thump, making Callie jump, which I regret. I'd rather be on the beach right now with the kids, enjoying the sun and water. And I know she's struggling with all this as much as I am, but I can't seem to let her in right now. "I never should have agreed to this. I should have shut Jake down from the start."

"Technically, the shoot was safe and successful. Jake's the one who messed up after the fact."

"That doesn't do a thing to make those parents feel better, Callie. They trusted us to keep their kids safe. And we failed." My voice grows more emphatic as I finish my words. Right now, I wish we had a punching bag installed with the workout equipment.

Callie crosses her arms and seems to sink down further into her chair.

All I'm doing is making things worse.

"Have you talked to Nick today?" Her voice sounds soft, almost sad.

"Yeah, he's hanging in there. Still in a fair bit of pain. He's trying to get in to see an orthopedist this week to see if he needs surgery."

A knock sounds on the door. Callie jumps up and opens it.

Graham's burly form fills the doorway. "Jake Ward is outside. He said he'd like a word."

I come around my desk and sit on the edge, arms crossed. "I don't think there's anything left to say."

"He said he didn't want to leave town before saying good-bye. To Callie."

Callie looks over her shoulder at me. "I'll go talk to him. I want to make sure he plans to help Nick."

I push off the desk. "I'll go with you."

Jake's sitting at one of the benches under the pavilion, dressed in shorts and a polo, hands clasped in front of him.

He jumps to his feet when Cal and I approach. "Thank you for seeing me. I didn't want to barge in." He gestures toward headquarters. "I didn't feel right walking in."

"Smart move. For once." I sneak a glance at Callie.

She keeps a blank expression as she faces Jake. "I hear you're leaving town?"

"Yeah. Time to go back to LA." Jake gestures down at the training area. "Small group today?"

"Most of the parents pulled their kids from the program." I want him to know just how much his rash actions impacted the program, the town, everyone.

The guy's face twists with genuine remorse. "I'm so sorry for the trouble I've caused. And I do plan to make amends. I've already talked to Nick and told him to forward all his medical bills to me. Steve knows I plan to take care of it all. And I'll make a public statement, taking responsibility."

He's staring at Callie as he says all this, like a child trying to get back into his mother's good graces again. I'm glad my arms are crossed so no one can see how tightly my fists are clenched.

"That's a start, Jake." Callie brushes back the strands of hair blowing into her face.

She's way more forgiving than I am at the moment. Everything I've worked for has fallen apart. And he gets to walk away with a slap on the wrist while we're left to pick up the pieces.

Jake holds his hands out. "Thank you both for allowing me to crash your party…" He shakes his head. "Sorry, bad choice of words. If there's anything else I can do, please let me know."

Neither of us replies. I can't tell where Callie's thoughts and feelings sit right now. Only that her body language is tense and somewhat closed off. As is mine, I'm sure.

Jake brings his hands together in front of him. "Okay, I guess that's it then. Oh, one more thing." He points his fingers toward Callie. "Steve asked if you'd reconsider the offer he emailed you. We both agree it would be great to have you back on the show, Callie. We really do need you."

Offer? My chest grows tight. Callie never said anything about getting an offer to go back to work on the show.

I stay silent long enough for Jake to swagger away, then I turn to face Callie. I have to unclench my jaw in order to speak. "What offer?"

"Steve sent it with the shoot information. I meant to tell you about it, but—"

"But what? You wanted to keep your options open?"

"Zane, I already replied—"

I hold my hands up to stop her. "You know what, I think you should take the offer, Cal. Sounds like you'll wind up in a better place than here."

She blinks, but that does nothing to wipe the hurt from her face.

The fire in my chest winks out, leaving me tired and drained. I turn around and walk back into headquarters without even looking back.

When Graham notices my warpath toward my office, he stops talking to one of the other lifeguards and heads in my direction.

I hold my hand out. "Not now."

Takes everything in me not to slam the door, but we've had enough drama around here to last a lifetime. I collapse into my chair, prop my elbows on the desk, and hold my head.

Callie kept her options open, which means that, once again, I was never going to be enough of a reason for her to stay in Sarabella. After watching her over the last six weeks and seeing how gifted and talented she is, I should have known better than to believe she could actually be happy here. Especially now with the likelihood that the youth program will be shut down.

I slam my hands on the desk.

As angry as I am, I know she deserves to be in a place where she can thrive and grow, doing what she loves. Even if it means I have to let her go.

Again.

The reality makes even breathing difficult. I thought we had a chance at a future together this time.

Clearly, I was wrong.

CHAPTER 37
Callie

To say I'm devastated is an understatement. I don't understand why Zane said what he did—why he pushed me away like that. He didn't even give me a chance to tell him I turned the offer down. Maybe he blames me for bringing the whole *Wave Watchers* debacle down on the youth program.

After Zane walked away, I thought about going after him. But I couldn't walk back into headquarters and face the rest of the team in the middle of an ugly cry. So I drove straight to Emily's and told her everything. I didn't want to go home—to Zane's parents' place.

If Sally saw me, she'd know right away how bad things were. And I can't bear to tell her I might be leaving again after all. Not yet, anyway. I'm still trying to figure this whole mess out and decide if it's salvageable. So I texted her that I was staying at Emily's for the night because I was too tired to drive home.

Since Emily and Aiden had already started turning the spare bedroom into a nursery, she offered me the couch for the night and some clean clothes so I could shower. I think I fell asleep last night crying and woke up crying. My face must look like a pufferfish by now.

And I don't know how many times I picked up my phone to call or text Zane, but I just can't seem to do it.

"What are you going to do?" Emily sets a box of tissues on my lap as she sits next to me on the couch.

Even though it's probably ninety degrees outside already, I huddle under the blanket, determined to hide for as long as possible. "I don't know."

"What about the offer? Sounds like they really want you back." She looks ready to puke just saying it, and I'm pretty sure it's not because of her pregnancy.

"I don't want to go back to LA."

"Well, that's good." She sounds so hopeful, but there's a big BUT to this situation.

"But I can't stay in Sarabella."

"Noooo…why not?" Emily shifts into full pout mode.

"You know perfectly well why."

"Mango Key isn't the only beach in Sarabella. Can't you just go back to lifeguarding?"

I groan. "I still believe in a youth lifeguard program. However, after what happened, no one will probably be interested in hiring me anymore. Maybe I *should* go back to LA. At least they want me there."

I don't really mean it. That's just my pain talking, but I may not have a choice if Zane doesn't want me to stay anymore.

The ugly cry sets in again.

Emily does her best to console me, but I can tell she's doing her best not to join me in this blubber-fest. "I still think Zane was just speaking out of frustration."

"I guess. He didn't even let me tell him I turned the offer down."

"You already turned it down?"

I nod.

"You need to tell him that."

"I know… But even if Theo doesn't cancel the program, we're going to have a hard time rebuilding trust and confidence in it. I'm pretty sure Zane blames me for everything." I stuff a wad of tissues to my nose and blow like a broken horn.

"He can't blame you for something you didn't do."

"Jake weaseled his way into the youth program because of me."

"And there wouldn't have been any youth program at all if it weren't for you."

She's right. I hadn't thought of it that way. "True."

"Then quit blaming yourself and push back. Fight for your place and your program. Fight for what you want."

I stop mid-blow and drop my hands to my lap, tissue and all. "You're absolutely right."

"I know I am." Emily giggles and hugs me again.

The heaviness inside me lightens when I smile at her. Feels good to do something besides cry. "I'm just not sure how to fight back."

Emily's phone buzzes on the coffee table in front of us. She leans forward and picks it up. "Aiden says to turn on the news." She swaps her phone for the remote and changes the channel.

Like a time warp, I feel like I'm shot back in time to the day before I left LA, and my roommate insisted I stop packing so I could see Jake proposing to Debra on TV. Only this time, Jake isn't proposing. He's apologizing.

I lean forward. "Turn it up."

Emily points the remote and ticks up the volume until Jake's voice fills the room.

He's standing in front of The Sand Piper Inn, surrounded by press holding out their smartphones. "Like I said, the youth lifeguard program here is the best in the country. The woman who created it, Callie Monroe, is one of the best lifeguards in the country. That's why we consulted with her for *Wave Watchers*. What happened is entirely my fault. We'd finished the shoot, and I got a little too curious with the boat."

I snort. "Too curious? Try cocky."

Emily hushes me.

"...plan to cover whatever costs are involved in Nick Lawless's recovery. He's a great guy, and I consider him a friend."

A reporter to his left asks, "What about the rumor that they may shut down the youth program?"

Jake looks away for a moment, and his Adam's apple convulses a bit.

Could the guy truly be upset and regret his carelessness for once?

When he faces the camera again, he appears genuinely moved. "I think that would be the biggest mistake Mayor Stringer could make. I wish everyone could see how committed and caring the Sarabella lifeguards are. I had the chance to watch young lives changed and impacted in amazing ways that will only make Sarabella an even greater community than it already is."

I fall back on the couch. "Wow. I'm sure Theo will love that."

The interview switches to talk about *Wave Watchers* and the upcoming new season, so Emily turns the TV off. "Okay, I can't tell if you're serious or being sarcastic."

"Both. Theo will love the way he talked up Sarabella, but he kind of put Theo in a corner, too. If he cancels the program, he'll be the bad guy." My brain kicks into gear. "That could work for us, actually."

I grab my phone.

Emily watches me as I type. "What are you doing?"

"Texting Jake that we need to talk. ASAP." I hit send.

"Why? I thought you said you're not going back to LA?"

"I'm not. Jake did that interview in front of The Sand Piper, which means he's still in town." I stare at my phone, waiting for those three dots and praying I'm right.

Emily narrows her eyes. "What are you up to?"

"Fighting for what I want." I throw off the blanket and grab my clothes and shoes.

Emily pats my shoulder. "That's my girl. Go get 'em!"

The drive back to Sally's place gives me more time to plan. When I walk in the door, Sally takes one look at me and rushes over to hug me.

"Zane texted me this morning to see if you were here. I told him you stayed at Emily's last night." Still holding my shoulders, she leans back to search my face with almost the same shade of blue eyes as Zane has.

And it hits me how much I miss him.

"Are you okay?"

Tears sting my eyes as I shrug.

"Aww, hon, it's going to be okay." She hugs me again.

I don't know how much she knows about what happened between Zane and me, but I'm so overcome by her compassion that I hold onto her for dear life. "Thank you."

"Of course. What else can I do to make this better for you? It's like everyone's gone out of their minds over it."

"I know, but I have a plan."

"Nothing better than having a good plan, is what I always say." Sally's eyes crinkle at the corners as her smile deepens.

I'm struck by how much Zane is like his mother. Even to the plans and mottos, it seems. I don't know why I never really noticed this before.

I glance away and nod. "I better get cleaned up. Lots to do today."

Sally cups my cheek and gives me one of her knowing looks. "No matter what happens, I want you to remember we love you and that you are always welcome here. Understood?"

Now, I'm wondering what Zane may have shared with her. Does she think I'm leaving? I brave a small smile for her benefit. "Thank you."

Sally swipes at her eyes. "I was just in the middle of moving the laundry around before I head to my shop, so I better get to it."

She zips down the hall toward the kitchen, a bustle of

energy. I love that woman like a mother, and the thought of not being here tears me up, too. But I told Emily I'm going to fight for what I want, so no backing down now, or she'll behead me with those pregnancy hormones of hers.

Once I'm cleaned up, I text Sally, letting her know I may be late tonight. I have a lot of people to see and talk to.

And Jake Ward is going to help me.

"THAT WENT BETTER THAN I HOPED." Jake follows me down the walk to my car.

We've "dropped in" on all the parents of the youth enrolled in our program. Even the ones who still showed up on Thursday and Friday.

But I saved Isaac for last because I know Mrs. Richmond will need more swaying than Jake's pretty TV star face.

"What did you expect, a roast?" I roll my eyes at him.

"Maybe." He chuckles, more at himself, I think, than my joke. He pauses by the car. "Thank you, Callie-girl."

I open my door. "I told you to quit calling me that."

"Sorry. Slip of the tongue."

Once we're in the car, I wait to start the engine. "What are you thanking me for?"

"The chance to help make things right. I don't want to see the program shut down because of my stupidity."

I have to say, I'm kind of impressed with Jake. He's really stepped up and tried to make things right. Old Jake would have defended himself with his last breath.

"You did good today. But we still have one more to convince. And she's a tough one."

"Let me at her." Typical Jake exuberance.

I wag my finger at him. "That won't work with this one."

"Oh, okay. Then tell me what will."

"Genuine humility. Think you can handle that?"

He gives me a nervous look. "I'll do my best."

When we pull into Isaac's driveway, his mother is outside, watering her flowers. A frown covers her face as she tries to discern who's in the car.

I put my hand in front of Jake to stop him. "Stay here a sec, okay?"

He only hesitates for a moment before taking his hand off the door handle. "Sure thing."

The driveway is wet from the hose, as is the grass where Mrs. Richmond is standing. "Hello, Callie."

"Hi, Mrs. Richmond." I tuck my hands into my back pockets.

"I think I know why you're here. Not sure it's worth your time. Or mine." She continues to water her flowers—marigolds and periwinkles.

"Your flowers are beautiful."

"Thank you." She glances at me. "I don't think you're here to talk about flowers either."

I bring my hands up in front of me. "No, I'm not. I'm here to ask what it would take for you to let Isaac come back."

The front door opens, and Isaac starts to come out.

Mrs. Richmond points at him. "Back in the house."

He ducks back in and closes the door. Mostly. I still see an eye peeking out of the cracked door.

Mrs. Richmond releases the handle, stopping the water flow. "I don't know if that's possible."

I wave to Jake to get out. "I've spent most of the day visiting all the other parents with Jake. He wants to make things right, Mrs. Richmond. Would you be willing to hear him out?"

At this point, I'm not sure it's going to work at all. Mrs. Richmond looks as if she's ready to turn that hose on Jake and teach him a lesson herself. Honestly, I'm ready to jump out of the way if she does.

Glancing at the hose in her hand, Jake holds his hands up as if she were holding a gun. In Jake's world, she might as well be.

That hose would demolish the thick swatch of hair piled on top of his head and the linen shirt I know he chose for its tropical pattern.

"Mrs. Richmond, I'd like to apologize for being an idiot."

I jerk my head to Jake, shocked at his bluntness. He's obviously figured out Mrs. Richmond isn't someone he can sweet talk. I'm impressed again.

She gestures the hose at him. "Go on."

"What I did was stupid. I wasn't thinking of anyone but myself. I should have been looking out for your son instead of putting him at risk."

"Sounds like you may have learned your lesson, Mr. Ward."

Jake lowers his hands. "Jake, please. I'm trying. Callie's been a big help. She's great with the kids. And with idiots like me. You can trust her with Isaac."

Mrs. Richmond bounces her dark eyes between us before landing on me. "Will he still be involved?" She gestures at Jake with the hose nozzle.

"No, ma'am." I cut Jake off before he can put his stylish flip-flop in his mouth.

After a tense nod, she finally nods. "Okay, he can go back next week."

The front door flies open as Isaac flies out onto the lawn to hug his mother. "Thank you!" Then he runs over and hugs me. "Thank you, Callie."

As he heads toward Jake, his mother grabs his collar. "That's enough thanking. Now go back inside."

"Yes, ma'am." Before he goes back into the house, he gives a low, short wave to Jake and me.

All I can think about is how much this will mean to Zane. It's all I can do not to let out a big squeal. "Thank you, Mrs. Richmond. Zane and I will make sure Isaac is where he needs to be each day."

"That's a good start. Then we'll talk about what's next." She turns her hose back on and continues watering.

I signal to Jake to get back in the car and tell her goodbye.

Once we reach The Sand Piper Inn, I pull up front to drop Jake off. "Thank you for doing this."

He turns in his seat. "Are you kidding? Thank you for letting me help." He glances at the Inn. "Can I buy you dinner?"

I shake my head. "Not a good idea, Jake."

Disappointment clouds his face, but he nods his understanding. "Have you reconsidered coming back to the show?"

"Nope, and I don't intend to. I'm staying in Sarabella." I shrug, feeling more certain than ever. "This is my home now."

"I get it. I hope you and Zane will be very happy." He climbs out of the car and goes inside without looking back.

That's my hope, too. Somehow. And I'm glad this part of my past is finished.

My next challenge?

Convincing Zane that I want him more than some glitzy Hollywood contract.

CHAPTER 38

Zane

When Callie didn't show up at headquarters today, I couldn't bring myself to text her and find out what was going on, so I texted my mother to see if she was at the house. She promptly replied that Callie had stayed at Emily's last night. Then my mother asked if everything was okay.

I almost replied, 'No, because your son is an idiot.' But I didn't. It's enough that I know it for now. I'm sure Callie needed time to think about her options, which still hits me in a raw place.

All night long, I replayed our conversation over and over again. But in the light of day, I'm convinced Callie shouldn't take that offer because she belongs in Sarabella. And Sarabella needs her. The youth program, if it even stands a chance, needs her.

And more importantly, I need her not just for the program but in my life.

But I may have blown it for good this time. I spoke out of exhaustion and frustration. The worst part is I told her I would try harder, and all I seem to do is fail her.

I check my phone to see if Theo tried to call. I've left messages and sent texts, but still no word back from him. I think he's avoiding telling me he's shutting down the program after we finish up next week, which I'm expecting to end with little fanfare.

Two more of the youth showed up today, making the number attending six now instead of four. But neither of them was Isaac, which hits me like a gut punch. He's the reason this program fell into place so fast to begin with, which makes me even madder at Theo since he's the one who pushed so hard to get things going. Maybe we rushed in when we should have put on the brakes and planned things better.

But as they say, hindsight is always 20/20. Jake was the wild card we could never have planned for. I realize that now that I've had time to cool down. None of us could have predicted what he'd do, not even Callie. In fact, she was completely up-front about Jake's self-centered and reckless nature.

As I stare at my phone, my mother texts. Jake's face fills the small picture above a link. I tap the headline and turn up my volume. True to his word, Jake did a decent job telling the press he was responsible. I'll give him that.

Just not sure how Theo's going to react. Could work for us, though. If the man doesn't get back to me soon, I plan to get in my Jeep and drive over to City Hall and barge into his office.

Arms braced on either side of the doorframe, Graham leans in. "You have a visitor."

My first thought is Callie, which sends a surge of anticipation through me. My chance to apologize and make things right with her. I hope.

Graham moves out of the way, and Nick walks in. A sling that wraps around his midsection holds both his arm and shoulder in place.

I jump up to greet him. "Hey, man, didn't expect to see you today."

He gives me a lopsided grin. "Had to see the crew. Surgery is Monday, and I'll be laid up for a good four weeks."

Graham's still standing in the doorway. "And he's going to need a lot of PT, which means he'll be working with my sister."

"Yeah, small world, right?" Nick shrugs, then winces. "I really need to stop doing that."

Graham nails him with a threatening look. "And remember, hands off."

Nick raises his free hand. "I'm only interested in getting better so I can get back on the beach."

A chuckle rumbles up from my gut and breaks off some of the tension I've been carrying. "Let us know what you need help with. We can take turns driving you to PT."

Nick shakes my hand, then we fist bump. "Sounds great."

Come to think of it, how did he make it here? "How'd you get here?"

His expression turns sheepish. "Jake's taking care of some things for me before he flies out Monday."

I clench my jaw. "Be careful, man. He's done enough damage to you."

Nick tilts his head. "He's genuinely sorry, Zane. He knows he has to make things right. Seems only right I give him a second chance."

Just like I'm hoping Callie will do for me. Here I am calling the kettle black. "Nick, you're a better man than me."

Nick grins. "Man, I hope not."

After he leaves, I return to my office and check my phone. Still no word from Theo…and nothing from Callie.

As much as I hate to say it, I need to take a lesson from Jake. The man is as imperfect as they come, but at least he's making an effort.

And so can I. Starting with Callie.

ONCE I FINISH MY SHIFT, I head to City Hall. I need answers so I can make what could be the biggest decision of my life.

And no, I don't mean proposing to Callie. Obviously, that's on hold for now, but I think I know what I need to do to prove to her I'm willing to do more than just try.

I approach his receptionist's desk. "Is he in?"

"Yes, but he's in a meeting right now."

"Tell him Zane Albright is here to see him. It's important."

Instead of calling on her phone as I expected, she gets up and goes into his office. The rumble of thunder sounds in the distance, matching my mood.

Finally, she comes out again and leaves the door ajar. "He has five minutes."

Five minutes? We've been friends for ten years, yet this feels more like something he'd do with a constituent.

As I walk in, Theo stands and greets me with a handshake. "Good to see you, Zane. I'm sorry I don't have more time, but as you can imagine, I'm in the middle of putting out fires, thanks to what happened Wednesday."

Just two days ago, yet it feels so much longer. "I understand. My phone's been blowing up too, but don't you think we should work together on this to find the best solution?"

I need to give Callie credit for that one. Her talk about being partners and working together seems to finally have sunk into my stubborn brain.

Theo leans against his desk and holds his hands out. "I'm in charge of this city, Zane. You run a beach program."

"A program you used to believe in."

"And I still do, but I have bigger issues right now."

"Like your re-election." I know that probably hits a little below the belt, but I'm pretty sure it's true. "Correct me if I'm wrong."

Theo crosses his arms and turns his head to face the window that overlooks Mango Lane. "I'm trying to do what's best for our town. And right now, I'm not sure the youth program is a good idea anymore."

"Theo, your silence has more than communicated that." I

sigh. "That's pretty much what I wanted to know. So...in light of that, I'm giving you my resignation."

He shoves away from the desk. "What? I'm not canceling the entire program, just the youth aspect."

"And you know how important that part has been to me. That it's always been a part of my dream for Sarabella and Mango Key. Callie and I wanted to expand the program to run year-round. That way, kids like Isaac don't fall through the cracks."

Now, he looks embarrassed. "I just don't see how we can bounce back from this, Zane."

That's it, then. I've put everything on the table that I can. "I'll keep running the program until you decide who you want to replace me. Nick's a great candidate and could probably run things once he's recovered from his surgery and doing PT."

"Zane, please don't do this."

"It's already done." I turn around to leave, then remember Jake's video. "In case you might have missed it, Jake Ward made a public apology this morning. Quite elegant, actually. You might want to watch it."

I catch a glimpse of Theo zipping behind his desk and grabbing the mouse by his computer as I leave. He'll figure it out soon enough. And who knows, maybe he'll change his mind.

But I'm not changing mine.

CHAPTER 39
Callie

After I dropped Jake off, I drove to the beach to walk and think.

And plan.

Which makes me sound like Zane. Guess he's rubbed off on me a little.

But also, I wanted to relish what I accomplished today. Talking to the parents, even with Jake in tow, made me realize just how important Zane's dream—our dream is.

There has to be a way we can make this work.

That was my conclusion when I left the beach just after sunset to head back to Sally's. As I pull up to the curb, my heart starts pounding like a drum.

Zane's Jeep sits in the driveway, which makes my stomach plummet to my feet. I'd hoped to have the weekend to figure things out more, but I might as well get this over with now. If Zane still doesn't want me to stay, then the sooner I know, the better.

As I walk in, he rises from the couch. "Can we talk?"

I nod as I shut the door. "Guess we should."

"Have you eaten yet?"

"No." My stomach growls as I say this.

He tilts his head toward the kitchen. "Mom made spaghetti again tonight. There's plenty left over."

I follow him into the kitchen and wait for him to say more, but he's intent on making me a plate of food first.

The thing is…I want to feel his arms around me more than I want that food. I want to go back to the way things were before everything blew up. I want to know that a future in Sarabella means a future with him.

And yet, I can't say any of this. My heart is still reeling, and I think I may be lightheaded from not eating all day.

At the beep of the microwave, he slides the plate out and sets it on the placemat at the end of the table. "What would you like to drink?"

As I slide into the chair, my mouth waters instantly at the tantalizing aromas filling my nose. I shove half of a meatball in my mouth. "Wawer, pease."

He chuckles as he takes a glass out of the cabinet and fills it with water from the fridge. "You must really be hungry."

I swallow. "Starved. Been a busy day." I'm hoping he'll ask me what that means so I can tell him what happened.

Zane pulls out the chair to my left and sits. His eyes look dull and tired, which makes my heart ache even more. "Tell me about it."

After I swallow the other half of that meatball, I take a sip of water to wash it down. He's being so caring and attentive—not at all what I expected. "Well, I spent my day with Jake Ward."

His immediate frown tells me that's what *he* expected. But that's okay. I'm all about the impact at the moment.

"Jake?"

"Mm-hmm." My mouth is full of spaghetti at this point.

"Why?"

"Because he wanted to help fix things, so I took him up on his offer. We visited all the parents of the youth so he could formally apologize to every one of them."

"Wow. I'm impressed. That's amazing, Cal." His reaction makes me smile. Just a little.

"And the best part…they're all coming back Monday. Even Isaac."

He runs a hand over his mouth as he drops his gaze. Like he's searching for the right words. "I'm so glad to hear that."

I thought that was the best part of my day, but he seems sad about it. I put my fork down. "I thought you'd be happy that he's coming back to the program."

"I am. Very. It's just that I, uh…"

"What? Now you're worrying me, Zane. Just spill it already."

"I talked to Theo today. He wants to cancel the youth program."

My respect for Theo drops yet again. The man has turned into a complete idiot. I spear another meatball with my fork, imagining it's Theo's head. "Then we'll fight him."

"But I already resigned."

I drop my fork. "You what?"

"Resigned."

"Why?" I push my plate away. Forget the food. This is juicier.

"The youth program was my dream. Our dream. I don't see the point of staying if we can't finish what we started."

"But to quit?" Has he lost his ever-loving mind? He loves the lifeguard program—he IS the program. I press my fingers against my eyes before I look at him again. "I don't understand. What are you going to do?"

He shrugs, but the corners of his mouth creep up a smidge. "Explore my options. Maybe it's time for a change."

My mind races, trying to believe that Zane actually said this. Who is this man sitting next to me?

Zane looks near tears as he holds his hand over his heart and works his mouth to form words. "None of it matters if I'm not with you, Cal. If you're going back to California, then count me in. Because I'm not staying in Sarabella without you."

I blink. Did he just say he'd leave Sarabella to be with me? "But I don't want to go back to LA."

He frowns. "You don't?"

"No. I turned down the offer the day I got it. I tried to tell you yesterday, but you wouldn't let me finish." I may sound a tad frustrated, but watching the play of emotions on his face as he processes what I said is totally worth it.

He tilts his head back and groans before he looks at me again. "I assumed you wanted it."

I can't resist throwing one of his mottos back at him. "You know what you say about assumptions..."

A goofy grin spreads on his face. "Makes a lifeguard sloppy."

"I think it applies to men, too." I nab another meatball, which is hard to chew when you're smiling, by the way.

He stares at me with those gorgeous blues that are telling me everything his lips aren't saying.

I swallow my food and reply with a gaze I hope tells him everything he needs to know.

"Callie." He growls my name as we jump up from the table and into each other's arms at the same time, lips joined in a hungry kiss that has nothing to do with spaghetti and everything to do with love.

I could live in this moment forever, I think. Nothing matters other than that Zane and I are together. Whatever happens next, we'll do it together. We'll make our own way somehow.

When we finally part, I take a shaky breath and then exhale, willing my heart to stop crashing against my chest.

He kisses me again, tenderly this time, as he runs his hands into my hair, holding my head as he explores my lips with his. "Mmm, spaghetti."

I drop my head against his chest in a fit of giggles. His chest vibrates against my forehead as he laughs with me. I wrap my arms around him and snuggle in closer.

This moment, right now...feels so right. So meant to be.

We're meant to be.

He kisses the top of my head. "We're going to fight for this program with everything we've got. Even if we have to ask Jake Ward to fund it."

I blurt out a laugh at the ludicrousness of his statement. "You must really be desperate."

He laughs as he speaks. "I am. I'll do whatever it takes."

I prop my chin on his chest so I can see his face. "*We'll* do whatever it takes."

His eyes and smile fold me into a sea of love. "Partners."

"Partners."

We spend the next few seconds just staring at each other, lost in this thing between us that makes me believe we can accomplish anything. Together.

Finally, Zane breaks the staring contest and clears his throat. "Then I guess I'll see you Monday at headquarters."

"I'll be there." My voice lilts with my words.

"And before then?" His grin makes me want to kiss him silly.

I know he's asking me to spend the weekend with him, but this playful interchange that we do is too much fun. "Hmm, I don't know. Maybe I'll go hang out with Emily and Aiden and help them work on the nursery."

"Nursery?"

I cover my mouth. "I don't think I'm supposed to tell anyone."

If I could capture the look on his face, I would frame it with a caption saying, 'This is the face of a man with a soft spot for kids.'

"I won't tell a soul. But that's amazing news." He searches my face. "Have you ever thought about it?"

"About what? Kids? I work with them all the time."

"I mean...your own."

My brows just hit my hairline. "What are you asking me, Zane Albright?"

His smile turns mysterious. "Nothing, nothing at all." He dips his head for another kiss. "Yet."

CHAPTER 40

Zane

You know that saying, 'go out with a bang'?

Callie and I spent the entire weekend planning the final week of the youth program so we could do just that.

Our plan?

Make every day we had left memorable.

Our end game?

Make it so memorable that the demand for it outweighs the nay-sayers.

Our hope?

A second chance at building a year-round youth program that's in constant motion and development.

I picked up Callie first this morning so we could drive together to get Isaac. And the excitement buzzing between us in anticipation of seeing him is like some kind of confirmation that we can save the program.

When I pull into his driveway, he's already outside with his backpack, ready to go. Callie gets out so he can get in the back.

"Hey, Callie." His grin is almost broader than his shoulders.

"Hi, Isaac. Ready for a great day?"

"You bet."

Once everyone's buckled in, I back out of the drive. I'm

tempted to ask Isaac how his mother was feeling about him going today, but I don't want to make him uncomfortable. Better to assume—not the sloppy kind—that she's still on board. After all, he's in my Jeep and on the way to the beach with us.

When we reach the parking lot, there's a lot of commotion at the pavilion. Several news trucks line the sidewalk that's filling with more and more people.

As we reach the pavilion, I approach one of the waiting reporters, who's scribbling notes on a piece of paper. "What's going on?"

"We got word that Jake Ward would be here this morning. Still no sign of him yet." He lifts his head. "Hey, aren't you the guy who runs the lifeguard program?"

He genuinely seems interested in who we are. This could be an opportunity to make our case public.

"Zane Albright." I gesture toward Callie, who's next to me. "Along with Callie Monroe, the brains behind the youth program. And this is Isaac, one of our best youth lifeguards and hopefully part of a year-round program Callie and I are trying to create."

He tilts his head and leans in. "Trying?"

Now that I have his attention, I go in with guns blazing. "The program's at risk of being shut down. We have an opportunity to support the youth of Sarabella by providing a program that teaches integrity, compassion, and responsibility, but sadly, we may never get it off the ground."

The reporter signals to his cameraman. "Mind if we tape this?"

"Not at all." Callie smiles at me. Excitement gleams in her eyes.

The reporter positions himself next to us as he faces the camera and introduces himself, and then explains the situation and who we are, including Isaac. Though brief, the interview is powerful. If aired, I think we could get a lot of support from the community, which could, hopefully, sway Theo into changing his mind.

But then the best part happens. One by one, the kids start showing up. Callie and I stand by the door to headquarters to greet each one.

And every single one showed up. The entire group is back, and they're all wearing the team T-shirts Callie had made. We follow the last one in, then stand there, taking it all in.

I tilt my head toward Callie. "Did you ask them to wear their shirts?"

"No, didn't even think of that."

Hit with a thought, I wave Isaac over. "Are you the mastermind behind the shirts?"

He grins. "Yeah. Mom and I called everyone over the weekend. Thought it would be cool."

We bump fists. "Well done, man."

After he rejoins his friends, Callie leans her head against my shoulder. "This is going to be a great day."

I couldn't agree more. "One of the best."

FRIDAY COMES WAY FASTER than any of us wants. The entire team has joined Callie and me in this state of holding our breath over the future of the program. The interview wound up broadcast that evening, and several news outlets picked up the story as well. But still no comment from Theo. I'm at a complete loss to understand this change in him. I guess politics can do that to a person.

And the funny thing? Jake Ward never showed up. When Cal texted him to ask about it, he replied he had a change of plans. Callie thinks he's the one who leaked the tip to get the press there to help us. Initially, I wasn't convinced as I don't see how the guy would miss a photo op, but I'm beginning to believe she's right.

As usual.

We filled the week with mostly fun activities for the youth to celebrate our last week, but the one we have planned today is a BBQ and a DJ. I, on the other hand, have something planned just for Cal.

Something that involves a ring and a proposal. And I have the entire team in on it, as well as the DJ. But that's for later.

I blow my whistle to alert the teams that it's time to shift gears. "Head over to the volleyball courts. It's the final playoff, and the winning team gets trophies." I hold one up. The youth tear off toward the courts.

This is also to keep them from seeing what we're setting up under the pavilion.

Cal joins me by the courts and tugs my shoulder down so she can whisper in my ear, which makes concentrating on what she's saying extremely challenging.

Her lips brush my ear even as her peachy scent floods my senses. "The food truck arrived, and the DJ's setting up now. Several parents arrived already with desserts, too."

Another one of Cal's brilliant ideas—to involve the parents. When she made the suggestion, it just made sense.

Nodding, I twine my fingers with hers and sigh. "We did what we said we would—gave them a great week. Can't wait to see their reaction."

"They're going to have a blast." She gives me a reassuring smile.

About a half hour later, Graham lets loose on his whistle and waves to let us know everything is ready.

I wave back, then return my attention to the volleyball court. The Lifeguardians of the Galaxy and the Skimmers are playing for the win. The score is fourteen to thirteen, respectively. The volley starts. Isaac slams it over, and the Skimmers miss. The Lifeguardians shout their victory and jump up and down, holding onto each other as they do.

This is a perfect picture of what we've worked for all these weeks. These kids understand what it means to work together as a team, and that's something they'll take with them wherever they land in life—the value of 'we.'

I blow my whistle and clap along with the other two teams who've been on the sidelines, watching and cheering. "The Lifeguardians of the Galaxy are the champs. Great job, Team. Now, everyone, head up to the pavilion. We have a little celebration set up for all of you."

As if to punctuate my words, the DJ starts the first music track, sending the youth into a frenzy as they take off for the pavilion.

Cal and I take our time getting there, holding hands along the way. My heart is pounding in my chest as I think about what I have planned to go into action in about thirty minutes, after everyone has at least one hot dog in them.

The music blasts us as we get closer. The kids are eating or dancing, or both. Several parents are manning the food, drink, and dessert tables. And I recognize several of the local business owners involved as well, including my parents.

"Your mother looks like she's having a great time." Cal points in her direction, where she and my father are dancing along with the kids.

I chuckle. "They know how to have fun. Always have."

Cal puts her hand on my chest. "Hmm, what would it take to get you to have some fun?"

"Hey, I know how to have fun."

"Okay, prove it. Dance with me."

"Bossy much?" I growl my words for effect.

Just as I'm about to show her my moves, I stop and clench my jaw. Theo's walking up to the pavilion from the parking lot. "He is not going to ruin this celebration. I'll make sure of it."

Callie holds onto my arm. "Maybe he's here for Isaac, Zane."

"Not likely."

Callie continues to hold my arm as if she's trying to keep me from losing my cool as Theo reaches us. And it's working.

"Can I talk to you two for a minute?" He slips his hands into his trouser pockets. His tie is loose, and no jacket. I think this is the most casual I've seen Theo in years.

I cover Callie's hand on my arm with mine for support. "Sure, but not if it's bad news. Don't ruin this day for us, Theo."

Theo drops his gaze as he rocks back on his heels. "No bad news. I promise." He looks at Cal first, then at me. "I have a stack of letters and a petition on my desk, demanding the youth life-guard program be fully funded and supported. So, consider your-selves notified that it's a go. That is, unless you're still planning to resign, Zane. But as your mayor, I'm asking you to stay on."

I can't stop the grin spreading across my face. "Then I with-draw my resignation."

He gives us a curt nod. "Good. Glad to hear it." He holds a knuckle to his mouth. "As your friend, I'd like to apologize. I...I guess I lost sight of what really matters."

I glance at Callie.

She smiles at me. Like she's encouraging me to be the man she sees. And I want to be that man, too.

"Thank you, Theo. I appreciate that." I hold my hand out to him. "Fresh start?"

He shakes my hand. "Thank you."

"There's plenty of hot dogs. And Isaac probably has a great story to tell you about how he won the volleyball championship with his team."

Theo glances over his shoulder at Isaac. "He looks happy."

Callie pushes her sunglasses up onto her head. "He's a great kid, Theo."

Theo manages a tight smile. "Thanks to both of you. Thank you for looking out for him."

He joins Isaac at the food table. When Isaac sees him, he launches into a demonstration of his winning spike.

"Cal, are you the one behind those letters and petition?"

"Nope, but I have a feeling I know who is."

I follow the direction of her wave, which turns out to be Mrs. Richmond, who's putting a hot dog on Theo's plate. She waves back, then holds her hands up, glances at Theo, and then gives us a knowing look.

Laughing, Cal looks at me. "Never underestimate the power of a mother. Especially when she's the mayor's sister."

I make a one-eighty so I can face her. "Callie, you did it. Talking with all the parents. You saved the program."

"No, we did it." She twines her fingers into mine.

I lift her hands and hold them against my chest as I lean in closer. "I have a little surprise for you, too."

"You do?" She eyes me with suspicion.

I give the signal to the DJ, who gives me two thumbs up. When the current song ends, the theme from *Wave Watchers* starts blasting. I know, cheesy, right? But its rescue theme fits perfectly with what I have planned.

Callie's shocked expression is priceless. As she's about to say something to me, the other lifeguards break into a flash mob dance, strutting and acting out the song. Graham's imitation of Jake Ward has everyone laughing.

As the song ends, the guards freeze in various ridiculous poses. The youth burst out with shouts and laughter, high-fiving the guards as they break their poses.

The whole crew then gathers around us.

Callie holds her hand to her mouth before speaking. "That was incredible! I love it. But you guys know I'm staying in Sarabella for good, right?"

Several of the guards nod. Several glance at me.

Cal turns to me. "What's going on?"

Thanks to Kade's resourcefulness, he finished the ring in record time. I don't know how many times I tapped my pocket today in anticipation of this moment. As I slip my hand into my pocket, I go down on one knee. Several of the teenagers of the female persuasion gasp.

Isaac pumps his fist. "This is righteous."

And Callie is staring at me with her hands covering her mouth and her eyes full of tears.

I hold the ring up. "Callie, you turned my world upside down when you came back. Like a wave that took me under and tossed me until I didn't know up from down. But then you jumped in and rescued me. I can't imagine life without you. Will you marry me?"

A sob slips out behind her hands, and then she nods as she lowers her left hand to me. "Yes!"

I slip the ring on her finger, then stand and hold her against me as we kiss. Her lips are wet from her tears, salty like the ocean, and I know nothing can come between us now so long as we keep operating not only as a team on the beach but in life as well.

Everyone around us is cheering and applauding as we finish kissing.

Callie's hazel eyes gaze up at me, and in them, I see a future filled with a whole lot of love, an abundance of sunshine, and enough sand to last a lifetime.

CHAPTER 41

Callie

EPILOGUE

FOUR MONTHS LATER

Never in all my days spent working on the beach did I ever imagine getting married on one. I know. Everyone else was surprised, too, including Sally and Zane, who cooked up this idea to have the wedding at sunset and the reception at The Turtle Tide.

And when you plan a wedding on the beach in November when the humidity and heat won't snatch your breath away, you can put a wedding together pretty quickly. Zane's the one who suggested using the tower closest to the restaurant as a staging area.

His motto?

When you catch the woman of your dreams a second time, marry her fast.

I'm not complaining. Quite the opposite, actually. Getting married like this makes sense for us. Our romance started on this beach, and now we're making it official. Personally, I can't wait to start this new adventure together. He even planned our honeymoon around exploring other beaches around the world.

First stop? Fiji!

"Are you ready?" Emily looks stunning with her red hair piled in curls on top of her head. And the simple dress Sally found for her, with soft splashes of aqua and pale green, accents her precious baby bump to perfection and flares around her calves.

I rub her tummy and bend over. Gotta get a jump on this baby-talk stuff, you know? "Yes, Aunt Cal is as ready as she'll ever be. Isn't that right, Gemma?"

Aiden and Emily found out they're having a girl and chose that name to honor Aiden's mother, who passed away when he was a teenager, which I find incredibly heartwarming. And I love being 'Aunt Cal.' I can't wait to teach this little monkey how to swim and build sand castles.

I'm going to spoil her rotten.

Kade walks up the steps and opens the tower door. "The music's about to start." As he says this, the sound of the violin seeps in from behind him. He holds his elbow out for Emily. While they make their way down the steps, I make a final adjust-ment to my dress to make sure the square neckline of the embroidered bodice is even, and the soft, tea-length skirt is smooth. I love the feel of the fabric as it swishes around my legs.

And then I touch the heart on the necklace I'm wearing— the one Zane gave me over eight years ago. Doesn't really matter how long it took us to get here. I'm just so happy that we did.

Jacob appears at the top of the steps, waiting for me to come out. I would have liked to have my parents here, but Dad is stationed out of the country at the moment, and Mom, well, she doesn't like to travel without him.

But honestly, I'm okay with all that. Sally and Jacob feel like parents to me already, so having him give me away seemed the best solution.

I step outside just as the sun has dipped enough to paint the sky in gorgeous shades of pink and purple that cast a soft glow of color on my white dress. The effect is dazzling.

When Zane sees me, he puts his hand on his chest and closes his eyes for a moment. He looks amazing in a pair of tan slacks and a white linen shirt. I can tell he's trying to collect himself, which makes my attempts to hold myself together really difficult.

He better not lose it because the last thing I need to do right now is ugly cry my mascara all over my face.

The violin continues to play softly as Jacob leads me down the stairs and across a path lined with solar lanterns and flowers—all designed and arranged by Amanda. I grin at the sight of the youth from the program sprinkled among the attendees as everyone rises from their seats.

Emily and Kade stand on either side of the flowered arbor set up near the shoreline. Kade has his hand on Zane's shoulder, which I think is what's keeping him from losing it.

I make the mistake of looking at Amanda and Sally standing at the front of the seats to the right. They're both trying their best not to cry but failing miserably. I give them a watery grin of appreciation for all they've done to make this day happen.

Can I say I adore this man more than I ever imagined possible? If you'd told me the day I left LA that I would marry him before the end of the year, I would have said you were crazy.

But here we are. We've waited for this moment for over eight years, and now it's finally happening. The start of a perfect partnership.

Zane takes my hand from Jacob and dips his head to whisper in my ear. "You outshine the sunset."

His words and the caress of his lips send tremors down my body.

I cup his face and whisper, "I love you."

We face the minister and say our prepared vows as the sunset continues to blaze the sky in full color. And as we're announced husband and wife, we kiss, just as the sun kisses the ocean and disappears over the horizon.

The perfect ending to the perfect romance in my playbook.

And just the beginning of our best adventure yet.

Ready for more of the Messy Love on Mango Lane series?
He's always played the field. But when an off-limits beauty is running his rehab, will this injured beach patrol hero flee or swim to friendly shores?
Start reading Tamed to Be Messy today!

Not ready to say goodbye to Zane and Callie? How about a bonus epilogue, featuring their next big adventure?
Grab your free epilogue today when you join my newsletter! (I have some additional goodies for you, too!)

(If you're already on my list, no worries! You can still download Zane and Callie's next sweet adventure.)

Before You Swim Away...

Dear friend,

If you enjoyed *Rescued to Be Messy*, please share it with your friends and leave a review on Amazon so other readers can enjoy Zane and Callie's story, too.

And thank you for reading!

~*Dineen*

Follow me on Amazon to get book alerts as they happen!

Join My Facebook Reader Group!

ABOUT ME

Dineen Miller is an Amazon bestselling and award-winning author of both fiction and nonfiction, but only recently discovered she has a sublime addiction to writing and reading romantic comedies. In addition to these, she's been known to write romantic suspense and has dabbled with thrillers and fantasy.

Needing additional outlets for her creativity, she's designed several coloring books under her own name and under Hue Manatee Art, and has crocheted too many afghans to count. No, she does not have cats, but she is a dog-mom to two furry rescues that answer to wiggle butt and snuggle boy. And she's married to a punny guy, who thinks she's unique.

Visit my website at DineenMiller.com for more information about me and my books.
And please connect with me on these social media platforms:

Acknowledgments

Growing up in a small beach town like Sarasota is my inspiration behind creating the fictitious town of Sarabella. And lifeguards are just part of the beautiful beaches here. Very grateful for them!

So, naturally, they had to wind up in my stories at some point, right? And I had an absolute blast creating this imaginary lifeguard program and culture that's an integral part of Mango Key Beach (modeled after our famous Siesta Key Beach, of course).

The research alone was so fascinating. Did you know they even have their own TV channel online? Lifeguards train hard, work hard, and take their jobs very seriously.

With that said, I'd like to express my sincere appreciation and respect to all the lifeguards out there, at the beach or by pool. You truly are lifesavers.

Special thanks to my beta readers Trisha Ontiveros and Charity Henico for once again being on the front lines of my stories. Especially for helping me see that first draft Callie needed some work.

To my Author Ad School coach, friend, encourager, and master blurb creator, Phoebe Ravencraft for always believing in my ability to succeed at this gig of being an author. I am so very grateful to you, Phoebe! You're a rockstar!

I want to thank my Facebook group, Dineen's Rockstar Readers, and my email subscribers for continuing this journey with me. *Rescued to Be Messy* flew onto the pages faster than I expected and taught me something new about myself. That I can write faster than I thought!

As always, thank you to my editors, Alice Shepherd and Judy DeVries for your keen eyes and encouragement.

And to you, dear reader, thank you for diving into the Messy Love on Mango Lane stories. I hope Zane and Callie's story made you laugh, swoon, and find a little time of peace and joy in your corner of the world.

Live authentically, love fully, and laugh often.

~Dineen

Printed in Great Britain
by Amazon

47255304R00182